Avenging Angelina

Avenging Angelina

Peter Tinucci

Other Books by Peter Tinucci:

Angelina's Fate
Saving Angelina

The end of the week came and they needed to deposit the week's proceeds in the bank. Usually, Dominic does this but because Angie has been learning about running the shop, she wanted to make the deposit. This had been a busy week with a few big jobs completed so they had an unusually large amount to deposit.

Angie took the checks and verified that they were all signed. Then she verified each was listed on the deposit slip and slipped the checks into the bank pouch. Then she counted the cash and verified the number on the deposit slip and put the cash into the bank pouch. She also put the deposit slip in as well. Then she put the pouch into her purse, told her father she was leaving and left for the bank. When she arrived at the bank, she parked and went in. She got in line for one of the tellers and patiently waited. As she waited, she had an odd feeling that something was going to happen. But she didn't know what. She felt alert as if adrenalin was pumping into her veins. She scanned the room and saw nothing out of the ordinary. She saw people talking to tellers and others waiting in line. A few were filling out deposit or withdrawal slips. But still she felt adrenalin. She turned and looked towards the person in front of her. Then she had an image flash in her head of someone with a ski mask. Then she had another flash image of a gun kicked out of a hand. She thought it was odd. The images flashed in her head so fast she was just barely able to recognize what they were. As she waited, two guys, both with guns and ski masks came running into the bank. "DON'T ANYONE MOVE!" One screamed. Then they both started to push everyone to move together. They got everyone together at the end of the teller counter. One of them went looking for the security guard. He didn't see him.

"WHERE IS THE SECURITY GUARD?" He screamed at one of the tellers while pointing his gun at her.

She was so scared she almost couldn't answer. "I don't know. He is here somewhere."

Angie scanned the lobby and watched these guys. The first guy screamed, "NOW, EVERYONE MOVE TO THE BACK OF THE BANK. C'MON, MOVE!" Everyone began to walk around to towards the back of the bank. The other guy went to the door to keep a lookout.

"MOVE IT. LETS GO!" The first guy used his gun to wave everyone to the back." C'MON, LETS GO! MOVE IT!" He screamed.

Angie was moving slowly and ended up following the last of the people. The guy was behind her aiming his gun at her. Angie waited until they were out of sight of the first guy and she spun, grabbed the gun on the barrel and pushed it away from everyone and herself. Then she grabbed the rear and twisted it up and pulled it from his hand. The guy groaned because this broke his finger. She tossed the gun aside. This only took a couple of seconds. She then hit him with a palm heal punch and broke his nose. When he grabbed his nose and she did a reverse 360 degree round house to the side of his head and his head slammed against the wall, which was brick and he fell. He did not move.

When everyone heard something happening, they turned to look and the guy was laying on the floor already. All they heard was a grunt. Angie picked up the gun and handed it to one of the tellers and told everyone to go into the back room out of sight and stay there. Everyone went fast.

Angie grabbed the guy's legs and dragged him into an office and put him behind the desk. She left the office and stepped around the corner and waited. Within a minute or two the other guy came looking for his partner. He had his gun in front of him and was walking slowly, looking around and he called out to his partner, "Where the hell are you? This isn't what we planned, where are you?"

He was walking slowly, and the bank guard ran out of the back room pointing his gun and the robber shot him. The bank guard's gun went off and shot the ceiling. Angie saw this and immediately came out from around the corner and kicked the gun out of the robber's hand. He was shocked at the move as he did not see her. She got into her stance and he threw a punch and she expertly blocked it and broke his arm with the usual Aikido move. He screamed and he looked as if he didn't understand what happened. Angie's moves have been increasingly faster due to her training. She followed with a few kicks to his side which likely fractured a few ribs. He grabbed his side from the pain and bent over some. He stood up and went to punch with his other fist and screamed, "You're gona die bitch!" She blocked it and then kicked out one of his knees and he fell hard. As he tried to get up Angie said sternly, "Get up and they will take you out in a body bag." He stayed down.

Angie turned and found a couple of patrons were trying to help the guard. He had been hit in the side of his abdomen. She scanned the area and spotted a sweater on the back of a chair. She rushed over and grabbed it, wadded it up and had the guard hold it on the wound to help stop the bleeding. One of the people screamed, "He's getting up!"

Angie turned and saw that the guy had pulled himself up and was trying to get to his gun that was on the floor across the room. She jumped up and ran at the guy then jumped, cocked her leg and snapped her foot in his chest and he flew back over a desk and his head crashed against a post and he fell limp.

Sargent Hernandez came running around the corner just as Angie had jumped. He saw her mid-air kicking the guy in the chest with her foot. He was shocked at the power of her kick. He couldn't believe this had been Angie when he saw the guy fly over the desk. He was kind of a big guy and he thought, "She can't be more than 110-115 pounds."

When she landed, Angie saw Sargent Hernandez and screamed, "Call an ambulance, the guard was hit."

Sargent Hernandez called for an ambulance. Angie said, "The other one is laying in the office over there." She pointed at the office and another officer ran to check. Both guys were out cold, and one had a broken arm and knee.

Sargent Hernandez was shocked. He had never believed Lieutenant Edwards when he told him about Angie. Now he saw it firsthand. Angie, "I just saw what you did and I can't believe it. What happened here?"

"These two guys tried to rob the bank and ushered everyone to the back. I didn't know what they were going to do. As soon as we were out of sight of the first guy, I engaged the first one, took his gun away, broke his nose and kicked him and he hit the wall and was knocked out. Then I dragged him into the office out of sight. I hid around the corner. And when the second one came looking for him, the guard ran out of the back room and got shot by the second guy. I came out and ended it sir. I kicked his gun out of his hand and he tried to punch me and I broke his arm. Then I kicked him in the ribs a few times which likely broke a few of his ribs. Then he did not back down so I broke his knee and he fell. As I went to help the guard, and someone screamed the guy started to get up and go for his gun, so I ran and kicked him in the chest and he flew over the desk and his head slammed into the post and he went down as you saw."

Sargent Hernandez stood there shocked and in awe at what Angie had done. He was shaking his head in disbelief even though he witnessed her kicking this guy. He thought, "Maybe she can fight like Joe Singso."

Soon news trucks pulled up and people jumped out and began to set up. They all were in front of the bank trying to find out anything about what happened. As they were setting up, an ambulance pulled up and the paramedics took the gurney and went into the bank. The news tried to follow but were held back by the police. The officer said, "The scene hasn't been secured yet. No one will be allowed inside."

All the news channels set up outside and began their broadcast. There were radio station news people there as well.

Dominic was in the office working when Jack came in a little riled up. "Dom, didn't Angie go to the bank?"

"Yes, why?"

"The news on the radio said that there was a robbery in progress at the Arizona Bank on Oracle. I hope Angie wasn't there."

"She left a while ago, so she likely missed it. At least I hope she did." He reached and turned on the radio he had in the office.

"We're here at the scene of an attempted bank robbery at Arizona Bank at 7130 N. Oracle Rd. This is the scene of a bank robbery gone wrong. We were told that two gunshots were fired and a bank security guard was hit. There have been rumors of a young woman defusing the situation but that cannot be confirmed. The paramedics are rolling out the security guard now. He has an oxygen mask on and they are holding something on his side. It appears that he has been shot."

As he was speaking the paramedics rolled out the security guard and put him in the ambulance. As it pulled away another ambulance pulled up. The paramedics pulled out the gurney and entered the bank. Everyone waited for additional information.

"Oh my God, it had to be Angie!" Dominic said.

The radio newsman continued, "They are bringing out someone now on a gurney and it he appears to have been beaten. One arm is bandaged up in a splint along with one leg. He is holding an ice pack on his head. An officer is getting into the ambulance with this person. There is another person holding an ice pack on the side of his head being helped out with two officers. He doesn't appear to be able to stand on his own. Officer, can you give us an update?" He just went by and didn't answer. "There are many people coming out from the back of the bank along with a few officers that we can see through the windows."

Dominic and Jack were staring at the radio waiting for anything more. The person on the radio continued talking this whole time.

After about 15 minutes the police were letting people leave the bank. Sargent Hernandez told Angie, "Maybe you should leave with the crowd so you don't get stopped by the news. Make sure you go to the station to make a statement."

"Yes sir. I will drive there directly, thank you, sir." Angie mixed and left with the crowd.

As this was playing out, Johnny was watching TV. He had called in to work sick today. He wasn't paying too much attention until they said that there were rumors of a young woman defusing the situation. At that point he was glued to the TV. He was watching as everyone was leaving the bank. "Is that Angie?" he said out loud. "That's her. She did it again. Dam it! She is always on TV."

Even though she had not been interviewed or identified he knew it was her. "Why do they keep focusing on her? Dam it!" He stood and almost kicked his TV again. Now he was beyond angry. His face was red and he was looking for something to kick so he kicked the wall and put a hole in it and screamed. Then he picked up the chair he was sitting on and threw it down. One of the legs broke.

The news guy stopped another officer and asked, "Can you give us an update officer?" All the news people gathered around.

"There was an attempted robbery and one of the patrons defused the situation. The bank guard was shot but it is not life threatening. He was sent to the hospital. We have the two suspects in custody."

"Who was the patron that defused this officer?"

"I cannot release that information at this time."

"Can I have your name, for the record sir?"

"My name is am Sargent Hernandez."

"They cannot release that information? Why not? They have done it every other time. It had to be Angie. Who else could it have been?" Dominic said.

After another ten minutes they decided they would not get any additional information about the attempted robbery. They just went back to work, although Dominic was pre-occupied thinking about Angie.

After another hour and a half Angie was able to go back to the shop. Dominic saw through the front windows when Angie turned onto 2nd St. When she pulled into the back lot, Dominic ran out to meet her. "Are you OK? You are not hurt? We heard about it on the radio."

"I am fine father, but I was not able to make the deposit because of this." Angie was angry. She got out of the CUDA and locked the door. They walked in together. As they walked in everybody asked her if she was OK. "I am fine." They could see that she was angry.

When they got up front Dominic wanted to go into the office and talk. He closed the door. Right away Angie said, "I cannot believe this, I finally get to make the deposit myself and two fools had to disrupt it." She reached into her purse and pulled out the bank pouch and handed it to Dominic. "We need to wait until the bank reopens. Possibly tomorrow."

"That is what you are worried about? They said two guys with guns tried to rob the bank."

"It was not a big deal. The first guy wanted everyone to go in the back of the bank and followed pointing his gun at us. As soon as we were out of the sight of the other guy I turned and took his gun away. I do not know what he had planned but I did not let him do anything. Then I broke his nose and did a 360 degree reverse roundhouse and his head hit the brick wall and he fell. I dragged him into an office. Then I went and hid around the corner. Everyone went into a back room. When the second guy came looking for the first guy the guard came running out of the back room and the second guy shot him and the guard's gun went off and he shot the ceiling. I took that as an opportunity to end it and kicked the gun out of his hand. Then he tried to punch me and I broke his arm and kicked him in the ribs. He wasn't stopping so I broke his knee. He went down. I ran to the guard and found something for him to hold on his wound and someone screamed that the guy was getting up. I turned and he had pulled himself up and was trying to get to his gun. I ran and jumped and kicked him in the chest and he flew over a desk and hit a post. Just as I jumped Sargent Hernandez came around the corner and saw me kick this guy. He was shocked. I was not in any danger at the point I stopped these two, father."

"Angie, this was a big deal. You are talking about it as if it was just a normal thing."

"It could have been a big deal, but I stopped it beforehand. "Maybe he was planning on shooting everyone, I do not know. But I did not want to wait to find out." Angie was beginning to get used to these situations now that they were happening more and more. "Father, I just refuse to be a victim. I will fight until the end if necessary."

"Angie, each time something such as this happens all of us become very worried. I always think, what if this is the time you do not make it.?"

"Father I will be fine. If I had waited more people could have been shot. The security guard was too much in a hurry to confront this guy and that could have gotten many of us shot. I waited to be out of the second guy's sight before I acted. I wanted to take them one at a time. This is all part of my training. If I would have been in real danger the guys would not have survived."

"What do you mean by that?"

"If I felt my life was in danger, I would have taken them out with the first or second kick."

"You could do that?

"Yes father. There are certain moves I would use that would kill them instantly. And father?"

"What is it, Angie?"

As I was standing in line and a few moments before these guys came in, I felt somewhat panicked had pictures flash in my mind of someone wearing a ski mask then of a gun kicked out of someone's hand. At the time I glanced around the bank and everything appeared normal. I thought the feeling was strange. The first was the guy that ushered us to the back and the second was the second guy. I saw myself kicking the gun out of his hand. But I did not know it was me at the time."

"You saw it before they came in?"

"Yes father. Only an instant, however. It flashed in my mind and maybe a few moments later they came in."

By the time the evening news came on they had more information about the botched robbery along with the two guy's names and mugshots and that Angelina Tucci was the one that defused the situation.

The next day, Saturday, Angie went to work as usual. The guys asked her about what happened, and she told them about it. It was late morning when an elderly lady walked into the shop. She walked up to the counter and asked, "Young man, is this the place where Angelina Tucci works?"

Jack looked at her for a moment, "Yes ma'am. She works in the shop."

"She works in the shop? What does she do?"

"She is an auto mechanic."

"She is? Her? That sweet girl? Could I see please? I can't believe it."

Jack looked at her and thought it would not be a problem to point her out. He walked her around the counter to the entrance of the shop and pointed to Angie. She was bent over the fender of a car and looked up and saw the lady with Uncle Jack. "Oh, I see, that's amazing! I have something to say to her. I believe she saved my life yesterday and I wanted to thank her if I may."

Jack walked the lady back to the front and asked her to wait. He went in back, "Angie, there is someone here to see you."

She looked up and put the wrench down that she had in her hand, took her gloves off and set them on the bench. She walked up front. "Who is here to see me Uncle Jack?" Jack glanced to the elderly lady. Angie walked over and said, "How may I help you Ma'am?"

"You are very polite dear. I came here to thank you personally for saving my life. I believe if you did not do what you did, we all may have been killed. I had a bad feeling that they were going to shoot all of us. Then I saw you kicking that last man and I was shocked. I was going to try to help the security guard and I happened to look up and saw you. You are a hero!"

"Ma'am, thank you for your sentiments but I just did what was necessary to keep everyone safe. I do not believe that makes me a hero. I just stopped anything further from happening."

Dear, you did a heroic thing. At least it was from my point of view. I don't know how you did what you did. It looked like you were from a movie. I didn't know that kind of thing was real. But you did save all of our lives. I just wanted to thank you in person dear." She reached out and grabbed Angie's hand and squeezed it. She smiled, turned and left.

Uncle Jack said, "That was very sweet of her Angie. She came here just to thank you. You touch so many people in such unique ways. I hope someday you can acknowledge how many people's lives you have changed."

Angie smiled, turned and went back to work.

Johnny finally returned to the Dojo in mid-August 1976. His sensei did not want him back there until his arm was completely healed and he could fight again. Johnny wanted to learn more ways to fight because of how easily Angie hurt him but his sensei did not agree. Johnny had gone to this Dojo to learn karate and train for competition. His sensei thought other training would easily disqualify him. His sensei did not believe that Johnny would be able to keep other kinds of fighting out of competition.

His sensei concentrated on the same abilities as he has been working on. "Johnny, you work get black belt. This best way advance."

Johnny didn't like this. "Getting a black belt is just practicing. I need to learn to fight better. It was too easy for that bitch to beat me. I need to learn defense for that."

"Johnny, you learn competition. Other kind fight disqualify you. Best get blackbelt."

"I need to learn to defend myself from other kinds of fighting. That's what I need." Johnny was defiant. He wanted to learn so he could beat Angie. He thought that then the TV would show him and not her. He was so obsessed with beating Angie it was all he could think about. 'How does he know what I need. I need to beat Angie and show her I'm better. She deserves this.' As he drove home, this was all he could think about.

As days passed, Johnny continued to become more arrogant bragging about being a champion to people outside of the Dojo. He was picking fights with anyone he could provoke to show that no one can beat him. His arrogance built fast and this got back to his sensei.

His sensei called Johnny into his office for a talk. "Johnny, hear you pick fight outside dojo. You no pick fight people. Not what this about. You continue disgrace Dojo and I. I not teach this. It not right. You stop. Understand?"

"You can't tell me what I can and can't do outside of here. I do what I want." Johnny said.

"You do this you get blackballed here. All I say." He dismissed Johnny. After this talk Johnny began to get arrogant even in the Dojo. He stopped pulling kicks and punches during sparing and a few students end up hurt, fortunately not seriously, but hurt none the less.

By the end of August Johnny's Sensei called him into his office again. "Johnny, you disgrace Dojo, I and students. Hurt students for fun. You hurt them and laugh. Not good. You leave. You no welcome here. You train in Tucson no more. End Karate for you. Go."

Johnny was angry. He left the office and slammed the door so hard the glass window broke. He grabbed his things from his locker and walked out knocking other students aside. "Asshole! I'll show him. He can't do this to me. This is all Angie's fault. It started with her, bitch. I'll show her, I'm going to get back at her somehow." He was screaming out loud as he walked through the Dojo and to his car. He got in and sped away.

Johnny's Sensei was worried. He thought Johnny was becoming very aggressive and he did not like that he was picking fights. He thought about Johnny's fight with Angie, the girl from his brother's Dojo. He decided to call his brother to discuss the situation, especially because Johnny left saying he wanted to get back at her.

"Kotomi, Akio, I kick Johnny out. He blackball. No teach more. I worried he say he get back at girl that that beat him. That Angie. We need work more. Angie need prepare. No want see hurt, not right."

"Akio, I understand. We prepare Angie. I talk with her."

While Johnny was at work the next day, he began to start trouble with his boss and one of his coworkers. Johnny works at a warehouse. He drives a forklift loading pallets of product onto trucks. Lately he has had verbal fights with coworkers but today he was very arrogant and decided he wanted to use a specific forklift. Usually, each of the guys there just use a forklift that no one is using. But Johnny wanted the one that a Larry was using. He liked this one because it was new.

Johnny walked over to the forklift and told Larry, "Hey I wana use this forklift, get off."

"No, I'm using it now. Use the other one." Larry said feeling a little annoyed. He drove away.

Johnny went after him. "I want this forklift now, asshole."

"What's the problem? Just use the other one." Larry said as he lifted a pallet.

"I WANT THIS ONE NOW!" Johnny screamed.

His boss heard this and looked over to see what the screaming was.

Larry ignored him and kept working.

Johnny reached over and grabbed Larry and pulled him off the forklift and threw him on the ground. He got on it and started driving away.

Johnny's boss ran over to Larry, "Are you ok Larry?"

"Yea." He replied angrily while brushing off his shirt and pants. He was just angry and shocked at what Johnny had done.

"What happened Larry?" his boss asked.

"Johnny just came over and said he wanted that forklift and when I said he should just use the other one he pulled me off and took it." Larry said.

His boss shook his head and screamed, "Johnny! Johnny! Come here!"

Johnny drove over and said, "What?"

"Why did you pull Larry off of the forklift?"

"This is my forklift, that's why. He should know better." Johnny said.

"Johnny, you don't own this forklift. And I never told anyone that any forklift is theirs. Turn it off and get off now." He called Larry. Larry came over. "Johnny, use the other forklift. Next time you do anything like this you will be fired. I am sick of your disrespect and causing trouble around here." He was already tired of the trouble Johnny had been causing there lately.

"Make Larry use the other one."

"I said get off." His boss said.

"No, it's mine." Johnny said in a snotty way.

"OK Johnny, you're fired pick up your stuff and leave now."

"The hell I will." Johnny said.

"I'll just call the police then." His boss walked away.

"Johnny got off the forklift, looked at Larry and punched him in the chest. This knocked him down.

"What did you do that for?" Larry asked.

"Fuck you." Johnny said. He went and grabbed his things and left. "Bitch gets me fired now. She is ruining my life. I need to kill that bitch." He said as he was walking to his car.

Johnny's boss went back to Larry and asked, "Are you ok Larry? I saw him punch you."

"I'll live." He was ribbing his chest and got back on the forklift and continued working.

Johnny was livid. He was almost screaming and beating on the steering wheel with his fist as he drove home. Then he had an idea. He had remembered that one to the TV news reporters joked and suggested that maybe Angelina was psychic because they thought she found those girls so quickly. He mumbled, "Yeah, we can kidnap the bitch's mother and use her as bait. Angie will know and come for her. We will be ready and we can kill her mother in front of her and then beat her to death, that bitch. I got to call Andy, Lenny, Rick, Donny and Jake. They will help."

Later that day Johnny called Andy told him how he wanted to get that bitch Angie for ruining his life. He told Andy about his idea. He knew Andy wanted her dead too because she killed his brother while his brother and his friends were robbing Dom's Auto. He knew Andy hated her for that.

The next night Angie went to the Dojo as usual and changed into her Gi. Her sensei called her to the office. "Angie, time work different exercise. You do isometric. Begin tonight. This work on strength and speed. You make equipment." He stood up. "Follow." He took her into the exercise room and showed her some equipment she had always seen but never saw anyone use. One was a wood frame with two uprights with holes every 3 inches up to the top. It had a dowel rod that fit through the holes across the two uprights. It also had a plywood base to stand on. The other was a piece of 2 x 6 about 3 feet wide with a chain hooked to an eye bolt in the center and it. It had a 2" dowel rod on the other end which also had an eye bolt in the middle. The chain was attached with an s-hook on each end which made it adjustable and there was a heavy spring at the lower end. This was also attached to a plywood base.

He showed Angie how to use it and explained, "Angie isometric exercise tense muscles no movement. You tense muscle and hold 15 sec. relax. Do three time then move another hole and repeat. You do full range of arms, legs, back. We work on all muscles. In short time you increase strength. Speed increase too."

He worked with Angie through the session. Angie said. "I will make these for home and begin these exercises. Should I stop my regular workouts?"

"No keep. Add these to work out every other day."

"I will. I will make this equipment tomorrow after work and begin." She dried her sweat and went to the meditation room. She always ends workouts with meditation.

Afterword's, she changed into her street cloths and went home. She explained to her parents what she would need to build tomorrow for new exercises and showed her father a sketch of how it will look when finished. Then she went and took a shower and ate dinner with her mother and father. As always, she helped her mother clean up.

The next morning Dominic went to the lumber yard. He bought the wood, chain, hardware and he also picked up a Forstner wood bit slightly larger than the dowel rod diameter. He brought all of it back to the shop. Now Angie would have everything necessary to build the new equipment.

After work Dominic went and helped Angie build the new exercise equipment. When they finished, they put it in the back of the pick-up and went home.

When they got home Dominic helped Angie carry everything into the garage where her other equipment was. They set it up. Then Angie demonstrated how it was used and explained to him what isometric exercises were. Then they went to have dinner.

Angie went out to exercise at about 8:00 as usual. Her regimen now took longer as she added the isometric exercises. When she finished, she sat down her meditation blanket and meditated. Afterword's, she went into the house, took a shower and got ready for bed. Tonight, she sat with her mother and father and watched some TV. After about an hour, she said good night and went to bed.

On Saturday night Angie and her friends met at the Bum Steer. It had become a weekly thing to go out and eat, sing and dance. They went in and got their usual table. They briefly talked about the bank robbery attempt. These incidents were happening more and more, so the discussions were becoming brief.

"Angie, like, don't you get tired of needing to fight? I don't know how you do it." Denise asked.

"Well, I do not have a choice, Denise. I feel as if these situations find me. They just happen." Angie said.

"Like, I think I would get crazy. I dunno."

"Angie, it seems like you aren't bothered as much by these fights anymore. I don't understand how you do it. Then you see things too on top of that?" Gina shook her head in disbelief."

The waitress came and they ordered beer, cheeseburgers and fries.

Angie was becoming more comfortable with the usual crowd and would now occasionally dance with some of the guys. It appeared that she really enjoyed it. Gina thought it was about time. She was beginning to worry about Angie because she said she didn't want to date. She never understood that, but now that she was dancing with some of the guys, she thought that possibly she would start going on dates.

They all danced and ate. All of them really liked the cheeseburgers and fries there. They thought that they were better than they could get anywhere else. The cheeseburgers were big and usually none of them would finish a whole burger.

As they were eating, an image of what appeared to be a letter opener in someone's neck flashed in Angie's head. Somehow, she knew it was shaped like a sword. She thought that was odd. She said, "A letter opener?" making an odd face. She thought she just thought it but Janet looked at her and said, "What about a letter opener?"

"Oh, excuse me, it was just an image that flashed in my head. I did not realize I said that out loud."

"That's so weird." Janet said.

"I see many images. Usually, I never determine what these are."

"I still think that would be weird to see things like that." Janet looked a little flustered.

Angie and Gina usually sang karaoke. The others didn't really like singing karaoke, so they just watched. Occasionally one of the guys would ask Angie out but as usual, she politely declined.

When they were all sitting Gina said, "There's this guy at school that keeps asking me out. He seems nice. You think I should go out with him?"

Denise said, "Like, why, don't you go out with him? If he seems nice. What's his name?"

"I think I would if someone seemed nice and asked me." Janet said.

"I'd be afraid if I didn't really know him. But that's just me." Karen said.

"Maybe I will. It's just one date, right? His name is Jeff."

"Follow your feelings, Gina. What does you first thought tell you? That is the one I always follow. It is usually the correct one." Angie said.

Gina thought for a minute, "Yea, I guess I will go out with him, if he asks me again."

"You could always ask him, Gina." Angie said.

"I couldn't do that. I'm not that confident."

"Just ask him. It is that easy. You could possibly say something such as, 'Hi, I have been thinking, I will take you up on your offer if it is still open.' He will likely like that." Angie said.

"I don't know, maybe. Oh look, the karaoke is open again." Gina jumped up to sing.

Janet looked at Angie, "You are so confident, Angie. I wish I could be more like that. I usually feel self-conscious and freeze up."

"You freeze up? You are usually forward with people; I would not think that. I believe that self-consciousness begins with worrying about what someone will think about you. If you can stop worrying about what others think, your confidence will rise. Worrying about what others think is something you cannot control. It is unreasonable to worry about something you cannot do anything about. People will either like you or not."

"That sounds so reasonable but it isn't that easy." Janet said.

Gina waited at the stage to sing. She had to wait for the current person to finish. Then she stepped up.

"Gina's going to sing." Janet said. They all turned to watch.

As Gina was singing, they continued eating.

Gina came back and they all continued to eat and talk.

"There's a guy at work that is kind of cute. I catch him looking at me a lot. I think he likes me. We talk a little during work." Karen said. "Maybe he will ask me out."

"What's his name? What does he look like?" Janet asked.

"His name is Curt. He's a little taller than me, has short blonde hair and blue eyes."

"Like, do you like him?" Denise asked.

"I guess. I don't really know much about him. Just that he has worked there a couple of years. He's a salesman. You know, he gets shoes for people to try on and puts them on them."

"Does he have a car?" Janet asked.

"Well, he leaves in an older I think Duster."

"So, he has a car! Cool!" Paula said. "You think he'll ask you out?"

"I don't know. Maybe."

"You could just ask him, like Angie said." Paula giggled as she said it.

"Yeah right. Me ask him. I still get embarrassed just talking to customers."

"I'm just kidding. I couldn't do that either." Paula said. "Janet, anyone at you work that you like?"

"No one I noticed. I guess that's the problem working in the Women's Clothing department."

"There have to be guys working there in other parts of the store aren't there?" Sherri asked.

"I guess. I just haven't paid much attention, that's all. How about you, Sherri?"

"Since that Jason thing, I haven't felt like having a relationship. I don't really look at any guys like that at school. Paula?"

"There isn't anyone my age at the lawyer's office." Paula said. "Every so often someone comes in but who knows what they are there for. For all I know they are murderers or thieves."

"Really, like, you think every young guy that comes into the lawyer's office are a murderer or thief?" Denise asked.

"No. but I'm not supposed to talk to the clients so how would I know." Paula smirked and bit into her cheeseburger.

"Like, I wish some guy would just sweep me off my feet. Maybe he would have lots of money too."

"Is that what you want Denise?" Gina asked. "I would have guessed you would want someone that likes to do fun things and hang out with you. I don't know. I never thought of you as the romantic type."

"You're probably right. Like, I can dream, can't I? Dreams don't have to be real."

"No, they do not need to be real. Denise." Angie said. "I think I am going to sing Angie Baby." She took a sip of her beer and went up to the stage.

When the intro to the song began everyone turned to see who was going to sing. The crowd clapped when they saw it was Angie. At the end the crowd roared. Then Gina took the mike. She sang "Born to be bad." Lots of guys screamed because Gina looks hot and she moves seductively when she sings. She finished and the guys screamed. Gina loves the attention. She went and sat down.

"Gina, your singing has been improving significantly." Angie said.

"You really think so?"

"I think it has." Sherri said. "Everyone is screaming a lot for you now."

"Like, have you been practicing? It sounds like it." Denise said.

"Has Angie been teaching you? We know she helps you with your math." Paula asked.

Angie looked at them kind of unbelievingly and rolled her eyes. "I would not know how to teach someone to sing."

"How did you lean to sing so well?" Paula asked. "You took lessons, right?"

"Of course not. I always sing along with songs when I hear them. That is all. It is just how I sing." Angie said.

They all got up and went to dance.

During this night a guy asked Angie to dance, and she danced a fast song with him. Then the guy stayed to dance a slow song with her and put his arms around her. She did not like this particularly but went along so as not to make a scene. She thought, "it is only one dance." So, she stayed. Gina thought that maybe she would rest her head on his shoulder or kiss him. She didn't and when the song was over, she was going to turn to go sit down, he reached out with his hands to grab her head to kiss her. Immediately Angie grabbed one of his hands and put it in a wrist lock. He immediately went down on his knees. She didn't do it too hard, just enough to show him she could break it if she chose. She didn't notice but his buddies were laughing hysterically when they saw this. She said, "I just danced with you. That does not give you permission to try to kiss me."

Some other people saw this but not everyone because the next song was playing. "OK, OK I'm sorry, I didn't mean anything."

Angie let him go and walked to the table and sat down. She was somewhat angry from this. She sat down next to Paula and said, "I cannot believe that guy. He tried forcibly kiss me."

"I wasn't really watching, what did you do?"

"I just grabbed his hand and put him into a wrist lock. He went down on his knees. I told him that dancing with me does not give him permission to kiss me."

"What did he say?"

"He said he was sorry. I did not believe him."

"You would think everyone would know about you by now. I guess not." Paula giggled.

"Hopefully no one saw, and we will not get kicked out. This is what I worry about when we go out, someone trying to take it further. I do not want to fight when we go out."

"I bet he won't ask you to dance again." Paula giggled again.

The song ended and Gina came to the table to drink some of her beer. "Angie, what was that guy doing down on the floor? I saw him get up. Was that part of his dancing?"

"No, he tried to forcibly kiss me. I put him in a wrist lock."

Gina laughed. "I bet you surprised him. I bet he didn't expect that."

Paula said, "I bet he won't try that again for a while on anyone else now." she giggled again. Paula giggles a lot when she drinks.

"He could have easily ruined tonight. This could get us thrown out. This is what I always fear when we come here. I feel as though sometime someone will want to go further and try to fight."

Gina said, "Angie, don't think like that. I don't think any of the guys here are going to want to fight. Well, at least with a girl."

"But fights seem to find me. I continue to have the feeling that somehow, I am attracting them."

"C'mon Angie. Lighten up. We're here to have fun. Nothing's going to happen. Let's go dance, C'mon." Gina reached out and grabbed Angie's hand.

"Alright." Angie got up and went with Gina to dance.

When the song was done Angie went to sit down. As she was walking to the table the guy came up to her and she was ready. He said, "Angie, I'm sorry. I shouldn't have done that. My asshole college buddy's bet me I couldn't kiss you. They knew what you can do and wanted to see you do something to me. I don't think that was funny. That was stupid of me to do. Some other guy saw what you did and told me about you. If I knew I wouldn't have done that. I'm really sorry, it was stupid."

She thought he sounded sincere. "I accept your apology." She went and sat down.

Paula asked her, "What did he say? I thought you were going to hit him."

"He apologized. He said his college friends made a bet that he could not kiss me. He said some guy that saw what I did told him about me. Then he said if he knew he would not have tried. He sounded sincere."

"Wow! I didn't expect that. I would have thought with all of the news everyone would know. I guess not." And she giggled a little more.

None of them were aware of this, but a few tables away from them, some people were sitting watching Angie to see how she looked and how she acted. There were five friends. Olive, her boyfriend Georgie; Alex and his girlfriend Ally, and Jose. "See that girl that used a wrist lock on that guy?"

"Yeah, What about her?" Ally asked.

"She's the one. That's the bitch I want to get back!"

"Olive, you mean beat up right?" Ally asked.

"NO, I want to kill her."

"What did she do to you?" Ally didn't understand. She thought they had all gone there for some fun. She didn't know they were there to scope out Angie.

"She killed my brother and now I want to kill her." Olive said.

"Won't you get in trouble? Aren't you on probation?" Ally didn't understand why she would do something like that.

"I have a foolproof plan. There is no way I will get caught." She flashed a snide smile. Olive thought she planned this out so well that nothing could happen. She thought she was the smart one between her and her brother. She thought, 'That's why he got killed because he was stupid. I am so much smarter.' She sat there basking in self-praise. She always thought she was better at most things than her brother. Even in Karate. Olive was a brown belt when she stopped training. She thought that was more than enough to defend against anyone. 'Pabby was just a blue belt working on his Purple.' But she still missed him.

Angie got up and went to the disk jockey and asked him something. She took the mike and turned to the crowd. "Today is the birthday of one of my friends. Could everyone join me singing Happy Birthday? This is for you Gina." The disk jockey played happy birthday. Angie began, "Happy Birthday to you." And everyone followed.

When she went to sit down Gina went to Angie and said, "Thank you Angie, that was really nice." Angie saw that she had tears in her eyes. They hugged and sat down.

Then Angie opened her purse and reached in and pulled out an envelope. It said Happy Birthday Gina on it. "Happy Birthday Gina." Angie said as she handed it to her.

"You got me a birthday Card? I can't believe it." She opened the envelope and pulled out the card. It was plain on the front and said, "Open me." Gina opened it and it was a pop-up card with a birthday cake, balloons and fireworks. And the cake said, Happy Birthday."

Gina got tears in her eyes and hugged Angie again. "This is so sweet! Angie. You are such a good friend!"

Then everyone else pulled cards out of their purses and gave them to Gina. "I can't believe this! Everyone got me a card?" She was a little overwhelmed. You guys are all so great!" She opened each one.

She didn't notice Angie got up and walked to the door to the kitchen. She talked to the waitress and came and sat back down. A few minutes later the waitress brought a cupcake with a birthday candle in it, lit it and said, "Happy Birthday!" She handed it to Gina.

Gina didn't know what to say. They all said, "make a wish and blow out the candle!"

Gina thought for a minute and blew out the candle. "You guys are too much. I can't believe you did this for me. Now she had tears rolling down her cheeks. "I never cry. I don't know what to say. Thank you everyone! If this was bigger, I would share it with everyone." It was a small cupcake maybe an inch and a half in diameter. She ate it in two bites.

Georgie leaned to Olive and said, "That girl sings really good, doesn't she? And that was nice singing for her friend."

Olive looked at him with disgust and elbowed him in his side.

"What did you do that for?"

"Georgie, that's the girl! How can you say that about her?"

"What, that's her? She seems so nice."

"That's the bitch that killed Pabby."

"Really? She's the one? She doesn't look like she could hurt any-body." Georgie said.

"Didn't you see what she did to that guy? He just wanted to kiss her and she put him in a wrist lock." Olive said.

"That's what she did? I thought he fell."

"Don't you see good? Alex and Jose, did you guys see?"

"We saw. She's the karate girl? The one that killed everyone and your brother?" Jose asked.

"Yeah. That's her. Take a good look. Under those looks is a cold-blooded killer."

Ally looked at Alex and asked, "She killed Pabby. Why didn't the police do anything then?"

"The police said it was justified because he was going to shoot her." Alex said.

"Won't Olive get in trouble? Isn't she on probation already?" Ally was kind of an airhead. She didn't understand most of the things Olive and the guys did. She thought they were just friends.

"Yeah, but Olive want's revenge. She says she doesn't care. Besides, she has a plan so she won't get caught."

"What plan? You're not gonna help, are you? I don't want you to. She's gonna get you in trouble." She had tears in her eyes.

"Don't worry, I'm not gonna get in trouble. Her plan is fool proof." Alex said.

"But didn't that girl kill all of those guys? The news said they all had guns and she killed all of them. Everyone says that girl is deadly. They say it doesn't matter if you have a gun. I'm scared, I don't want to lose you, Alex."

"Don't worry. I will be fine. She can't do anything with Georgie and I both pointing guns at her together. And if she moves, we'll all shoot her. It's fool proof."

Ally was afraid. She knew what everyone said about this girl. Ally's other friends have told her that this girl fights just like Joe Singso from all of those karate movies. 'And Joe Singso never got shot,' she thought. She was afraid. She gulped down her beer and wanted another. She had a feeling something bad would happen.

Angie and her friends danced and drank. Angie and Gina sang a couple of more songs. By about 11:00 they left.

After last year's July 4th celebration, everyone decided that Dominic and Lizzy's house was the best for it. Besides the pool area was perfect for party's and the location of their house gave everyone a good view of the fireworks.

Everyone was there. Lizzy and Angie made the roast beef, gravy and mashed potatoes. Aunt Lilly brought salad, rolls and vegetables. Grandmother Kristina brought fruit cocktail and she baked cherry pies and brought the whipped cream. Maria brought a large decorated Cannoli cake. Jack and Sofia brought a couple of bottles of Chianti and Carol, John and Sherri brought home made Hors d'oeuvres.

As now has become family tradition, Lizzy hired a server. Lizzy introduced her to all of the ladies. "Everyone, this is Ana our server for today."

All of the cousins and Sherri had changed into their swimsuits and had gone outside and into the pool. All of the men had also gone outside and were talking and drinking beer.

Lizzy had taken out a bottle of Cabernet Sauvignon and poured some for each of the ladies. "Dominic and I had this with dinner some time ago and we loved it. I bought a couple of bottles." She handed a glass to each and raised her glass and said, "Salute!"

Each took a sip. Maria commented, "Elizabeth, this has a wonderful flavor."

"Thank you, Maria."

Lizzy asked Ana to bring the Hors d' oeuvres outside. Then all of the ladies went outside to join the men.

All of the cousins were hitting a small beach ball to each other around the pool. They were screaming and having fun. After a bit they got out, grabbed their towels and dried off. Then they went into the house to get something to drink. They all sat at the table in the kitchen. They weren't worried about getting the chairs wet because this was the same dinette set that Dominic and Lizzy brought from the house on Yavapai. It was the one that Dominic's mother brought from their house when Dino, Dominic and Maria's father, had died. It was a classic 1940's set and the tabletop was Formica and the chairs were upholstered in vinyl. Each of them put on the t-shirt they each brought because if felt chilly in the air conditioning.

Angie took the pitcher of iced tea out of the refrigerator and put it on the table. Then she took out tumblers for each of them. She poured iced tea in each tumbler and handed them out to each of them. Then she put the pitcher back in the refrigerator and sat back down.

"Cuz," Shelly said, "Are you going to show us another self-defense move?"

"If everyone is interested I will."

They all said they were.

"Alright. Let us all go into the Arizona Room. We have an area rug in there so if anyone falls you won't just hit the tile."

Everyone got up and followed Angie into the Arizona Room. "Who would like to play the aggressor?"

"I will." Edward said.

"Edward, reach out and grab my shirt with both hands as a bully would."

Edward reached out and grabbed Angie's t-shirt one hand on each side just below her shoulders.

"Watch what I do, I will do it slowly for you all to see."

She put one arm under his arm inside and pushed it up then wrapped it around his arm tight and pulled his arm down and in from his elbow. Then she reached with her other arm and grabbed the other side of his head and pushed his head as she pulled his arm down and in.

This made him bend to that side and with her pushing his head he almost fell over. "Did you see what I did? Anyone that grabs you this way will not expect you to do anything, much less something like this." She let Edward stand up. When you do this, you do it fast and hard. The person will fall over. And when they fall, you would have pulled their arm in and they will not be able to cushion their fall. It is likely they will hit their head hard on the ground."

"That looks so easy." Shelly said.

"Now, each of you can try this. Shelly, come here." She came over. "I will grab your shirt and then you can try what I just showed you."

She came over and Angie grabbed her shirt. "Now take your arm and push it under mine." She did that. "Now wrap it around my arm and start pushing it down."

She tried and Angie used her other hand to help her move her arm in the correct position and pushed it down. "Put your other hand on the side of my head and push while you are pulling my arm down."

She did that and Angie started to fall to the side. Shelly stopped. Can I try that again?"

"Of course, Shelly." Angie grabbed her shirt again. Shelly tried it again herself and got her arm in the correct position and pushed Angie's arm down and reached out and pushed her head to the side. Angie started to lean over and almost lost her balance.

"That is easy!" Shelly said.

Edward said, "I want to try." He walked up to Angie and she grabbed his shirt. He moved his arm just as Shelly did and wrapped it around Angie's and pushed down. Then he reached and pushed her head to the side. Angie almost fell again. "This is so cool!"

Bella went next. Angie grabbed her shirt and Bella did the move. Again, Angie almost lost her balance. "That is easy!" she said.

Rosa did it next. She almost knocked Angie down as well. "That is so easy, cuz!" Rosa said.

Angie said, "Sherri, your turn." Sherri walked over and Angie grabbed her shirt. Sherri tried it and needed a little help from Angie to get her arm in the correct position. She pushed Angie's arm down and pushed her head with her other hand. Again, Angie almost lost her balance.

"If someone does this to you, you do this fast and as hard as you can. They will fall over and likely bang their head on the ground. And if you are on something hard such as a sidewalk or tile floor there is a good chance it will either knock them out or make them dizzy. This gives you time to run."

Edward said, "Wow! Now we know two cool moves. Thank you cuz. After you showed us the move last year it made me feel, aahh, I do not know. Not so afraid. I am not so afraid all of the time."

"Edward, I am happy it helped you. How about everyone else? Anyone else feel more confident?"

The cousins were talking along with Sherri. Shelly said, "Maybe that is it. I think we all have felt somewhat more confident. That is it."

"I am delighted that it has given all of you more confidence. Why do we not go back outside. I see the server has brought out the Hors d'oeuvres. Sherri, your mother's Hors d'oeuvres looked wonderful! I wish to try some." Angie led the way back outside. All of them went over to the table to try some Hors d'oeuvres.

Edward went over to his father. "Father?"

"Yes Edward."

"Angelina taught us another cool move."

"She did? Do you want to show us?"

"I don't know if it is a good idea here because we are on concrete. Angelina showed us in the Arizona Room because it has an area rug. She said if anyone fell it would be better on the rug. And this move makes you lose your balance."

"Is that so. Perhaps you can show me when we are back home then." Lilly and Carl have plush carpet in their Arizona Room.

"OK, Father." Edward was excited about showing his father.

About an hour later Lizzy went to ask Ana to begin to bring out the food. She cleared what was remaining of the Hors d'oeuvres and began to bring out the meal. When everything was out on the table Lizzy announced it was time to eat.

Everyone got some food and sat down. Dominic opened a bottle of Chianti and poured for everyone. When all of the adults had wine and the kids had iced tea, Dominic said grace. "Our Heavenly Father, please bless the feast we are about to partake, may it nourish our bodies. Thank you for the country you have given us and bless all those that made the ultimate sacrifice that our country could be free. Please bless those that are less fortunate than us. Amen."

Lizzy said, "Thank you Dominic." Everyone ate.

Everyone finished and Ana took all of the plates and silverware inside. Then she washed everything and stacked it on the counter.

After another hour Lizzy asked Ana to bring out the cake and pies. She had decided to have Ana cut pieces and place them on plates. Everyone had some of each.

"Maria, this cake is wonderful! Just as last year. Could you possibly give me the recipe?" Kristina asked.

"Of course. It is a recipe I found in a magazine."

"Really? It is from a magazine? I would never have guessed!"

Dominic, Carl, Enzo, Joseph and John were talking cars and about drag racing. "I have been proud of how Angie has been driving. It is almost unbelievable. It is as if she knows exactly when the light is going to turn green. I never have seen anyone so fast out of the hole. It is uncanny!" Dominic said.

"I agree. It is almost as though she leaves an instant before the light turns green. I have watched many times and it still amazes me." Jack said.

"It also appears that this has caused some damaged egos." Dominic said.

"There is that guy with the gray 427 Camaro that gets angry every time he races against her because he always loses to her. I kind of feel bad for his girlfriend." Jack said.

"Why do you feel bad for his girlfriend?" Carl asked. "Seems like an odd thing to say."

"Every time he races against Angie, he red lights. Then when I see him in the pit's afterword's, he throws things around. I have seen him scream at his girlfriend and push her. It is saddening. She usually cries."

"Really? What a jerk! That is terrible." Carl said. "Do you feel like doing something about it?"

"I usually want to, but what can I do?" Jack said.

"I have seen him do that as well. It is sad. He loses fairly, if that makes sense." Dominic said.

John said, "I would like to go with all of you sometime. I have never seen any drag races. I just hear about it from all of you. And now Sherri talks about it at times. Possibly we could all go as a family thing."

"We could do that. Lizzy has gone a few times and she has said that she enjoyed it. Possibly we could all go on Labor Day weekend. You would not see Angie and I race but it is a big weekend, and you would be able to see Top Fuel, Funny cars, gassers and usually they have wheel standers doing exhibition runs."

"What are wheel standers?" John asked.

"These are vehicles that are built for the purpose of running the whole quarter mile with the front wheels up. It is a thrill to see." Dominic said.

"Really? The whole quarter mile? That almost sounds impossible." John said.

"Later on, we could suggest it to everyone." Dominic said.

Shelly asked Angie, "Are you going drag racing on Labor Day? You always go that weekend, right?"

"Yes, we always go on Labor Day. It is one of the biggest racing weekends of the year. They call it the Winter Nationals."

"Why do they call it that?" Shelly asked.

"It is a weekend when all of the pro racers run. And it is almost winter time. They have all of the big names. And all year they race against each other and get points. At the end of the year the highest point car wins each class. And they have Nitro Funny cars. Those are my favorite."

"Why are they your favorite, cuz?" Shelly asked.

Then Edward asked, "What is a Nitro Funny Car?"

"Edward, Nitro Funny Cars are specially built cars that have engines that burn nitromethane fuel and make over six thousand horsepower. They have fiberglass bodies. The nitro engines are so loud that you can feel it in your chest. You need to see them to understand. I do not know if I can explain them. There is nothing else to compare them to."

"You mean like Uncle Dominic's car?" Edward asked. He has heard the Nova running at the shop a couple of times.

"No Edward, they are much louder, and you feel the concussions each time a plug fires." Angie was becoming excited just talking about them.

"Louder? I cannot imagine anything louder that Uncle Dominics car."

"There are many types of cars on Labor Day. Father and I do not race on these weekends. It is too busy, and I always want to go into the pits and see the cars close."

Sherri said, "It must really make you excited, Angie. I can see you are excited just talking about it. Maybe sometime we could go with you."

"That sounds like it could be fun!" Rosa said.

"I agree!" Bella said. I believe my father would enjoy it as well. He has said he would like to race his Impala sometime to see how fast it is."

"Yes, he has said that a few times. Mother said she would like to see that. Possibly we could all go sometime. It sounds like it could be fun!" Rosa said.

"I think it would be cool!" Edward said.

"How do you feel about this Shelly and Sherri? Would you be interested as well?"

"I have already thought about asking you Angie. I think Gina would want to go sometime as well. She told me she wanted to see you race."

Shelly said, "I want to go."

"I did not know any of you would be interested. We should talk to our parents. This could be a large outing for all of us. I do need to warn you, the nitro cars do scare some people the first time you see them." Angie said.

Were you scared the first time? I know you went when you were eight or ten years old. I remember you telling us." Shelly said.

"I was nine years old. I remember it very clearly. Father took me close to the starting line I was extremely excited. I was almost dancing. I could not believe the sound and how powerful the cars were. I was so excited I had tears in my eyes. Likely from the excitement and if you are close the fumes from the exhaust burn your eyes somewhat. That is one of the best memories from that time."

It was beginning to get dark, and the fireworks would begin soon. All the men went to get chairs for everyone to sit on while watching the fireworks. They brought the loungers over. All the parents used them. All the men sat down, and the women sat in front of them and leaned back on them. Angie always smiled when she saw this. Usually, she would get a tear or two from this. She dreamed about the time when she would be doing that as well.

Rosa saw this and asked Angie quietly, "Is there a problem?"

"No Rosa, I am just thinking of the time when I will have someone to sit with like all out parents. Thank you for asking, you are sweet." Angie hugged her. Out of all of her cousins, Rosa always could see when Angie was the slightest emotional.

"You are welcome, cuz."

Everyone sat and soon the fireworks began. From where they sat, they could see the fireworks from Marana and from A-mountain in Tucson. There were always a few others they could see from a distance, but Marana and Tucson were close enough to see well.

Angie watched and remembered when she was much younger, and they used to go close to A-mountain to watch. She remembered how her father would put her on his shoulders so she could see better, and she smiled.

When the fireworks were finished, they all went inside. By this time the server had finished washing the dishes and packaging the remaining food.

Everyone went into the Arizona room. "We were talking shortly before dinner and thought that possibly one of the days during the Labor Day weekend we could all go to the drag strip as a family get together. Then everyone could see what drag racing is about. Labor Day weekend is the Winter Nationals and there will be many types of racing that you do not see during the normal weekends." Dominic said.

"Father, that is a coincidence. We were talking about this same thing earlier."

"Really? What does everyone thing about this?" Dominic asked.

"Uncle Dominic, all of us want to go." Shelly said.

The ladies talked a little. "We think it would be fun." Maria said.

"We can plan this for Sunday or Labor Day." Dominic said. "What day is best for everyone?"

The men and ladies talked a little and they decided on Monday. They thought it would be a fun thing for Labor Day.

Everyone talked and by about eleven o'clock everyone decided to leave.

7

Sherri had called Angie one evening, "Angie, hi. I wanted to tell you that Driftwood is going to be here at the Arizona Stadium on August 27. I was thinking we could all go. Wouldn't that be great!"

"That would be wonderful! Have you told anyone else?"

"No, I just found out. I wasn't paying attention but today I saw the posters on the wall at school. There are also a few other artists are playing too!"

"Why do we not call everyone to see if they want to go?"

"Yeah. Great. I'll call Karen, Janet and Denise. Can you call Gina and Paula?"

"Oh course. I will call them now. When we know who can go, we can go and buy tickets."

"Ok Angie. Bye."

Angie immediately called Gina. "Hello Gina, how are you today?"

"I'm good. What's going on?"

"Sherri just called and told me that Driftwood is coming to Tucson."

"Yeah, I just heard it on the radio! Cool! I wana go. They said a few other artists are playing too! Tickets are eight dollars. Who else is going?"

"Sherri and I. She is calling Karen, Janet and Denise. I still need to call Paula."

"Paula will want to go. She loves Driftwood. We can get together and buy the tickets then."

It turned out everyone wanted to go. They bought the tickets and Angie took off work on Saturday August 27 for the show. Lizzy and

Carol Winston (Sherri's mom) drove everyone and dropped them off about 12:30 PM. Lizzy and Carol thought it was far too early. The performance started at 4:30 PM but when they got close to the U of A they were surprised. There were so many people. They wondered if they would even get in.

They all walked towards the entrance and waited in line. The temperature was in the 90's but the breeze was west Northwest at about 6-8 MPH. It wasn't too bad. They finally got to their seats shortly before the concert began.

They loved the concert. It ran until around 11:30 PM and they all got home long after midnight. They found out on the radio the next day that there were an estimated 67,000 fans there and it was the largest concert in Arizona history. And all of the proceeds went to the Arizona Heart Foundation. They also said on the radio that the sales manager for Rock radio who was the student producer for the concert, stood on the 50 yard line the night before the concert and was there for a four song sound check at 8 PM. He said it was a dream come true.

Driftwood had just released their new album which ended up on the Billboard chart for 31 weeks! Angie and her friends couldn't stop talking about the show.

8

It was Sunday, the day before Labor Day, and Angie; Dominic and Jack went to watch drag racing. It was Labor Day weekend and the AHRA Winter Nationals were here. This was one of Angie, Dominic and Uncle Jack's favorite weekends. They would be going Sunday and Monday. And on Monday, the whole family was all going as well for the first time. On these big weekends they went as spectators due to the large crowds and huge number of cars.

Angie was bursting with excitement, and she could hardly be still. She couldn't wait. All the big-name drivers would be there, Sherley Muldowney, Gene Snow, Bill Jenkins, Jim Liberman, Tom McEwen and many more. They will be seeing fuel altereds, Alcohol and Nitro funny cars, top fuel dragsters, gassers, Pro Stocks, etc. She was somewhat disappointed because Bill Jenkins had retired as driver of his cars, but he was still going to be there. He had hired Larry Lombardo and Ken Dondero to drive. Ken Dondero would be driving this weekend.

They got up early Sunday morning and left. They stopped and picked up Uncle Jack and drove directly to the track. For these races, all three of them rode in the truck together. The drive was uneventful. They talked about many things. During the times when no one was talking Angie had images flash in her head. She saw someone screaming. It appeared that a woman was being held against her will. She also kept seeing Cholla cactus that appeared driven over. And she also kept seeing a split rail fence. These didn't make sense to her. When she saw images such as this it was never enough to understand. They were just images.

As usual, they also bought Pit passes. Angie wouldn't be happy unless she could be in the Pits. This way she could see everything up close and maybe talk to some of the big-name racers.

Angie was very excited because she would get to see Shirley Muldowney race Top Fuel again. Shirley switched to Top Fuel in 1973 giving up her Funny Car. And she became the first female to win a NHRA Pro title at the 1976 Spring Nationals so Angie was all hyped up.

They walked around the pits between rounds when some of the bracket racing was going on. She knew some of the bracket racers and would see them when she was racing. Now she wanted to see everything else.

During the racing, they went and stood as close to the starting line as they could. Just before the AA/FC (nitro funny cars) started, Dominic asked Angie, "Do you remember the first time you saw a funny car?"

"Of course, father, how could I forget? I was 9 years old. We stood right here and I was holding your hand. If I remember correctly, I was almost dancing when I saw the first burnout. It is one of my best memories as I child. I remember feeling it in my chest and watching the tires smoke. And hearing the sound of a screaming nitro motor, it was the best thing ever!"

Just then they started the first two funny cars and they pulled up to the burnout area and BURRRRAP! Angie still thought it was the best sound ever! She was screaming "Yeah!" as they did the burnouts. No one could hear her over the sound of the engines. The smoke from the exhaust and the tires burned her eyes a little but that was a small price to pay for standing close to the starting line. She got a rush not much different that when she raced herself. As they backed up the cars, the idle sound was just as invigorating for her. The impulses she felt from each cylinder popping, for her, was just amazing! She always told her friends that there is no way to describe the sound and feeling. She said you have to be there to experience it.

They watched a round of Funny Cars and then a round of Top Fuel Dragsters. She thought Top Fuel was cool, but there was something about Funny Cars that she just loved!

Between rounds they walked around the pits. Angie stood at the barrier that was around Sherley Muldowney's Dragster and watched as they tore down the engine for a rebuild. She was always amazed at the speed at which they were able to do this. She was also surprised at the condition of the pistons. They are usually badly scored showing spots that were burnt. Just from a couple of runs.

Angie turned to Uncle Jack, "I recently read an article where a racing team leader was talking about some facts about a top fuel car. A top fuel engine at full throttle will consume 11 gallons of nitro methane per second. Each cylinder is filled just short of hydraulic lockup when the plug fires. The flame front in the combustion chamber reaches 7000 deg. F. The magnetos supply 44 amps to each spark plug. By half-track, the electrodes are consumed, and the engine is dieseling on the glow of the remaining tip of the plugs and the glowing exhaust valves. And what really amazes me is that a top fuel engine only turns just over 900 rpms under load from the burnout and the ¼ mile run. And a top fuel dragster accelerates faster than any other land vehicle on earth and faster than a jet fighter plane."

"Angie, you sound like an encyclopedia!" Uncle Jack said.

Angie was running this through her head watching when someone said hello to her. She turned and it was Shirley Muldowney herself. Angie turned and said "hello, ma'am. I am one of your biggest fans. I also race here but my car is nothing like yours. I only have a HEMI CUDA."

"A HEMI CUDA is nothing to laugh at. The engine in my dragster is based on the original HEMI."

"Yes, ma'am. I am aware of that."

"Angie, Is that Shirley Muldowney?" Dominic asked.

"Yes father."

"Ma'am, would it be alright if I took a picture with you and Angie?"

"Of course." Shirley walked around the barricades and stood next to Angie.

Dominic aimed and snapped a picture then another.

Angie said, "Thank you so much ma'am. You just made my day."

"You're welcome, Angie." Shirley said and turned and walked behind the barricades again.

Angie was so excited. She got a picture with her favorite driver. She just hoped the pictures came out clear. She stayed there watching the team putting the engine back together then start it. It was so loud! But she loved it. She could feel the exhaust pulses even stronger while standing this close. The exhaust fumes burnt her eyes more as well. Once they were finished and shut off the engine, she, Dominic and Uncle Jack walked around more. They came across Bill Jenkins and his team and car. Angie said to her father and Uncle Jack, "Bill Jenkins is not driving anymore. He retired but is now using his time for research and development. Ken Dondero is supposed to be driving this weekend."

"How do you know that, Angie?" Uncle Jack asked.

"I read about it. Bill is still building 331 small blocks but spending his time in research and development. See, there he is!" Angie pointed towards the Bill Jenkin's Car trailer. "Cool! There's Bill Jenkin's car, father." They walked up to it and watched the team led by Bill Jenkins himself. "This car is famous. It runs one of his famous 331 small blocks. See, this is Bill Jenkin's XII car a 1975 Monza. See this car father? It has clear headlight covers. The NHRA will not let him use them, but the AHRA does. This car has all the innovations he used in his XI car, the Vega." They were looking at the car. "See, he was the first to use McPherson Struts in a Pro Stock along with dry sump oiling. He was also the first to build a complete tube steel chassis and cage assembly. He did this in the last Vega and then used all of it in this Monza."

Uncle Jack said, "You still sound like an encyclopedia, Angie."

"As I stated, I read all the time about racing in National DRAG Magazine. This is why I am up to date on so many teams."

They watched the team for a while then walked away. Angie wanted to see Jim Liberman and his new Monza funny car. When they found him, Angie almost ran over. They were just starting it. She had to see it running in the pits. Dominic and Uncle Jack caught up. "Father, this car is so cool! I cannot wait to see him run. I love his burnouts. He is such a showman."

They shut the car down and readied it. It was about time for the next round of funny cars then top fuel dragsters. They went and stood at the starting line again. They watched a couple of races then Jim Liberman pulled up. Angie was excited. He did his famous 1000-foot burnout. The crowd went wild! He backed up, and as usual, Pam his girlfriend, was in front guiding him. He staged against Don Prudhomme.

The lights came down and the cars slingshot towards the finish line. Don Prudhomme won. Angie was loving it! A few more rounds of funny cars then the top fuel began.

"It is too bad they crashed the HEMI Barracuda wheel stander. I think it happened at US 30 Dragstrip in Indiana in 1975. It would have been nice to see the car run again." Angie said.

Dominic said, "Which car was that? It does not sound familiar."

"Father, that was the 1967 Barracuda with the injected HEMI in the back seat. It did ¼ mile wheel stands. Do you not remember it?"

"OK, yes. That was pretty cool watching the car do a wheel stand full track. But now there are others, aren't there? Is there not one called the Little Red Buggy? A VW Bus?"

"Yes father. But I really liked the HEMI Barracuda wheel stander. Maybe because it was the first one."

They spent the day there and left in time to get home for dinner.

As they were driving home, Angie was thinking about everything that happened throughout the day. She smiled when she thought about getting her picture taken with Sherley Muldowney. She couldn't believe how fortunate she had been. As they drove, she thought about the burnout that Jim Liberman did. She thought it was so cool! She smiled.

Then she had a vision of an old, dilapidated shack. She thought this was odd. Then she saw a rope shot or cut somehow and it had frayed ends. Then the vision of a bowie knife slashing at someone came into her head. She could not make anything of any of them. She thought about these visions, along with what she saw while on the drive to the track, most of the way home.

When she got home, they parked and went into the house. Angie went and took a shower before dinner. She passed her mother on her way to the shower. "Hello mother."

"Hello Angie, how was today?"

"It was amazing! I was able to get my picture taken with Sherley Muldowney! She drives a top fuel dragster and is my favorite driver. Hopefully the pictures turn out. Father took them."

"It sounds as if you enjoyed the day."

"Yes, mother. Very much. I am going to take a quick shower before dinner."

"OK, Angie."

As she took her shower, she thought about the visions again. They didn't make any sense to her. She decided to put them out of her mind for now.

Dominic came in and went up to Lizzy. "Hello sweetheart." He went up and kissed and hugged her.

"How did you enjoy the day Dom?"

"It was a wonderful day of pro racing. I got such a kick out of Angie. She gets unbelievably excited. Each time it reminds me of the first time I took her to see drag racing."

"Angie was excited about getting her picture taken with Sherley Muldowney. She said she is her favorite driver." Lizzy said.

"Yes. We were watching her team freshen up the engine in her dragster and she walked over and said hi to Angie. Angie told her that she races as well. They talked a little and then Angie asked if she could get a picture with her and she walked out from around the barricades and stood right next to Angie, and I took a few pictures. Angie was so excited about it. She shows excitement just as she did when she was young and began going along with me to watch." Dominic had a big smile on his face. "I would like to take a shower before we eat. Is there enough time?"

"Of course, Dom."

He kissed her again and walked away.

During dinner Angie dominated the discussion talking about everything that happened throughout the day. Lizzy was enjoying her excitement. She could see how Angie was excited just as she had been the first time we went with Dominic. She reminisced about how Angie couldn't stop talking about it the first time she had gone with Dominic. She remembered that she had felt that Dominic had been pushing her to like cars but by the time she had returned from racing the first time, she knew Angie had been hooked. And it seemed as if it wasn't all that long ago. When she thought about it, she realized it was already 12 years ago. How different everything was then.

As Lizzy was cleaning up after dinner, she thought about this more. How their lives had changed since then. They had still been living on Yavapai in that small house and they had just opened the business. And Angie, she had been so much like a tomboy and for her 18th birthday she had wanted to dress in a gown for the first time. She was smiling and getting tears in her eyes. She thought she could never have guessed that Angie would have turned out as she had.

As Lizzy stood there, she prayed and gave thanks for what she had been blessed with. She finished cleaning up and went to the bedroom. Dominic was sitting back on the bed reading. She sat down and said, "Dom, I love you so much." And reached and hugged him.

Dominic saw that she had tears in her eyes. "Is there a problem?" he asked looking concerned.

"Of course not, Dom. I was thinking about how excited Angie had been when she went with you to the track the first time. Then I thought about how different everything was at that time. And how much Angie has changed since then. And I thought about how she dressed for her 18th birthday and tears came to my eyes. I thought that I never could have guessed how much she would change. I prayed for what we have been blessed with." She had turned and laid against Dominic.

Dominic marked his page and put the book he was reading on the nightstand and put his arms around her. "I love you too Lizzy. And I agree that we have been blessed with many things."

After a few minutes, Lizzy got up and changed for bed. As she was sitting down on the bed there was a knock at the bedroom door. "You may enter Angie."

"I came to say good night to you both and tell you how much I love you." She went and hugged each of them smiling.

"Good night, Angie." Dominic said.

"Good night." Lizzy said. "We love you too honey. More that we can describe."

Angie turned and left closing the door behind her.

Dominic and Lizzy looked at each other, smiled and turned off the lights and they laid back and feel asleep. As Lizzy laid there, she thought about how the whole family would be going tomorrow and she wondered how the day would go. She drifted off to sleep.

9

The whole family along with the Winstons gathered at the Tucci's house early Monday morning. Then they left for the track. When everyone arrived, they met in the parking area. Then they all went and paid. Everyone also got pit passes. Angie wanted everyone to see the cars up close. Angie acted like a tour guide telling everyone about each of the cars they stopped to look at. She told everyone much of what she told her father and Uncle Jack the previous day.

"Angelina, you sound as if you are reading from a book. You know everything about these cars! I am amazed!" Shelly said.

"I read about the cars and the drivers in a monthly magazine I receive."

"But you know everything, cuz!" Bella said.

Angie smiled and continued. They went from car to car, and they came up to the first Funny Car. "These are my favorite! They are amazing." Everyone working on the car was rushing, as if choreographed. "They are going to start the engine now. Everyone put your hands over your ears. It is going to be loud."

They started the car. Most of them jumped! They held their hands over their ears. As it warmed up, they blipped the throttle. Sherri jumped. She was a little scared. Shelly stepped behind Sherri. Bella, Rosa and Edward had big smiles on their faces. They loved it. After a couple of minutes, they shut it off.

"That was scary! I jumped! I never heard anything so loud!" Sherri said.

Shelly was shaking. "It scared me as well!"

"When we sit in the stands it is not quite as loud because it is open all around." Angie said.

Lillian, Kristina and Carol were a little startled. Joseph, Carl and John smiled and put their arms around them. "It was not that bad, was it?" Joseph asked Kristina.

"It scared me. I never thought anything could be like that." Kristina said.

Lilly agreed.

"I am a little used to it since I have been here before." Lizzy said. "I have come a few times with Dominic and Angelina. I knew how it would sound. Angelina is correct, there really is not something you can explain. You have to hear it."

They all walked around the pits and Angie explained about all the cars. "Angelina, what kind of car is that? Wow! It is cool!"

"That is a Top Fuel Dragster, Edward.

These and the Funny Cars are so fast they need to use parachutes to help them stop."

"Parachutes? How?" Edward asked.

"You will see. When they pass the finish line and shut the engines off, they pull them. We should head to the stands. Racing is going to begin soon.

Everyone walked and found a place to sit together. Soon, they announced racing would begin with Pro Stock.

Angie was excited. Aunt Maria could feel how Angie felt and it made her feel excited as well. The first two cars pulled into the burnout area and did burnouts. The tires smoked.

"Why do they do that Angelina?" Bella asked. Rosa was waiting to hear as well.

"They do that to heat up the tires. When the tires are hot, they grip the pavement better. Otherwise, when the lights turn green, they would just burnout. You will see." Angie replied.

The cars moved forward and stopped. Each did a couple of short burnouts, then pulled up to staging. "Watch the lights when they pull up. See the first turns on then the second. This is called staging. This puts the front tires in line for each car. It also determines if they red-light." Ange told them.

Then the last yellow then the green lit and the cars slingshot away. They saw the lights at the end of the quarter mile come on for the winner and the times and speed. "That was so cool!" Edward was excited.

The next two cars pulled up and the lights came down and they slingshot forward. One red lighted. "Angelina why did the red light come on for one car?" Shelly asked.

"That one red lighted. That means that he left just before the green light came on. That means he automatically loses."

"I think I understand. I never thought there would be so many rules." Shelly said.

They watched Pro Stock, then Super Stock, then Stock eliminations. During Stock eliminations Angie told everyone, "This is the class I run in. These are basically street cars like mine. Notice how usually one leaves before the other."

"I see that. Why, I don't understand." Sherri asked.

"For Stock and Super Stock, you do a few practice runs to see how fast their car runs. Then you decide what your dial in time is. Say you run 12:50; 12:52 and 12:48. You decide what you think you will run and then you write it on your back window. You need to have a number just slightly faster than you run. If you run faster than your dial in time, you break out and loose. What this does is make each run as equal as possible so that everyone has the chance to will. The faster car doesn't leave at the same time and the slower car. If each car runs the exact time that they wrote on their rear window, both cars would tie."

"I get it now. This is interesting. There is a lot to racing. I thought you just raced against each other. I guess I never thought about it." Sherri said.

After about an hour of Stock they announced the Nitro Funny Cars were beginning. "These are my favorite. I am excited. They will still be loud" Angie said. "They also do burnouts differently."

The first two were started and they dropped the bodies down and locked them in place. They began to move and, BRRRAAAPP! They did a big burnout maybe 700 feet. Then they backed up. "Why is there someone on front waving one way then the other?" Shelly asked.

"They are guiding the driver, so they are on the burnout marks they made during the burnout. The burnout lays rubber on the track surface and it helps the tires grip when they leave the line." Angie told them. The cars staged. "Maybe you should cover your ears."

Everyone did this. The lights came down and Sherri and Shelly jumped! It almost appeared as if they got an electric shock! It was still very loud! "Wow! They are so fast! It makes the last cars look slow." Shelly said.

Edward said, "Wow! I see how they use the parachutes! That is so cool! Is that two hundred thirty-eight miles per hour? That is unbeliev-able!"

"Yes Edward. Top Fuel cars go even faster."

This whole time Dominic was describing the same things to every-one else. Lilly, Kristina and Carol jumped just like Sherri and Shelly.

Eight Funny cars ran. Then there was a little time, and it was time for Top Fuel.

The first cars did their burnouts. One was Shirley Muldowney in her magenta car. "See the magenta car everyone? That is my favorite driver, Sherley Muldowney."

"Really a woman? That is so cool!" Rosa said.

The cars staged. Angie stood. They left. Shirley Muldowney won! Angie screamed and jumped. Lizzy was watching her. She couldn't be-lieve how excited Angie was. She heard about it all the time but seeing her was so much different.

The Top Fuel was done for now. The next round would be in about two hours. They all decided to go and get some food.

They all got their food and drinks and found a couple of tables next to each other and sat. They ate and talked about what they just saw. Kristina had no idea what drag racing was but she found that she loved it. She said, "This is so exhilarating! I cannot believe how much adrenalin I felt during this. I do not think someone with heart trouble should come and watch this!"

"I thought you would enjoy this, sweetheart." Joseph said.

They continued to eat and talk. All the cousins could not believe how much fun this was. Shelly said, I thought I would just be seeing what you do, cuz. But I never would have thought I would like it! This is amazing!"

"I agree." Bella said.

"I as well." Rosa said.

Sherri said, "Angie, we need to bring Gina here sometime. I know she will love this. Maybe we could bring all our friends!"

"We could do that sometime. I agree Sherri, Gina would love this." Angie said.

Everyone finished. The adults stayed at the tables and the cousins and Sherri went to walk around the pits again. They looked at other cars this time. They saw the Stock and Super Stock cars and more of the Pro Stock cars. Edward was asking Angie about lots of things. "Angelina, what are those bars with the little wheels for that stick out the back of some cars?"

"They are called Wheelie Bars. They keep the car from pulling the front wheels too far. They put quite a bit of force onto the rear wheels as well. It helps with traction."

"When they do the burnouts, how do they keep the cars from moving forward?" Edward asked.

"That is a good question, Edward. You are very observant. There is something called a line lock. You install it in the front brake lines. You step on the brakes and push the lever and when you let go of the brake pedal the front brakes stay locked. When you are ready you flip the lever, and the brakes unlock and the car moves forward. This is used to make it possible to heat up the rear tires."

"I get it. Cool!"

They watched racing all day. When the last of the Funny car and Top Fuel cars were done, they decided to leave. It was about 4:30 and most of them needed to get up for work or school in the morning. Everyone said their good bye's and left. They all talked about the day during the drive home. Angie didn't have any more visions. When they got home Angie went and worked out then went in and showered before dinner. Lizzy prepared sandwiches because they ate quite a bit during the day. They ate and went into the Arizona room and sat for a bit watching the night sky. By this time, it was fully dark. After about an hour Angie said, I am going to go to bed. Good night. I love you both." She stood and reached and hugged her mother and father.

They both said good night we love you to Angie and she turned and went to bed.

Dominic and Lizzy stayed there watching the night sky. They talked a bit about how everyone had enjoyed the day. Lizzy had thought her mother and Lillian would not like racing, but they had become excited by the racing and stated that they had enjoyed it quite a bit.

10

Angie and her friends met at the Bum Steer on Saturday night. Angie told everyone about the races the previous weekend and how the whole family came on Monday.

Sherri said, "Since this was decided on the fourth of July, my parents and I went as well. It was really cool! Loud but cool. Angie, her cousins and I walked around the pits and Angie was just like a tour guide. She knows everything about everything there. She knows about the drivers and the cars and she explained how the racing works. It was very interesting."

"Sherri, I do not know everything. I only know what I read." Angie said.

"It sounds like you know everything."

Gina said, "What kind of cars did they have?"

"They had all the pro cars, Funny Cars; Top Fuel, Pro Stock and Bracket Racing cars." Angie said.

"What are funny cars?" Karen asked.

"Funny cars are a type of custom-built race car with tube steel chasses, fiberglass bodies and alcohol or nitro burning engines. They make as much as six thousand horsepower." Angie said.

"Six thousand horsepower? That sounds impossible!" Janet said.

Sherri said, "They are so loud you have to cover your ears. But they are so fast it is almost unbelievable!"

"Wow! Maybe we could go with you sometime Angie." Gina said.

"We could do that. Sherri said you would want to go, Gina."

"You did Sherri?" Gina said.

"You always say you like fast cars, so I figured you would want to see it." Sherri said.

"When Angie talks about it, she gets so excited. It makes me want to see it." Gina said.

"Well, we can plan on going sometime then." Angie said.

"Gina, not to change the subject but what ever happened to that guy at school? I think you said his name was Jeff. Did he ask you out?" Paula asked.

"Oh, I didn't tell you. I can't believe I took Angie's advice."

"What advice was that, Gina?" Angie was thinking about what advice she gave her and did not remember.

"You said I should tell him, "If the offer is still good, I'm interested. I can't believe I said that. You were right, he liked that! He smiled and said something like, "Really, Great!" then he asked if we go out Saturday night."

"See, it was not difficult was it not?" Angie asked.

"No, it wasn't. But I don't think I would have ever said that if you didn't suggest it, Angie. I should thank you."

"You are welcome, Gina. Did you go out with him?" Angie asked.

"Yea, we went out last Saturday night." She sounded excited.

"Like, what did you do?" Denise asked.

"We did something I never thought about doing. He took me roller skating. It was so much fun! I guess he skates a lot because he is really good. I kept falling and he kept helping me up. He's really nice!"

"What else happened?" Janet asked.

"He pulled me out when they did a waltz. I was afraid because I never skated before. He can dance skate."

"Really? You danced?" Janet asked.

"Well, no. I fell once and he fell with me. He ended up on top of me and then he kissed me. I wasn't expecting that. It was so cool!" Gina said.

"Wow! You going to go out again?" Karen asked.

"Yea. I don't know when but we are going to meet in the student union one day." Gina was very excited talking about him.

Angie said, "I am happy for you, Gina."

"Thanks. I even feel like I had more confidence. I think you gave me that, Angie!"

"That is wonderful! But I do not know how I did that."

"Hey Karen, anything happen with the guy at your work?" Gina asked.

"Curt?" Karen asked.

"Yea, him. Did he ask you out?" Gina asked.

"We talked a couple of times. I think I like him. He suggested we go to Tucson Burger for lunch some time. I told him OK."

"Cool! When are you going to go?" Gina asked.

"I don't know. It has to be a day when we can take lunch at the same time. We don't take lunch at the same time often. It depends how busy we are."

"That's cool." Gina said.

The waitress had come and everyone ordered food. They already had ordered beer. She had just come with the beer. Gina took a sip and said, "I'm going to sing." She got up and went to the stage.

She sang Dark Lady. When the song began the guys in the bar screamed. Gina always danced seductively when she sang. She finished and handed the mike to the disk Jockey and went back to the table.

The food was waiting when she got there. They ate and talked, mostly about Jeff, the guy that Gina went out with. When they finished Angie went up to sing. She sang Anticipation. As usual everyone screamed. Then she sang Rainy Days and Monday. The crowd roared. It didn't matter what she sang, they all loved hearing her sing.

Angie went back to the table. They drank more beer and Gina sang a few more times. Then they went home.

The next day, Sunday, Angie's parents had gone out shopping for patio furniture. Angie had decided to stay home and spend some time relaxing and listening to music. She doesn't take the time to do this often and she was fully enjoying it. She was lying on her bed with her head on her pillow. She had her eyes closed and was completely relaxed, feeling the music. She had her headphones on and was listening to her Pink Floyd Dark Side of the Moon album. She had it turned up loud. The song "Time" had just begun. She was getting into the rototom intro thinking that if she had more time, she would learn how to play the drums. When suddenly two guys kicked open her door and burst into her room each with guns pointed at her. She jumped up surprised and pulled off her headphones. One had a rifle the other had what looked like a 9mm automatic. They stayed at a distance because they knew she could easily disarm anyone. "Sit down!" One said sternly.

Angie sat down on her bed. "Who are you and what do you want?"

They did not reply and just stood there pointing their guns and stared at her.

Then a young woman walked around the corner and came in. She was Hispanic, medium build, a bit muscular and maybe 5'8" tall. She had short black hair and wasn't wearing any make-up. "Well, well, well, if it isn't the famous martial arts bitch. How does it feel not being able to fight your way out?"

"What do you want? Why are you here?"

"All in good time. If you try anything, Alex and Georgie here will shoot you." She moved closer to Angie. As always Angie was assessing the situation and looking for a way to subdue these people. "You think you can get out of this? Not this time sweetheart!" She sounded very sarcastic.

Angie started to move into a position for defense. "Ah, ah. Put your arms down. Angie put them down. Just as she did that the woman put her arm back and slapped Angie across the left side of her face hard. It caused Angie's head to turn a little.

Now Angie was angry. It showed in her expression.

"How does it feel not being able to defend yourself? Scared?"

"I am not afraid of anyone."

"You should be. You are going to sign your car over to us then we are going to kill you. I know how much you love that car, so I am taking it from you first. How does that sound? Do I have your attention?"

"You will not leave here alive. You know that do you not?"

The young woman just chuckled. "Why do you talk like such a bitch? Huh? Doesn't matter. You killed my brother, Pabby. It destroyed my mother and it left me alone. Now you are going to pay."

"Pabby? I do not know a Pabby."

"Yes, you do." She sounded angry. "You beat him to death. I am Olive, his sister." She put her arm back and slapped Angie in the face again hard. She wore a snide smile. She felt satisfaction being able to slap Angie.

"Do not do that again!" Angie said sternly. She was thinking that she should grab her and use her as a shield for bullets but could not think of how to subdue the guys with the gun's afterwords.

"You're in no position to demand anything, bitch. You trained with him at your dojo. He thought you were shit. He always told me that your sensei always treated you different than anyone else. Like you were special. Then you killed him."

Angie thought for a minute, "Pablo. Your brother was Pablo." Angie said in a disgusted tone.

"Good! You aren't stupid."

"You speak a bit as he." Angie said with disgust, "He pulled a gun on me."

"He should have killed you when he had the chance."

Angie was very angry now. "He cocked his gun and was about to fire. I did not give him the opportunity. That is why he is dead."

"Yeah, yeah, yeah. That's what the police said. Well, you're not getting out of it this time." She laughed a sinister laugh, "Ha, ha, ha. This time you're not gonna make it." Olive was smiling a sinister smile again. She knew in her mind that there was no way that Angie could get out of this. She knew her plan was fool proof. She laughed more.

Angie knew different. She just needed to formulate a plan to subdue them.

"Georgie, grab Angie. We need to take her to her mom and dad's bedroom. She is going to open the safe and get us the title to the CUDA." Georgie was a large muscular guy. He handed his gun to Olive and she pointed it at Angie. Then he grabbed Angie's arm and pulled her up. He put one of his arms around her neck. He did this tight enough to slightly choke her. Then he grabbed one of her arms and twisted it behind her back.

"Ahh." Angie groaned as Georgie twisted her arm. She coughed a little as well.

"MOVE!" Olive screamed as she pushed the gun into the back of Angie's shoulder.

Angie walked with Georgie's arm around her neck and her arm twisted behind her back. She was bent back slightly because of the way he was holding her. Georgie pushed Angie to her parent's room. When they got into her parent's room Olive said, "Open the safe, now!" Georgie moved her to the closet and over to the safe. He pushed her down so she could reach the knob on the safe door. All along Angie was running scenarios through her head planning her defense. She opened the safe door. "Take out the title and the cash."

Angie reached with the arm Georgie was not holding and grabbed the money and titles. There were titles for her father's truck, the Nova, her mother's Bonneville and the CUDA. Georgie pulled her up and pulled her out of the closet and over to a chair in front of a small table. He pushed her down onto the chair. He kept his arm around her neck. All along Olive had the gun pointed at her and Alex had the rifle pointed at her from across the room at the bedroom door.

Olive pushed everything on the table aside. She grabbed and pulled the titles and cash from Angie. She still had the gun pointed at Angie. She took the titles and cash and put them in the hand she was holding the gun with between her index finger and the gun.

Angie noted that Olive was holding the gun in a way that would make it difficult to shoot now and she was looking through the titles to find the one for the CUDA.

Then Olive pulled out the title for the CUDA with her other hand and slapped it down on the table. She was still holding the other titles and cash between her index finger and the gun. Angie saw this as a possible opportunity.

Angie had an idea when she saw Olive holding the titles, cash and the gun in the same hand. She had noted that her mother's letter opener was on the desk right next to the title. It was one that looked like a small sword with a blade maybe 8" long.

Olive then squatted down and grabbed a pen that had fallen onto the floor when she had pushed everything aside. It was obvious that she didn't think she would need to use the gun now as she didn't have her finger on the trigger. She stood and slapped the pen down. "Sign it. And don't try anything. I will shoot you."

Angie glanced at her then went to pick up the pen but grabbed the letter opener and swung her arm around and stabbed Georgie in the neck. All 8" of the blade went into his neck. The handle was all you could see. He immediately let go of her and grabbed at his nick and fell. Olive was stunned and before she could do anything, Angie turned and took the gun away from her and shot Alex. The other titles and cash flew all over. This took maybe two or three seconds. Alex fell and dropped his rifle. Olive was completely shocked. Her eyes were wide open. Now

Olive was unarmed and unguarded. She frantically screamed, "Jose!" and another guy came running with his gun pointed in front of him. He turned into the room and began to point his gun at Angie. As soon as Angie saw him, she shot him as well. He dropped his gun and fell. By this time, Olive had stepped back and kicked the gun out of Angie's hand. Angie had done all of this while still sitting at the table. Angie jumped up and the chair fell over. Olive got into a stance and said, "I'm going to warn you that I am a brown belt in karate."

Inside, Angie thought sarcastically, "Really, a brown belt in karate? Maybe I should be afraid." They began to fight. Immediately it was obvious Angie had the upper hand. Olive punched at Angie and she blocked them easily. After one block Angie hit Olive in the stomach with her knee so hard, she bent over and almost fell. She was coughing and it sounded as if she was struggling to catch her breath. She recovered in a few seconds and threw another punch. Angie blocked it and kicked Olive in the side with her shin likely fracturing a few ribs. She gasped for breath again and the thought came to her, "Shit, she's too fast." Then turned and ran out the sliding door to the deck. Olive thought she could get away by running down the stairs but quickly found that there weren't any. She then ran to the other sliding door on the other side of the deck, which was Angie's room, but it was locked. She turned around and Angie was already there in her stance, prepared to fight.

Angie looked at Olive and said, "You can back down or you may not make it out of here alive."

"The hell with you!" Olive said and kicked at Angie. Angie easily blocked it. She then tried to punch Angie and she blocked it and kicked her on her side. Olive screamed "Ahhh!" and fell then jumped up. Olive was angry. This wasn't supposed to happen like this. She had wanted to kill Angie. She did a 360 degree reverse roundhouse. Angie stepped back and ducked. She returned the kick with a side kick and Olive fell back and down again. She jumped right up. She screamed and ran at Angie to try to punch her, and Angie punched her in the face. Olive's head snapped back and she fell back down again onto her back. She was stunned for a few seconds then wiped her nose and saw blood. She looked crazy angry. She jumped up and tried to kick Angie but she just stopped it using the Muay Thai move. Angie kicked her again and she fell back down a fourth time.

Angie was trying not to hurt her too much. She just wanted her to back down. Olive stood and reached down to her cowboy boot and pulled out a bowie knife. She started slashing back and forth at Angie. Angie watched her moves and one time as soon as the blade went past her, she did a reverse 360 degree reverse roundhouse to her head. Angie's foot hit Olive on the side of the head and Olive fell to the side, hit the deck railing, and fell over falling about 20 feet onto the concrete stairs below. Angie looked over and Olive did not move. She just laid there face down. There was blood running from her head. The bowie knife was still in her hand.

Angie ran back into the bedroom, took the guns and rifle and slid them down the hallway. Then she called 911.

"911, what is your emergency?"

"This is Angie Tucci 7607 N. Chrisy Dr. I have been attacked by people that broke in and tried to kill me. There are at least four."

"Ma'am, can you get out of the house?"

"I am more worried that there are additional threats. I need to check the house and neutralize them. Please send an ambulance as well. I believe I killed at least one of them." She slammed down the phone.

Angie ran through the house looking to see if there was anyone else. She found no one. She went back to her parent's bedroom and found Alex and Jose were not dead. She told them not to move or she would kill them as well. She checked Georgie and he was dead.

Angie heard sirens coming. The Sheriff arrived along with Deputy Moody and two other cars with deputies. They all ran into the house, guns drawn. The front door was wide open. Angie called them upstairs. They ran up the stairs. When they got to the master bedroom Angie was there with two guys that had been shot. One in the shoulder and the other in the abdomen. They were sitting up against the wall guarded by

Angie. Then she pointed out Georgie. She heard the ambulance arrive. "Their guns are down the hallway. I slid them there to get them away from these guys."

"Angie, are you alright?" Deputy Moody asked, he saw she had a hand shaped welt on her cheek.

"Yes sir. A little shaken however."

"I can see that. Where are your parents?"

"They went shopping for some patio furniture for around the pool."

"When do you expect them back?"

"I do not know. Possibly any time now." Angie replied.

The sheriff looked at Georgie and said, "A letter opener?"

"I had to improvise sir. They had guns pointed at me."

The sheriff called the coroner.

Dominic and Lizzy saw all the flashing lights as they turned onto Cristy. Lizzy screamed, "Oh, no!" When they pulled into the driveway, they saw squad cars and two ambulances. Lizzy jumped out of the truck before it was stopped. She screamed, "Angie? Angie?" She ran into the house. She was crying. There were sheriff's deputies all over the house and paramedics were bringing a guy out on a gurney with an IV and an oxygen mask. Dominic caught up to Lizzy. They didn't know who this person was. When they got to the stairs other paramedics were bringing out another guy on another gurney. They didn't know who this was either. Lizzy was frantic. As soon as they got the gurney off the stairs Lizzy and Dominic ran up. "Angie? Angie?"

Angie was in their room. "I am in here mother."

Lizzy and Dominic turned the corner to see another man lying on the floor that appeared dead. They saw Lizzy's letter opener sticking out of the side of his neck. "Angie!" Lizzy ran to her and took her into her arms. "Your face! Oh, my lord!" Lizzy exclaimed. "What happened?" She was talking through her tears.

Angie's left cheek was badly bruised and swelling in the shape of a hand. She saw finger shapes in the swelling, and it appeared she was beginning to get a black eye. "Mother, I am fine." Then the realization was coming to her of what just happened and she began to cry. She said through her tears, "Mother they attacked me in our house. They said that they were going to kill me."

Then they noticed the Pima County Sheriff and Deputy Moody. "Mrs. Tucci, we just arrived. We have not talked to Angie to learn what happened yet." The sheriff said. "Where can we go and sit to talk?"

"We can go sit in the dining room Sir." Angie said. She was wiping her tears.

The sheriff, Deputy Moody, Dominic and Lizzy followed Angie downstairs and into the dining room. Angie opened the refrigerator and grabbed the pitcher of iced tea and set it on the table. Then she took out a tumbler for each person. Lizzy poured.

The Sheriff began, "Angie, what happened today?"

"Sir," She tried hard to talk. She was holding back more tears and her jaw was trembling. She cleared her throat. "I was lying on my bed relaxing and listening to some music. I do not have the opportunity to do this often. I had my headphones on. I did not hear anything because I was listening to Pink Floyd very loud. Then two guys with guns rushed into my room. I jumped and pulled off my headphones. I asked who they were and what was this about. One said, "Sit down!" Then a young woman came in and said, 'Well, well, well, the famous martial arts bitch. How does it feel not being able to fight your way out?' I looked at her and asked what she wanted and why was she here. She replied, 'All in good time. If you try anything Alex and Georgie here will shoot you.' She stepped closer then slapped me hard on the side of the face. Then she asked if I was scared, and I told her I am not afraid of anyone. She said, "You should be. We are going to make you to sign over your car to us then we are going to kill you. I know how much you love that car. How does that sound?"

"I said to her, 'You will not leave here alive. You know that do you not?' Then she said, 'Why do you talk like such a bitch? Doesn't matter.

You killed my brother Pabby. It destroyed my mother and left me alone. Now you are going to pay.' I told her I did not know a Pabby."

"She said, 'Yes you do. You beat him to death. I am Olive, his sister.' Then she slapped me in the face again and said, 'You trained with him at your dojo. He thought you were shit. He always told me that your sensei always treated you differently than anyone else, like you were special. Then you killed him.'

Then I remembered, Pablo. He was one of the guys that kidnapped those young ladies. I told her that he pulled a gun on me, cocked it and was about to fire. That is why he is dead. And she said, 'He should have killed you when he had the chance.' Then she told Gorgie, the big guy to grab me and take me to the safe. He handed his gun to her and pulled me up and put an arm around my neck almost choking me. Then he grabbed one of my arms and twisted it behind my back. He pushed me here to my mother and father's room. Olive had the gun pushed into my shoulder the whole time. Somehow, they knew there was a safe there. The whole time I had two guns pointed at me and one was on my shoulder. I was thinking of how to get free. Georgie pushed me down and I opened the safe. Olive told me to take out the money and titles and she grabbed them from me. Georgie pulled me over to the small table and forced me to sit in the chair. He kept his arm around my neck. Olive put the money and the other titles in the hand that she was holding the gun with and pushed everything on the table aside. Then she slapped down the title to the CUDA onto the table. She squatted, grabbed a pen that had fallen to the floor and slapped it down and said, 'Sign it!' I went to grab the pen but grabbed the letter opened instead. I immediately swung my arm around and stabbed Georgie in his neck. He let go and I turned and took the gun from Olive and shot the other guy that had the rifle. This may have taken two or three seconds at most. Olive looked shocked. She screamed for help and another guy came running and as soon as he turned into the room and raised his gun, I shot him. Olive then kicked the gun out of my hand, and I found she had some martial arts training. She told me she was a brown belt in karate, as if she thought it would scare me. We fought for a minute or so then she turned and ran out onto the deck. I believe she thought she could get away but quickly found that there are no stairs. She turned and I was there in my stance. I told her that she should back down. She decided to fight. We fought and I kicked her, and she fell four times. I did not want to hurt her. I just wanted her to stop. Then she pulled a knife out of her boot and started slashing at me, I ended up doing a 360 degree reverse roundhouse and she fell over the railing. I went to look, and she had fallen onto the concrete stairs below. I saw blood running from her head. At that time, she still had the knife in her hand. Then I ran and grabbed the guns and slid them down the hallway and called 911."

Deputy Moody stood up and went to look and sure enough there was Olive lying dead on the concrete stairs. She still had the knife clutched in one hand. He called the sheriff. "There is another over here."

The sheriff walked over. Olive's body was lying on the stairs. There was a large puddle of blood, and it was dripping onto the stair below.

Dominic followed and saw her as well. Angie walked over. "Sir, the ironic part is that the title for my car is in my parent's names. I would not have been able to sign it over. And I do not understand how she knew there was a safe in my parent's room and that the title would be there."

"She had to find that out somehow." The sheriff said. He turned to Dominic and asked, "Have you ever talked about putting your titles in a safe around anyone?"

Dominic was looking at the dead girl. Somehow, she looked familiar. "Sheriff, this girl was in my shop last week. We repaired a loose exhaust pipe. It was just loose as if someone loosened the nuts. If I remember correctly, she waited for the car near the front counter."

"Were you talking to anyone then? Maybe she overheard you?" the Sheriff asked.

Dominic was thinking. "I was talking to Jack."

"Who is Jack?"

"He is my service manager. He was asking me where I kept my car titles. He had said that he was always afraid he would lose his. I told him I keep them in the safe in the bedroom closet. Maybe she overheard? We were not speaking loudly. At the time I did not think it was an issue." Dominic said.

"If she knew who you were that is how she knew." the sheriff said.

"This is all my fault." Dominic was feeling bad.

"Dominic that just made it easier. She could have just asked Angie where the titles were. Things wouldn't have been much different.

Deputy Moody had gone to tell the coroner that there was another body they needed to bag up. They came and removed the body from the steps, put it in a body bag and carried it away.

Dominic looked at the stairs where Olive had fallen. He thought that he needed to clean it as soon as possible so it did not stain the concrete.

Angie had gone back inside of the house to the table and was sitting with her mother. They were talking about the details from this. The adrenalin was wearing off and Angie was becoming very tired. She put her elbow on the table and went to rest her head on her palm. When she leaned her head she said, "Aah!" She had not realized how much her cheek hurt until then. Lizzy got up and made an ice pack. She put ice in a plastic bag, wrapped it with a hand towel from the drawer right there and gave it to Angie. "Thank you, mother."

"You are welcome." She was sad when she looked at Angie. "I feel terrible that this happened. Can I get anything for you?"

"I am fine mother. Please do not worry. It will heal soon enough."

"I am just worried that you continue to attract these altercations. Some nights it takes me some time to get to sleep because I am thinking about it."

"Please do not worry mother. I will be fine. We need to clean up the blood before it stains the wood floor. The wood is so beautiful."

"Do not worry about that, honey. I will take care of it. I need to take care of you now."

"Mother, I am fine. I can help. I just have a bruised cheek. Why do we not get started?"

They went and got a bucket of warm water and some mild soap, sponges, towels and rubber gloves. They went upstairs. By now everyone had left except two of the deputies that were outside looking at the blood on the stairs. As he was leaving, the Sheriff told Dominic he would have the car towed in the morning. There was not much blood from the two guys Angie shot. Only two small spots. And the guy Angie killed with the letter opener must not have blead out much. There was only a small puddle maybe about a foot in diameter there. They scrubbed lightly so as not to damage the finish on the floor. It appeared that all the blood came off and there were no marks remaining.

Dominic went upstairs after everyone left. "You cleaned up the blood already? I was going to do that."

"It was not bad Dom. It cleaned up easily." Lizzy put the sponges in the bucket as Angie dried the areas on the floor with the towel. Lizzy took the towel from Angie and brought them and the bucket to the utility sink in the laundry room and rinsed everything out.

"You killed the guy with a letter opener? That almost sounds impossible." Dominic said.

"Yes father. I had to use what was available. If there was just a pen, I would have used that. I picked up the letter opener with my right hand and swung as hard as I could. I had this planed out before Olive put the pen down. She did not expect me to react as I did. I stabbed the guy with the letter opener then turned and took the gun from Olive's hand. The money and titles flew all over and I turned the gun and shot the guy with the rifle before he knew what had happened. Olive screamed and the last guy came running in and I shot him as he was raising his gun. Then she started fighting. I tried to get Olive to stop but she would not father.

Dominic went and hugged Angie. She hugged him back. She started to cry. "I do not want to kill anyone, father. If I did not, I would not have survived. I feel so bad. I feel as if I have sinned again."

"Angie, you have done only what was necessary to survive. It is not a sin to protect yourself." Dominic looked at Lizzy as if asking for support.

"Angie, would you care to talk to one of the priests at St. Augustine? I could set it up if you would like. Maybe this will help you."

"I do not know, possibly. I would be worried that they would cast me out." Angie cried more.

"Angie, a priest will not cast you out. He would help you to forgive to yourself. Possibly this is what you need, some spiritual support."

"Alright mother. Could you set it up please?"

"I will take care of everything." She went and hugged Angie from behind. Dominic was still hugging her.

By the time everyone had left it was late. They had not had anything to eat for dinner. Lizzy said, "I will go and make some sandwiches for dinner. I believe we have some chips as well." She turned and walked to the kitchen. Dominic and Angie followed.

Angie picked up the tumblers from when they served the sheriff and deputy iced tea and brought them to the sink. Then she reached and took out dishes and clean tumblers for each of them and placed them on the table. She also took some paper napkins and folded them and placed one at each dish. She also placed a clean tumbler at each place setting.

Lizzy finished making the sandwiches, cut them and placed them on a serving dish. She turned and placed it on the table. Then she reached into a cabinet and took out a bag of potato chips and placed it on the table.

They sat and Angie began to say grace. "Our Heavenly Father, please bless..." This was all she could get out. She began crying again. "I am sorry, I did not mean to.."

"Do not worry Angie. I am certain God understands how you feel. Father, please bless this food we are about to eat and may it nourish our bodies. Amen." Lizzy finished.

They each took a sandwich piece and some potato chips and began eating. They mostly ate in silence. "The sheriff told me he would have a tow truck pick up the car those people came in tomorrow." They finished and Lizzy and Dominic began to clean up. "Angie, I will help your mother clean up. Why do you not get cleaned up and get ready for bed. We will come and see you when we are finished here."

"Thank you, father." Angie said tears still rolling down her cheeks as she turned and walked to her room.

Lizzy and Dominic finished in the kitchen and went to Angie's room. Lizzy knocked on the door.

"You may come in." Angie said.

Lizzy opened the door and she and Dominic went in. Angie was laying on her bed with the comforter pulled up to her neck. It appeared that she was trying to hide under the comforter. "Angie, we are here if you need anything." Dominic said. He leaned over and kissed her on the forehead. Lizzy did the same.

"We love you, Angie." Lizzy said.

"I love you both as well. Thank you for always being here for me." More tears dripped down her face.

"Good night." Lizzy said as they left the room, turned off the light and closed the door behind them.

Angie laid there, tears running down her cheeks. She folded her hands and said, "Dear father in heaven, please do not forsake me. I did not mean to kill those people today. Please forgive me. I do not know if I can live without knowing you are watching over me." She could not say any more. Her crying cut her off. She eventually fell asleep.

Dominic and Lizzy went to bed. When they laid down, Lizzy said, "Angie is extremely distressed. I hope one of the priests can calm her down. I feel terrible, Dom."

"I agree, I hope they can help her. I do not like seeing her like this." He leaned over and kissed Lizzy. "Good night, I love you!"

"I love you as well Dom."

12

The next day when Angie went to work in the morning, she was feeling depressed. When the guys saw her, they were shocked. She had swelling on her cheek in the shape of a hand and a partial black eye. Eric couldn't hold back, "Angie, what happened?"

Angie looked at him and got teary eyed, "I killed two people yesterday."

He could see that she was upset. "I can see you are upset. Is there something we can do? If you don't want to talk about it that's fine."

"Maybe at lunch. I do not feel like talking now. I do not think there is anything you can do. But thank you for your offer, all of you are altruistic." She turned and went to up front to say hello to her father and Uncle Jack.

Eric and the others knew she was upset and preoccupied because she used the word altruistic. She never uses words like that around them except when she is upset or preoccupied.

"Altruistic? What does that mean?" Hector asked.

"I am not sure. But I think it was a complement." Eric said.

Angie came back and began to work.

That morning, Lizzy called St. Augustine's and made an appointment for Angie to sit with Father Lopez that evening after work. Then she drove to the shop to tell Angie. This was early in the day. She drove home. She needed to call her mother, Lilly and Maria to tell them what happened.

When she got home the phone was ringing. Lizzy ran and picked it up. "Hello?"

"Lizzy, this is Maria." Lizzy could hear she had been crying. She sniffled, "Something bad happened. I feel it. Someone was killed." She cried. "Is Angie alright?"

"Calm down Maria. Angie is fine. Well, as fine as she can be after killing two people. I was just going to call you, Lilly and my mother."

"Oh, my lord, what happened?"

"Angie was attacked in our house yesterday late afternoon."

"In your house? Why?"

"Well, evidently the sister of one of the people Angie killed while saving those young ladies came for revenge. She came with 3 guys that had guns. They wanted her to sign over her CUDA and then they said they were going to kill her."

"How awful! And in your house."

"Evidently Angie killed one of the guys with my letter opener. She stabbed him in his neck, then grabbed the gun from the woman and shot the two other guys. Then she fought this woman and when the woman realized she could not fight against Angie she turned and ran onto the deck outside of our room but could not get away. Angie fought with her trying to get her to stop but this woman pulled a bowie knife out of her boot and slashed at Angie. Angie used a 360 degree reverse roundhouse and the woman fell over the railing and onto the stairs below. The fall killed her."

"I now feel awful for Angie. I feel as if she is extremely disturbed by this. I had felt that she had been hurt physically but now understand I interpreted her pain incorrectly. Is there anything I can do?"

"I do not believe there is. I made an appointment for her to speak with one of the priests at St. Augustine's today after work."

"That was a wonderful idea. I know she has been feeling as if she has sinned terribly. I feel positive about this."

"Thank you, Maria. I need to call Lilly and my mother."

"I will not hold you. Will you tell Angie I love her?"

"I will Maria. And thank you for calling. Goodbye."
Lizzy immediately called her mother then Lilly.

A little later when Angie went up front, the guys talked among themselves. They were worried for her as she wasn't herself. They didn't know what happened and were worried that maybe she was in trouble.

Lunch time came and everyone went to the break room to eat. It initially was quiet. Then Angie said, "I was attacked yesterday. I had some time to relax and just listen to some music. I was laying on my bed with Pink Floyd blasting in my headphones and two guys burst in with guns. It startled me and I pulled off my headphones, stood and asked what this was about. They just screamed for me to sit. I sat on my bed. A young woman came in and was sarcastic and said something like 'Well, well, well, it's the famous martial arts bitch. How does it feel not being able to fight you way out?' Then she slapped me hard on my cheek. I began to move into defensive posture, and she said, 'Ah ah, put your arms down.' She said the two guys would shoot me if I tried anything. What it was about was I killed her brother during the child trafficking incident, and she wanted revenge. She told me I was going to sign over my car to her because she knew how much I loved it then she was going to kill me. I ended up stabbing one guy in the neck with my mother's letter opener, I took the gun from her and shot the second guy. Then she screamed and a third guy came running in and I shot him as well. She then kicked the gun out of my hand, and we began to fight. She immediately found out she was no match for me and ran out onto the deck. This was on the second floor. I believe she thought she could get away but there are no stairs. I told her she should just stop but she decided to fight. After I kicked her, and she had fallen four times she pulled a large knife from her boot and began to slash at me. I used a 360 degree reverse roundhouse and she fell over the railing and landed on concrete steps face first. That killed her. The guy I stabbed in the neck died as well."

Hector asked, "What happened to the two guys you shot?"

"They did not die and did not have serious injuries. I shot one in the shoulder and the other in the abdomen. I just feel as if I am going to be condemned to hell because I have killed so many people." She began to cry.

Johnny stood and went over to her and hugged her from behind. "Angie don't think like that. You did it in self-defense."

Miguel said, "It isn't a sin to defend yourself. You didn't do anything bad."

Angie wiped her eyes. She didn't say anything for the rest of lunch. She didn't eat much either. She got up and went back to work. During the afternoon she didn't say anything much. Everyone else could see she was hurting, so they didn't say anything to her. They didn't say much to each other either.

At the end of the day Angie cleaned up and said bye to everyone and left. Johnny said, "Man, I never saw her like this. I hope she will be OK."

"I never saw her like this either. It makes me feel bad." Hector said.

"Yeah, I hear ya." Eric said. "I'm going. See you guys tomorrow." The others said bye and left as well.

13

Angie drove to St. Augustine Cathedral directly from work. She parked and walked to the church to see Father Lopez. He met her just inside and he took her to his office. They sat. "Angelina, how can I help you. Your mother is very concerned."

Angie was fighting tears and her chin was quivering. "Father," She was fighting tears. "I feel as if I am destined to be condemned to hell." She began crying hard.

"Angelina, why do you feel as if you will be condemned?" He was quite shocked to hear that.

"Father," She paused to try to compose herself somewhat, "I, I, I have killed people in fights. It was while saving my life and the lives of many others. It is a grave sin to kill. I have thought about each time in an attempt to determine if there would have been another way to stop these aggressors without killing them, but I cannot. It is a sin to kill. And I killed two additional people yesterday afternoon that attacked me in my own house and said they were going to kill me."

Father Lopez reached and offered Angie tissues. She took two and patted her eyes. Father Lopez sat back to think. He rubbed his chin, "Angelina, I have read about the situations you have been in. I understand how you must feel. You need to focus on the fact that defending yourself is an act of self-love and self-preservation." He turned and reached for a book on the shelf behind him, turned back, opened it and found what he had thought of. "A quotation is from # 2265 in the first edition of the Catechism of the Catholic Church states," he began to read, "legitimate defense can be not only a right but a grave duty for someone responsible for another's life, the common good of the family or of the State." What this says is that you have done good by defending your own life along with many others. This is self-preservation and is very important. Think about all the young girls that you saved. They would have been used and most likely killed in time. I understand how you feel but the sacrifice was for your life and the lives of others. You could not have fought for a more noble cause. You will not be condemned for this." He sat and thought for a minute. "Think of the story of David and Goliath. The story shows the great courage David had confronting an advisory much larger than him to whom brandished a sword. He had just a sling and rocks. This is not unlike what you have been up against. You showed great courage being confronted by advisories much stronger than you and in greater numbers, most of which had guns or knives. You obviously did not use a sling and rocks, but you used your martial arts training. You have in a sense defeated your goliaths. And you did this for a most noble cause, self-love and the love, compassion and safety of others."

Angie sat there for a while thinking. He had shown her a different perspective. This made her feel much better. "Father, you have opened my eyes. I have been praying for forgiveness for these actions every night and many nights I have cried myself to sleep. You have shown me a point of view that never occurred to me. I had been stuck in self-blame for quite some time. I feel as if my eyes have been opened again. I have been praying to God for understanding and to help me to understand. I want to thank you so much for taking the time from your schedule to talk. You were the answer to my prayers. I need to reread the story David and Goliath again. I am going to open my bible soon after I return home."

"I am happy that I have helped you, Angelina. Let us pray," He crossed himself and Angie followed along, "In the name of the father, the son and the holy spirit.

Heavenly Father, thank you for giving me the wisdom to help Angelina. Please watch over her and guide her in her life. Show her the way as she has faltered in recent time. Bless her and keep her safe throughout her life. Angelina, please join me with the Lord's Prayer,

> Our father who art in heaven,
> hallowed be thy name,
> thy kingdom come,
> thy will be done
> on earth, as it is in heaven.
> Give us this day our daily bread,
> and forgive us our trespasses,
> as we forgive those who trespass against us,
> and lead us not into temptation, but deliver us from evil.
> Amen.

Angelina, go in peace. Remember to love thyself as well as others."

"Thank you, father." She wiped her eyes. She crossed herself as she left the Cathedral, walked to her car and drove home. She thought about what Father Lopez had said. The longer she thought about it the more she understood. She realized she was feeling much better. The loathing she felt was fading. Now that she had a new understanding, she thought that she may be able to sleep without first crying. She had to talk to her mother when she got home.

Soon she was home. She parked and immediately went to look for her mother. She had been in the kitchen preparing dinner. "Mother?"

"How did you talk go"

"It was very enlightening mother. I need to tell you what he explained to me. I feel so much better now. Thank you for suggesting this."

"Give me a minute and we can talk." She slid the pan she had in her hand into the oven and closed the door. "Would you care to talk here or in the Arizona room?"

"Here is fine mother." They both sat across from each other. "Mother, Father Lopez had already known about my fights. He said he had read about them. I had an extremely difficult time trying to say what was bothering me. I cried. I was finally able to tell him, and he had a very interesting things to say and a story to explain why I should not feel as if I will be condemned."

Lizzy reached out and took her hands. She had a concerned look in her eyes.

"Father Lopez equated what I have done, to the story of David and Goliath. He explained that David had great courage confronting Goliath. He only had a sling and rocks while Goliath had a sword. He continued that I was confronting my Goliaths, people much stronger than me, with guns and knives and in greater numbers. He continued that I had self-love and love and compassion for others and was defending myself and them. He explained that the young ladies would have been used and likely eventually killed and my killing of these adversaries was done with great courage. He also recited a passage from the Catechism of the Catholic Church which states that legitimate defense can be not only a right but a grave duty for someone responsible for another's life, the common good of the family or of the State. I am not certain I quoted this correctly, but I am certain it is close."

"How do you feel now Angie?"

"I feel as if a huge weight has been lifted from my back. I realized that the talk with Father Lopez was the answer to my prayers. Every night I have been praying for forgiveness and asked that God would show me the way and help me to understand."

"I am very happy for you Angie. You may not have known but I have been suspecting this may have been what has been bothering you. I have seen that you have been preoccupied at times recently and I felt that I should wait until you wanted to talk."

"It was that bad? I thought I had covered it up well enough that no one would notice."

"I am your mother, Angie. I see very subtle changes easily."

Angie stood and walked around the table. Lizzy stood and they hugged. Angie said, I love you so much mother." She was becoming teary eyed.

Lizzy said, "I love you more that I know how to express Angie."

Dominic came into the kitchen. "Did I miss something?"

"Dom, Angie talked to Father Lopez and he has helped Angie greatly."

"That is good to hear. How are you feeling Angie?"

"I feel so much better father. I feel as though this talk with Father Lopez was the answer to my prayers. He gave me more than I had asked for."

"I am happy to hear that. I could see that there was something bothering you. I did not want to push. I thought you would talk when you were ready."

"You saw it as well?" Angie said. "I have been fooling myself then thinking I was covering it up."

"Do not think about it Angie." Lizzy said. "You did what you believed was correct. It is not wrong or right, it is just how you have delt with your problem."

14

Angie and her friends met at the Bum Steer on Saturday night. They got their regular table and ordered beer. Angie wasn't her usual cheerful self. She appeared preoccupied. No sooner than they ordered, Gina began telling everyone about her last date with Jeff.

"I went out with Jeff last Saturday." Gina said.

"How did it go? What did you do?" Janet asked.

"You won't believe what we did! It was so cool!"

"What did you do? C'mon, tell us." Karen said.

"OK, OK. He said he was going to pick me up at about 10:30. He didn't say what we were going to do. He just said I should wear jeans and a sweater because it would be chilly where we were going. I couldn't think of where we could be going." Gina said.

"Don't keep us waiting, Gina. C'mon." Karen said.

"OK, give me a chance. He drove to the northeast side and he turned on Catalina Highway. He took me to Summerhaven and we ate lunch at the Mt. Lemmon Inn! Then we walked around the little town. It was so cool!" Gina said.

"That sounds as though it would be a wonderful date, Gina." Angie said. "I understand it is a long drive."

"Yea, it seemed like we drove all day to get there. The views are unbelievable but the road is a little scary." Gina said.

"Like, what did you eat? What is the place like?" Denise asked.

"We had fried chicken and fries. It was good. The place is cozy, kinda like a big cabin. There is a little general store and we went in and he bought me some fudge." Gina said.

"That sounds like it was fun." Sherri said. Do you like him?"

"I like him a lot. He is funny and sweet! We sat down on a bench outside of the general store and we kissed. Then he hugged me so hard. It felt so good."

"What is he studying at school?" Sherri asked.

"He is in the engineering program. He wants to be a mechanical engineer. Karen, has anything happened with you and Curt?"

"Um, yea. We went to Tucson Burger Thursday for lunch. I was going to get my lunch, and he came up to me and asked if I wanted to go for lunch. So, we went."

"So, what happened?" Janet asked.

"We went there and ordered. He paid for my lunch. He said that since he asked me, he should pay."

"That was gallant of him Karen." Angie said but without her usual enthusiasm. Her friends did notice she appeared as if there was something on her mind.

"We sat and talked. He has an older sister that goes to U of A. He lives at home. He said he doesn't know if he is going to go to U of A or not." Karen said.

"What else?" Janet asked.

"We only have a half hour for lunch and it went by fast. We walked back. He reached out and held my hand." She blushed.

"Why are you blushing?" Sherri asked.

"I don't know. I guess I'm a little embarrassed."

"Why are you embarrassed? You're with us?" Janet asked.

"I don't know. Then he kissed me when we walked in the back door, but our boss walked in. I had butterflies in my stomach, and I got all embarrassed when our boss walked in. I don't know if he saw." Karen said.

"That is so cool Karen! Are you going to go out again?" Gina asked.

"He asked me out for next Friday night."

"You're going to go, aren't you?" Gina asked.

"Yea. I think I like him. He's nice."

"I am happy for you as well Karen." Angie said.

Sherri asked, "Angie, is there something wrong? You don't have that positive and energized look you always have. And it looks like your cheek is swollen."

"You look sad. No, that's not it." Paula said.

Angie sat for a minute. She wasn't going to tell them about last Sunday, but now she felt she had to. "Well, last Sunday I was attacked in my home."

They all looked shocked. "Like, what happened?" Denise asked.

"My parents had gone shopping for pool furniture and I stayed home. I thought I could spend some time relaxing and listen to some music. Two guys burst into my room, and they had guns pointed at me."

"My God!" Gina said. "What was it about? What did you do?"

"It turned out that the sister of one of the guys I killed at the child abduction incident wanted revenge. She slapped me in the cheek hard twice and she said she was going to make me sign over my CUDA because she knew how much I loved it then she was going to kill me."

"She slapped you in the cheek. I didn't notice before but now I see your left cheek is swollen." Karen said.

"I tried to cover it up with makeup along with the black eye."

"I didn't notice either before you said anything." Janet said. Everyone looked at Angie and then could see it.

"I ended up killing this girl's boyfriend with my mothers' letter opener, then I took the gun from her and shot both guys that were there to guard her. They both were going to shoot. We began to fight, and she ran on to the deck outside of the bedrooms. I believe she thought she could get away, but there are no stairs. She turned and fought, and I kicked her four times and she fell each time. I wanted her to back down. Then she pulled a bowie knife out of her boot and slashed at me back and forth. I ended up doing a 360 degree reverse roundhouse and she fell over railing and landed on the concrete stairs below. That killed her." Angie looked as if she were going to cry.

"Oh My God, Angie! How terrible!" Gina said and went over and hugged her.

Everyone looked sympathetic. "I don't know what to say, Angie. I feel so bad for you." Paula said. She was sitting across from Angie and reached out and took one of her hands.

"I was extremely distraught and went to talk to a priest at St. Augustine Cathedral Monday after work. I felt terrible that I killed two more people. I had an enlightening discussion with Father Lopez and I feel much better about it now. However, it did not help me to forget about the people I have killed. That has been on my mind since."

"Now I understand why you are not your usual cheery self." Sherri said.

Paula said, "Maybe we should order. Maybe eating will help you to put this out of you head at least for tonight."

"Possibly. I did not want to bring tonight down. I was not going to say anything about it until you asked."

"Like, that is what we are here for. We want to help you. You do so much for us." Denise said.

"What is it that I do?" Angie was beginning to feel small again.

"Like, I don't know. You're always so positive and you say stuff in a way that makes us think and feel better about ourselves." Denise said.

"You gave me confidence to talk to Jeff. If it wasn't for you, I probably wouldn't have said anything to him." Gina said.

"And you are so caring. You care about everyone. You don't get mad either. I wish I could do that. I think we are all better people because of your influence." Janet said.

"You make me sound as if I were some type of role model. I am just a normal person. I am not special."

"You're special to us because you are our friend." Sherri said.

Angie thought for a minute. What Sherri said struck a nerve. That got her to thinking. "I am special because I am their friend." She thought. That made sense to her. "All of you are special to me as well because you are such good friends. I had not thought if this in that manor. Thank you everyone." Angie was feeling better.

The waitress came over and they ordered the usual cheeseburgers and fries. Then Gina went to sing. She sang two songs and came and sat down. "Angie, aren't you going to sing?"

"Yes, Gina. I have not decided what to sing yet."

Then Rick and his friends came in. As they passed the table Angie and her friends he said, "Hi Angie and friends. You're going to sing to-day?"

"Of course, Rick. I just haven't decided what to sing yet." Angie said.

"Cool! I always look forward to you singing." And they continued to a table.

A girl from the table behind Angie turned and said, "Excuse me, but I couldn't help but overhear. You're the one that fought all of those guys at that child abduction thing? Really?"

"Yes, that was me." Angie said.

"I almost can't believe it! You're a hero! Ah, I didn't mean to interrupt, sorry." She looked a little embarrassed.

"That is alright. Do not worry." Angie said.

The disk jockey played a couple of dance songs and they all went and danced. After a couple of songs, they came back and sat town. Then their food came. As they were eating Janet said, "Since we talked about some of us dating, I have kind of been watching the guys at work."

"And?" Gina asked.

"Well, there are lots of guys working there around the store. I haven't seen anyone that looks interesting though." Janet said.

"That whole store and there isn't anyone interesting? Really?" Gina asked.

Everyone was looking at Janet. Now she felt like she was put on the spot. "I don't know. It's a big store and I don't get around that much."

"Sooner or later, you will meet someone Janet. And likely when you least expect it." Angie said.

"Angie, you are always so upbeat and positive. Even with all of the fights you get into. I was feeling a little down because I haven't met anyone."

"I do not believe you need to worry." Angie said.

"See, you're always so positive. It kind of makes me feel better, I don't know." Janet said.

"Paula, is there anyone you like?" Janet asked. She wanted to get the conversation away from herself because she was feeling a little self-conscious.

"No, mostly I see lawyers. There are other offices in the building but I don't see anyone from those." How about you Sherri?"

"I'm not really interested. I don't look at guys like that since those jerks that wanted to rape and kill us. I guess I'm not ready yet."

"That makes me feel sad." Angie said. "I understand that what happened to you was traumatic, Sherri. You need to heal. Sometimes that means you need to get back up on the horse, so to speak."

"You make it sound easy Angie." Sherri said.

"I do not believe it will be easy, but finding someone new may help you move on. It will come soon enough. I have faith." Angie replied.

Sherri said, "How about you Denise?"

"Like, I don't really see anyone at the doctor's office so I dunno."

Gina said, "I'm going to go sing "Cherry Bomb." The guys always seem to like it when I sing that." She got up and went to the stage.

The disc jockey gave her the mike and began the music. When some of the guys recognized the song, they looked. One screamed, "Go Gina!" She danced moving seductively. She loved the attention. She finished and handed back the mike and Angie was waiting.

Angie stepped on the stage and asked for "The Right Thing to Do." Someone screamed, "Hey It's Angie!" Everyone turned. When she began, they recognized the song and screamed. When she finished, she handed the mike back and went and sat down. Everyone was screaming and clapping.

"I think you're getting better, Angie!" Paula said.

"You believe so?" Angie asked.

"Yes! Your singing is amazing!" Janet said.

They finished eating and Angie and Gina sang a couple of additional songs and they decided to leave.

15

Soon it was Thanksgiving. This year it was at Angie's Aunt Lilly's house. And just as she has been doing since her 18th birthday, Angie and Lizzy went and bought new gowns.

Angie bought a floor length burgundy satin gown with floral lace around the shoulders and v neckline. It also had floral lace three quarter sleeves. Lizzy bought a floor length bone colored satin gown that had traditional lace over the low rounded neckline, and it also had lace three quarter sleeves. They also went and bought new shoes. Both Angie and Lizzy chose satin covered shoes in a color that was close to the gown colors.

On Thanksgiving Day while Angie and Lizzy were dressing, Dominic took out the new suit he had just bought. He did not tell Angie or Lizzy. He had bought a black pinstriped suit and had it fitted by a local tailor. He bought a beige satin shirt and a dark burgundy silk tie. He also bought a new pearl tie pin and matching cufflinks. He finished with black suede Oxford shoes.

He dressed and went to the Arizona room and waited for Angie and Lizzy. When Angie and Lizzy were finished dressing, they went to look for Dominic. They went to the Arizona room they were shocked! "Dom, you bought a new suit! And you had it tailored! You look so hansom!" Lizzy said.

Angie said, "Father, I almost did not recognize you when I first walked in. I agree with mother, you do look hansom."

"Thank you both. Both of you are very beautiful. I love your new gowns. And Angie, you have perfected your makeup. It looks just as it did when you had it done by the makeup artist for your 18th birthday. I believe I have been blessed with the two most beautiful women in Tucson."

"Thank you, Dom." Lizzy went and kissed Dominic.

"Father, you made me blush. Thank you."

"Let's get the dishes we prepared and we can leave. Lizzy had prepared baked buttermilk biscuits and a vegetable dish. Angie had baked her first pies. She baked two pecan pies.

"I hope my pies turned out edible being they were my first."

"Angie, I am certain they will be wonderful, honey." Lizzy said.

They picked up everything and went and got into Lizzy's car and drove away. They were the first ones to arrive. Lilly opened the door and said, "Hello, my all of you look absolutely wonderful. And Angie, you look amazing again! You never cease to amaze me." They went and put everything in the kitchen. "Lizzy and Angie, this is Charlotte. She will be preparing everything and will be serving tonight."

The doorbell rang and Lilly and Lizzy went to welcome everyone. Everyone else had arrived. Grandmother and Grandfather Hall, Enzo and Maria with Bella and Rosa and Uncle Jack and Aunt Sofia.

Angie had been talking to Shelly and they walked into the living room. "Angelina! You continually astonish me! You look absolutely elegant!" Grandmother Kristina said. "Did you go to the makeup artist again?"

"No grandmother, I learned to do it myself."

"Did you?" She was amazed.

Shelly, Rosa, Bella and Angie went to Shelly's room to talk. "Cuz, I cannot believe it! You out did yourself! You are so beautiful!" Shelly said.

"Thank you for the complement, Cuz." Angie replied.

Bella said, "You look like a princess again Cuz."

"You do!" Rosa said.

"Each of you look amazing as well. It is not just me. I cannot describe how different it has been for me at our family holidays since I have been dressing in gowns. I feel different and our holidays have more meaning now."

They all discussed what they have been doing lately. They talked until it was time for dinner. Edward came to tell everyone it was time to go to the dining room. "Angelina, this may sound odd coming from me but you do look very beautiful." As he said this he blushed.

"Edward, you are sweet." Angie said and went and gave him a hug.

Everyone went to sit but as has happened since Angie began to dress in gowns, Dominic, Grandfather Joseph, Carl and Uncle Jack helped each lady to sit and pushed in their chairs. This began at Angie's 18th birthday with Grandfather Joseph helping her.

Dinner was the usual with a small fruit cocktail, then salad. Lilly prepared separate salad bowls this year instead of the usual family style salad. Then came the turkey, stuffing, gravy, biscuits, vegetables and sweet potatoes.

Lizzy had made the vegetable dish. It was a combination of new potatoes, baby carrots, fresh spinach, radish slices, mushrooms, chopped red and green peppers, chopped green onion greens and parsley. She baked this with light olive oil and fresh garlic.

They all talked and ate. When everyone had finished, Charlette cleared the dishes and trays and prepared the pies. Aunt Lilly had made two apple pies; Grandmother Kristina had made two pumpkin pies and of course there were Angie's pecan pies.

When everyone had their pieces of pie, they passed around whipped cream cans. Angie was a little worried that her pecan pies wouldn't be good, but she soon found out different.

"Angelina," Grandfather Joseph said, "your pecan pie is wonderful! Is there anything you cannot do? It appears that you excel at everything you do! You are immensely talented."

"He is not stretching it, Angelina." Sofia said. "Your pie is absolutely delicious!"

"Without equivocation Angelina, your grandfather is correct. Your pecan pie is wonderful!" Grandmother Kristina said.

"Thank you everyone. I was worried that they would not be good. I have not baked a pie until yesterday and I did not taste the filling. Mother showed me how to make the crust."

"I was wondering. It is flaky just as Elizabeth's crusts. You should be proud of yourself, Angelina." Lilly said.

Angie kind of forced a smile. When her Aunt Lilly said that she should be proud of herself she immediately thought about the people she had killed again. "Would everyone please excuse me? I would like to visit the lady's room."

Aunt Lilly said, "Of course you may."

Angie got up and went to the nearest bathroom and closed the door. She was fighting tears. She was feeling guilt again. "How can I feel proud of myself after killing so many people?" she thought to herself. A few moments later there was a knock on the door. "Yes?"

It was Aunt Maria. She had felt Angie's guilt. "Are you OK?" She said quietly so no one else would hear. "I feel that you are feeling strong guilt. Would you care to talk?"

Angie opened the door and stepped back to allow her into the bathroom and closed the door. "Angie, what is bothering you? I know it is not your pies. This feels different. It feels as if it is deep pain."

Angie was fighting tears. "Aunt Maria," She paused. "I am feeling guilt for killing all of those people. When Aunt Lilly said I should feel proud of myself, it hit me. I understand what Father Lopez explained me that what I have done was justified because I was defending myself and others. I understand his explanation that these people were my Goliath's, but from time to time I still feel guilt. I did not want to feel this way on my favorite holiday. I do not want to destroy Thanksgiving for myself as well as all of the others. Now I am feeling bad because I may make today a sad day." She was carefully blotting her eyes trying not to smear her makeup.

"Angie, I understand how you feel. Mostly because I am feeling your emotions right now. I do not want to try to minimize your feelings. And I understand how you feel about pulling today down as well. I believe you may be taking your confrontations far too personally. You are such a kind, caring and loving person. And again, I do not want to minimize your feelings. I just hope I may be able to help you understand these in a healthier way. I feel that in a way you are beating yourself up inside. That is not heathy. Possibly you could attempt to think of those young ladies you saved when you have these thoughts. Possibly even just thinking about Amy when you have these thoughts. You had had such an attachment to her afterwards. If you think of her possibly you could help yourself to substitute the people you have saved in place of the ones that you killed.

"You are right. When I feel the guilt, I ultimately concentrate the people I killed. That is good advice Aunt Maria, thank you. I already feel better. Could I ask you to get my purse so I can freshen up a bit please?"

"Of course, Angie." She reached out and hugged Angie. "If anyone asks, I will tell them you will be back directly. I love you, Angie."

"I love you as well, Aunt Maria."

Maria turned, opened the door, stepped out and closed the door. She retrieved Angie's purse and brought it back to her.

When Maria returned to everyone, Lizzy asked Maria, "Is Angelina OK?"

"She will be fine."

"Was it something about the pies? She looked as though she was going to cry."

"No, Elizabeth. It was something that she thought about. Do not worry. We talked. I believe she will come to you to talk as well. Under her strong confidence she has some intense feelings of self-doubt. She is just touching up her makeup."

"Thank you, Maria. I know she is very close to you and trusts you."

"Yes, she does. Fortunately, it appears no one picked up on her feelings. She was worried that she would destroy this celebration. I know that when she begins talking to everyone she will cheer up."

"How do you know?" Lizzy said. Then she said, "You do not need to answer. You feel it. I continue not understanding what you Angie and Sherri share." She smiled and turned to talk to Lilly.

Angie returned and Shelly walked up to her. "Are you alright? I thought maybe you were not feeling well."

"I am fine. Thank you for your concern, Cuz." She reached and hugged her. "Sometimes things go through my head that upset me."

"I still do not understand what you and Aunt Maria feel. But that is OK. Provided you are alright."

"I am fine, thank you."

By now Bella and Rosa had come over and they all went to sit in the living room and talk. Edward walked up. "Do you mind if I sit with all of you?"

"Of course, not Edward." Angie said.

"Everyone is talking adult things and I feel out of place."

"You will not feel out of place talking to a group of young ladies?" Rosa said and laughed a little.

"Sometimes I feel as if I do not fit in anywhere." Edward said sounding somewhat dejected.

"Edward, I was just kidding with you." Rosa said. "Come on lighten up." She reached out and gave him a hug from the side.

Edward smiled. "Angelina, do you know I went and bought a car model? After watching you race, I thought maybe I should try to learn more. It was truly fun seeing you race. I even bought a Hot Rod magazine because I saw that is what you have."

"Really? You bought a model? What did you buy?"

"He bought a CUDA like yours. I thought it was interesting." Shelly said.

"Why do you feel it is interesting?" Angie asked.

"Well, I read somewhere that imitation is the sincerest form of flattery. I thought that maybe he looks up to you."

Edward blushed. "Yes, I kind of look up to you Angelina. It looks as though your friends do and I can see why."

"Why do you think that, Edward?"

"You do everything so well. You make me feel as if I should try harder at everything."

"You should always strive to do your best, Edward."

"See, it is the things you say and how you say them, and the things you do."

Shelly was a little shocked. She didn't think Edward thought like this. "Edward, I did not know you thought things like that."

"I know you think I am not smart. But I am smart." Edward said looking a little dejected again.

Bella said, "Edward, we do not think you are not smart. Why would you think that?"

"I do not know. But it feels like that sometimes."

"Edward, I do not believe anyone ever thought you were not smart. You have told us that you recognize that my friends look up to me and you bought a model kit to build. Someone that is not smart does not see and do things such as that. Could it be possible that you feel this because you are the only young man at our family gatherings? I can easily see that that could make you feel left out. I promise none of us think you are not smart."

"And Angie never breaks a promise. You know that." Rosa said.

Angie went to Edward and hugged him. "I think you just needed a big hug." She saw that he was blushing. "I did not mean to make you blush Edward."

"That is alright." Edward said.

Carl, Edward and Shelly's father, came and said, "We are getting ready for the family photo. Come everyone."

They all went into the living room. Grandfather Joseph set up his camera and focused it. He called Carlette over to press the button to take the picture. She took two.

Angie loved this part. As usual, she wanted a copy for her family album. She had every picture from every Thanksgiving since she was 4 years old. That is when Grandfather Joseph began taking family pictures on Thanksgiving.

Afterwards, everyone talked. It became late and everyone began to leave. They all said their goodbyes and left.

16

It is March 1977 and Angie has been thinking about new things to learn. She decided that she needed to learn to weld better. She knew about welding and knew how it works. Dominic has showed her some basics with gas welding. This is what he uses for exhaust systems. She had bought the book "Modern Welding" which is used in welding classes and covers most types of welding.

She wanted to perfect gas welding and learn stick welding, MIG welding and TIG welding. She felt TIG would be last due to the initial cost of the machine so she would begin with gas and stick welding.

Since they already had gas welding equipment in the shop, she began with this. Dominic worked with her to teach her how to set the regulators, how to set up the torch; how to choose tip size. Then he showed her how to light the torch. He showed her how to do silver soldering and how to braze as well. She practiced many days after work had been completed for the day. After a few weeks she began to do very well. Just as everything she tries to learn, she learns quickly.

Next, she worked on welding exhaust pipe together. This will allow her to do some of the jobs only Dominic or Eric had been able to do which was exhaust system work. This would give Dominic much needed help with custom exhaust systems and hooking up headers.

Angie still wanted to learn stick welding and then TIG because she has ideas for chassis modifications and roll bars. She also was getting the bug to build something different such as a mid-engine car or possibly a kit car.

Dominic already had a Lincoln 225 AC/DC stick welder. Eric began teaching Angie how to use this when she needed to modify the A/C compressor bracket for her CUDA.

Dominic had a machine shop he used from time to time to get custom parts machined so having a TIG welder would open up the possibilities with work they could do at the shop. Eric already knew how to tig weld, but Dominic hadn't considered work that required a TIG welder and did not have one either.

Angie was already saving for a TIG welder. These are expensive but it was necessary as far as she was concerned. And along with this she would need a few additional metal working tools if she was going to build a chassis one day. Her list had a steel cutting band saw; sheet metal finger brake; Beverly sheer (throatless sheer); a notcher; a portable spot welder; disc/belt sander; bead roller; slip roll and a chop saw and possibly in time, an English Wheel. She wanted to learn to be a master fabricator and Eric was excited about mentoring her.

Angie had bought many of books on design and fabrication as well and this was stimulating ideas for different projects she had thought about. She had ideas for building a mid-engine car possibly using a Porsche 915 5 speed transaxle, but these are unreasonably expensive. There were limited options at this time. There was always the Pantera transaxle but those are rare and unreasonably expensive. She was thinking however about using a Turbo 400 transmission and engine rotated 180 degrees if she could figure out how to make-up something to turn the output 180 degrees. Maybe a 4-wheel drive transfer case would work but these are large and heavy. She had seen a quick-change differential and the gears in the back of it, and it got her thinking. Maybe she could design a case to bolt to the back of a turbo 400 or a 4 speed that would use quick change gears. Her latest idea was using a Tornado transaxle but removing the final drive and making an adapter to connect to a driveshaft. This way she could mount the engine and transaxle 180 deg and run a driveshaft to a conventional differential. But this would mean that the differential would need to be turned upside down. This would cause additional problems but could be done. Then she read about the V-drives used on inboard/outboard boats and thought one of these could work as well. She learned that a V-drive was used on the HEMI Barracuda wheel stander car. She spent hours thinking about this and making sketches.

Dominic used to snicker at the ideas Angie had but recently he looked at some of her sketches. And some looked very possible. He never could get over the different ideas she thought about and sketched out. It seemed like every day she had a new idea. He thought that one day she would actually build something.

Angie had bought the book, "Handbook of Fiberglass and Advanced Plastics Composites," to learn about fiberglass and how to make bucks and molds. Since she had made a fiberglass front bumper for her CUDA, doing a car body wouldn't be much different, just larger. She thought that maybe she could come up with her own exotic looking car body. Although she believed this would be a huge undertaking. She would need to find glass from existing cars that would work along with latches, hinges and everything for the suspension and steering. But this did not bother her. She believed that she could accomplish anything she put her mind to, and she could always design and build all the parts that were necessary.

She had also been looking at kit cars and there weren't many that caught her eye. Although there was one that was fairly new called the Cimbra SS. It was manufactured in Milwaukee Wisconsin and she thought the body design did not have the typical kit car look. It had gull wing doors and sleek styling and may be able to be built as a semi mid-engine, so she thought possibly she could buy just the body at some point and maybe stretch it enough to make it a true mid-engine car. She also was looking at the Fiberfab Avenger and Valkyrie and possibly the Kelmark GT.

She had been discussing these ideas with Dominic for some time now and he had initially thought of these as just daydreams. But lately he was beginning to understand that she was very serious. She discussed with him where she could set up equipment as she was able to procure it and where she could work without disrupting regular work.

The more Dominic thought about this the more he thought it could add to the business. He began discussing this with Jack, showing him some of Angie's sketches and they decided that they could clean out the back storage building behind the shop and that would make a very nice fabrication shop. Basically, he was just storing the trailer there and a few miscellaneous engines and parts. It was 30' x 50' (1500 sq. ft.) and had 2 overhead doors facing the fenced in parking lot. This would make at least 3 spaces for cars and plenty of space for the fabrication shop.

Dominic figured he would need to add power for the new equipment and lighting since there were only a few lights; possibly add another lift and have an access door installed through the brick wall into the main shop. Just as he did before he opened the shop, he decided to discuss this with Joseph. Joseph always had good input for any building or business project.

Dominic went to talk to Joseph to discuss the whole idea. "Hello Joseph, how are you sir?"

I am fine Dominic. It is nice to see you. Are you here to work on investments?"

"Actually, no sir. I wanted to discuss some of Angelina's ideas for the business and get your input. I value your thoughts and would like to get your opinion on Angelina's ideas as well. She is very committed to these already even though I have not told her yes about any of it as of yet." They walked and sat down in his office.

"This sounds interesting. Maybe you should have brought her along, Dominic."

"I thought about that but today is one of her nights at the Dojo and we both know how committed she is about her martial arts training, particularly since she has had to defend herself so many times."

"Yes. Angelina is an amazing woman. What are her ideas?"

"Well, originally, I just smiled about these but then she began to elaborate on her plans and went on in detail and showed me sketches. I then discussed this with Jack, and he feels as though this could be a very important addition to the shop."

"Angelina came to me recently about her plans to learn to stick weld along with TIG welding. She already is becoming proficient at gas welding, and she just began learning a few weeks ago."

"Really? Now that is something I would not have guessed she would have been interested in."

"That is not all sir. She proposed outfitting the shop with many metal working tools and stated that she wants to learn to be a master fabricator."

"A master fabricator? What exactly would that be?"

"A master fabricator is one that would design; engineer; build chassis and suspension systems; build linkages and frames; specialty exhaust headers and exhaust systems. Basically, fabricate anything. She had told me she wants to build a mid-engine car of her own design along with her own design fiberglass body. That would be a monumental accomplishment. Eric is as close to a master fabricator that I have met and he is excited about teaching and mentoring her. This could give us the ability to do major modifications to race cars and possible build race car frames and suspensions. Eric already has experience building and modifying race car frames as he worked for a stock car shop out of high school. This is one reason I hired him. I figured if we ever had the opportunity to do any work such as this, he would be a perfect fit. He was the one that showed Angelina how to modify the air conditioning compressor bracket for her CUDA."

"Angelina has already discussed this with Eric in detail and now she has Eric thinking about this. She never ceases to amaze me, Joseph."

"This is almost unbelievable. I never thought Angelina would top getting ASE Certified. Now I am thinking there is nothing that she could not do. Where in the shop would you set this up?"

"Jack and I discussed this, and we decided that the storage building behind the shop would be perfect. It is 30 x 50 feet and has 2 overhead doors facing the parking lot. All we would need to do is add some power, lights, an access door into the main shop and possibly a lift and it would be set. Not counting the equipment, we would need to purchase. And Angelina told me she is already putting money aside for the equipment. She showed me a list of what she would like, and I shared that with Eric and it shocked him because this would be everything he would have suggested."

"Now I am surprised she hasn't come up with a business plan Dominic."

"She may have already begun putting one together for all I know."

"I am amazed, more than I was when she told all of us what she planned to do after graduating high school on her 18th birthday."

"Sir, I am not asking for help for this. I just wanted to tell you about her idea and get your opinion. The business has been doing so well that I believe I may be needing to hire an additional mechanic. And if we add this, possibly two. If Eric and Angelina begin to do this, I will be short two mechanics."

"Dominic, when I told you I was going to give you the money to open this business, I never expected it to grow like it has, and in only 14 years! I knew you would put every bit of effort into it but the growth is phenomenal. More than I would have expected. Dominic, I knew from that day I met you that you were an amazing person, but I could not have predicted how this would turn out. I could write a book on your, Elisabeth and Angelina's accomplishments. I could not be prouder."

"Sir, that has to be the best and most touching complement I have ever had."

"Wait here for a minute Dominic. I wish to have Kristina hear this. Particularly since she spent so many years disliking the fact that you and Elizabeth married. This is something she needs to hear to show her your commitment to the business and our family. I am almost speechless."

He stood and walked out of the office and brought Kristina back with him.

"What is this about Joseph? Dominic, I was not aware you were here. How are you?"

"I am doing very well Ma'am." He stood when she entered.

"Always the gentleman Dominic. I don't know what my problem was all of those years dear." She walked over and hugged him.

"Dominic has something to tell you about expansion of the business and where the idea came from."

"I am listening, Dominic." She pulled a chair over and sat.

"Ah, well," He wasn't completely positive he was going to do this but now he felt Joseph decided it was a done deal. "I came here to discuss this with Joseph, and I believe he approves, Ma'am. Angelina has been pestering me about her idea to expand our capabilities at the shop. She has had idea after idea and this one caught my interest."

"You will be very surprised sweetheart. You think Angelina surprised us at her 18th birthday with her wanting to learn the business and take over when Dominic retires, wait until you hear this."

"Ok, I am intrigued."

"Angelina came to me to tell me that she wants to learn to be a master fabricator. A master fabricator is one that would design, engineer and build chassis and suspension systems and build linkages and frames, specialty headers and exhaust systems and more. She told me she wants to build a mid-engine car of her own design along with her own design fiberglass body. That would be a monumental accomplishment. Eric is as close to a master fabricator that I have met, and he is excited about teaching and mentoring her. This could give us the ability to do major modifications to race cars and possible build race car frames and suspensions. Eric already has experience modifying race car frames as he worked for a stock car shop out of high school. This is one reason I hired him. I figured if we ever had the opportunity to do any work such as this, he would be a perfect fit. He was the one that showed Angelina how to modify the air conditioning compressor bracket for her CUDA.

Angelina has already discussed this with Eric in detail and now Eric has been thinking about this and is excited to teach and mentor her. She never ceases to amaze me. I have discussed this with Jack, and we decided that we could set up a fabrication shop in the rear storage building behind the shop."

"Angelina wants to do this? I never understood why she would want to be a mechanic but then she became the first woman in Tucson to get ASE certification. I am finally over the shock of that. Is there anything she cannot do? I still have a difficult time believing she is a mechanic, particularly when she gets dressed formally. She looks and acts so feminine. I do not know how to feel. Then with all the terrible incidents she has been thrown into, saving all of those young ladies. I almost feel we have our own superhero! I feel as though this surreal!" She looked stunned. She was thinking that her granddaughter that looks like a model and drag races is going to be a master fabricator. This was making her teary-eyed. "I am completely speechless. And it is making me feel as I did when I finally listened to your story Dominic. I never could have believed that you could have a family that would make me very proud. I still feel deeply sorry for all of the years I missed Dominic."

"Mother," now Dominic was teary-eyed, "You are an amazing person. There are so many things you share with my mother, ma'am." He stood and hugged her. "Thinking about how I felt after my father and mother died, I could never have believed I would be here now with people that I love and feel as complete as I did while they were alive. The love and connection I feel for my parents cannot be replaced but what I feel for the two of you is more than I could ever have wished for."

Dominic never saw Joseph get teary eyed, but he thought he saw tears in his eyes.

"Joseph, you have my blessing for anything you decide to do to help Dominic and Angelina achieve this." Kristina said.

"I am touched ma'am. I wasn't here to ask for help, just advice and thoughts. The both of you have done more for Angelina, Elizabeth and me that I could ever ask."

"I appreciate your sentiments, Dominic. But I want you to know we will always be here to help in any way." Kristina said.

They all sat there for a few minutes. Then Dominic looked at Joseph and asked, "If we do this, I would ask for your help in choosing a contractor for the power, lighting, lift and adding an access door between the shop and storage building. And if everything works out, I believe it will be time to pave the lot in the back as well."

"I would love to sit with Angelina and have her show me and describe her ideas, Dominic. Thinking about her excitement when she told me she was going to add factory air conditioning to the Cuda and then she did. It looks as if it came from the factory. I am just amazed." Joseph said.

Dominic said, "I do not think that would be a problem. In fact, I believe she will be excited to tell and show you. I will mention it to her tonight when she returns from the Dojo."

Dominic went home to tell Lizzy about her mother and father's reaction. He walked into the kitchen and hugged her from behind. She was finishing cleaning up from dinner. He told her about their reaction and how it was just as she had expected. He also told her that her father wanted Angie to discuss this with him and show him some of her sketches.

"I would expect that Dom. I believe he has a special place in his heart for her because besides being very intelligent and beautiful, I think he had wished we had a boy. But Angie has given him everything he had hopped for and more."

"I believe you are correct." They walked outside and sat together on the deck. It was almost twilight and the view of the mountains was spectacular. They sat and relaxed until it was completely dark, then went inside.

One Saturday morning Amy and her mother stopped at the shop. Amy is one of the girls Angie saved from child trafficking and she was also the one that Angie had developed a strong bond with during the incident. They came in and went up to the counter. Her mother said, "Excuse me, would it be possible to see Angelina?"

Dominic was filling out a customer invoice, he looked up. "Hello ma'am, of course, I will go and get her." He turned and went into the shop and told Angie there were some people here to see her.

Angie took off her gloves and walked to the front. As she walked behind the front counter she looked and saw them. "Amy? How are you doing? I almost did not recognize you now that you have healed. You are a very beautiful young lady."

"Thank you, Angelina. I wanted to come to see you to thank you again for rescuing me. I brought you and Sherri each a gift." She handed Angie two small boxes. "I don't know how to give this one to Sherri, so I brought them both here. Maybe you could give it to her?"

"Thank you, Amy, you are a very sweet young lady." Angie opened her gift. She pulled the cover off of the box and then the cotton. It was a crystal angel. It was obvious she was touched.

"I got this because I think you and Sherri are like my guardian angels." Amy said.

Angie was terry eyed and choked up. She walked around the counter and walked up to Amy and hugged her. "Thank you, Amy. You are very compassionate. I know that every time I look at this, I will think of you. I will make certain to get this other one to Sherri. I am certain her reaction will be just as mine was." She looked at Amy's mother and said, "Ma'am, you have a wonderful daughter."

"I have you to thank for that Angelina. You didn't only save Amy; you saved our family. My husband and I were constantly fighting when we thought we would never see Amy again. We had been blaming each other for her abduction. Amy's sister had just closed herself off from everything and everybody. She just stayed in her room and was depressed. Now we are almost back to normal. You are an angel in my eyes too!"

Angie had tears in her eyes. "I do not know how to respond to that ma'am. I had no idea what I did would have such an effect."

Dominic was off to the side and heard everything. He was choked up.

"Angelina, you are an amazing person. I wish you and your family well. We will go and let you get back to work." Amy's mother said.

"Bye Angelina." Amy said and waved as she walked out of the door.

Angie looked at the crystal angel again and smiled. She was teary eyed again. She grabbed the other box and went and put it in her purse along with hers. She would give the other to Sherri the next time she saw her. She went back to work.

18

Angie went to talk to her grandfather. She brought her portfolio with her sketches and lists. She had also begun to write a business plan. She planned to show everything to her grandfather.

She pulled up and shut off the CUDA and walked to the front door. As she was walking to the door, she had a vision of an old dilapidated farm house. As with the visions she had been having recently it was just a flash, barely long enough to see what it was. She got to the door and rang the bell. Her Grandmother Kristina answered. "Hello Angelina," she reached and hugged her, "please come in. Your Grandfather is expecting you. Your father told me of your ideas and you continue to astonish me." She walked with Angie to her grandfather's office. She knocked on the door.

"You may enter." Angie went in. "Angelina, you are looking beautiful as always."

"Thank you, grandfather." She blushed a little. Angie still has a bit of an issue with people saying she is beautiful. "Father told me you wished to see my sketches and ideas. I brought everything for you to see. I also began to write a business plan, but I am not certain exactly what is required. I was hoping you could assist me."

"Angelina, I would be happy to help." He got up and pulled a chair over to the desk. "Sit down here and show me what you have there."

Angie sat and opened her portfolio and pulled out a stack of paper about one inch thick. "I have all of my sketches and layouts and the pad I used to begin the business plan. Since we need permits to make the changes necessary in the back building, I believe we need a business plan for modification of the business license."

"You are correct. Let us see what you have here." He began to look through Angie's sketches. She had two scale layouts for the new shop drawn on graph paper to scale showing where the equipment would go and where the vehicles would go that were being worked on. She had more scale drawings showing the lights and electrical and sub panel along with additional compressed air lines. These showed the lighting type with switches; receptacle locations for the welders and marked where and what would be necessary to bolt down some of the equipment. She also had another scale drawing for the placement of the door, the framing and support structure that would need to be added for access to the main shop. She had a separate stack of sketches for the things she would like to build herself.

"Angelina, I am highly impressed. I do not believe we will need an architect for any of this. You have included everything that is required. We will need to make copies, however. This is fantastic! What else do you have?"

"I have my sketches of some ideas of things I would like to build." She moved to her stack of sketches. "This one has my latest idea. I have been thinking about building a mid-engine car of some sort but have been struggling with the idea of what to use for a transaxle. The transaxles I can find are far too expensive. So, I thought of some alternatives. My first idea was to use a Toronado Transaxle, but this limits the axle ratios to the ones offered from the factory. Since these were not designed for performance cars the ratios are not optimal. Then I thought of this." She pulled out her sketches of a conventional transmission with her design of a method of changing the direction of the output. "I would use a Franklin quick change rear case using quick change gears and an extension housing adapter and custom-made shafts. This would allow use of a conventional rear axle, but I could turn the engine and transmission 180 degrees and place the transmission in the tunnel. Then I would have a method of changing overall ratios easily and quickly. I believe this could be done to a regular 4 speed transmission as well as automatic. I also had a thought of possibly using a marine V-drive like they used in the HEMI Barracuda wheel stander car. Then, you can see I designed an engine cradle that I believe I could adapt to many different cars that were not designed as mid-engine cars."

"Angelina, I am shocked. I feel as though I am sitting with an engineer. These sketches are amazing. Now I see why your father was excited. I can hardly believe this."

"Oh, I almost forgot, these are my beginning sketches of the body design I have been working on. When I finish this, I will need to design a chassis for it as well."

"This looks like an exotic car, somewhat like a Ferrari or Lamborghini but not exactly. I am shocked. Angelina, you are so talented."

"Thank you, grandfather. My plan is to make something exotic looking. But whatever I come up with I need to be able to find glass from cars already made. I do not want to think about what a custom piece of glass would cost. Then I would need to find or fabricate hinges for the doors, engine cover and front end and of course, everything else."

"I find your excitement about this amazing Angelina. I will help you with the business plan and then we will need to submit it for license modification from the city. I have to say it again, you amaze me!"

"Thank you, grandfather. Your complements mean so much."

"The excitement I see in you is amazing! I just cannot believe it!"

Angie said goodbye to her grandfather and went to look for her grandmother. They talked for a time then Angie went home.

19

The following Sunday Dominic, Uncle Jack and Angie went racing. Dominic ended up winning eliminations. He had raced against Angie and won. She did not tell him that she thought she had an unconsciously thought to let him win. She ran slower than usual, 12.60/ 121. This was slow compared to her 12.35 dial in. She drove back to the pits and parked.

"You lost? I was so positive you were going to blow him away. He never runs close to his dial in. But you always are only a few hundredths under your dial in. What did you run?" Uncle Jack asked.

"I ran 12:60 at 121." She sounded disappointed. I do not know what happened Uncle Jack. Maybe I was trying too hard to win, I do not know. I guess I am finished for today."

"Don't feel bad Angie. One slower run isn't so bad. It is just one time. You will get another chance against you father."

"I understand Uncle Jack. I just feel as it I was not doing my best and that concerns me."

"Angie don't be so hard on yourself. It was just one run. It isn't a big deal. Besides, you father probably thinks he really beat you. I don't think he ever thought he could."

"You are likely correct. I will let him think he beat me."

Uncle Jack hugged Angie. "Angie, you are such a unique person."

Later when the eliminations were over Dominic drove back to the pits where they were. He pulled up and shut the Nova down. "I cannot believe I beat you, Angie. It was a good run for me. I almost ran my dial in." It was obvious he thought he beat her. The thought of Angie running well below her dial in never crossed his mind.

Angie didn't say anything besides congratulating him. They put the Nova on the trailer and packed up. Then they drove home.

While Angie was driving home, she saw a few different images flash in her head. She saw someone screaming and swinging her arms. Then she saw someone beating on a steering wheel extremely angry. Then she saw a cowboy riding a horse. Then she saw a speedometer pegged. But nothing felt as if they were related. They were all just a few milliseconds. Barely enough time to recognize what was in the images. She saw other things such as cholla cactus that appeared that were driven over. None of this made any sense to her. She got home and parked the CUDA and went into the house. "Hello Mother." She had been sitting in the kitchen. "Dinner smells good. Pot roast?"

"Hello Angie. Yes, it is pot roast."

Angie hugged her mother. "I am going to take a shower. Father is dropping off Uncle Jack." She walked away.

While Angie was in the shower Dominic got home. He went into the kitchen and hugged Lizzy and kissed her. "Do you believe I beat Angie? I cannot believe it. I ran well that run. However, I wonder if she possibly let me win. I cannot believe I could beat her."

"Possibly this was an off day for her. I know that does not happen. But maybe it is possible." Lizzy said.

"Possibly. I am not going to say anything. It was a good day otherwise. There were not many cars today."

"How did Angie do otherwise?"

"She did well. There was a guy with a gray 427 1967 Camaro she raced against. I think this guy cannot take losing to a woman. He looked insanely angry afterwards. I think this is the second time she has raced against him, and he lost both times."

"Well, you have said she is incredibly fast at the light."

"She is. There have been many guys that redlight when running against her. But that is their problem. There are many egos that have taken a hit." He chuckled. "But there are also some that are impressed at how well she does. It does not seem to bother her, however. I am going to take a quick shower before dinner." He walked to their bedroom.

Lizzy just sat down and smiled. She picked up the LIFE magazine she had been reading when Angie got home.

Angie had finished her shower and changed into her pajamas. She had her hair wrapped in a towel. She came back into the kitchen and sat down at the table. Dominic came in a few minutes later.

Lizzy served dinner. As they ate Lizzy looked at Angie and asked, "How was racing today?"

"It was alright."

"Just alright? Something happen?" Lizzy looked slightly concerned.

"Well, no, mother. Nothing really. I got to race against father and he won. I had a slow time. I cannot figure out what happened. But on a good note, father won against me." She looked at Dominic. "That had to feel good. Winning against me?"

Dominic looked at Angie, "It felt good. I did have one of my best runs. I still cannot believe I won."

"Father, I am happy for you. I know the only other time I raced against you I ran my dial in and won by quite a bit."

"Yes, you did. And I thought this would have been a repeat of that."

"I think possibly I was not concentrating as I usually do. I have seen quite a few images in my head lately and it is possible this hurt my run."

"Really? What have you been seeing?" Dominic asked.

"Many different things. I have seen an old dilapidated farmhouse, someone screaming, a cowboy riding a horse. None of these make any sense. I do not think these are related. At least it does not feel like it. I just see them for an instant, barely long enough to recognize them. There have been quite a few. Maybe these were in the back of my mind today."

"I cannot imagine seeing things such as that." Lizzy said.

"Well, I am becoming used to these visions. I always have racing thoughts all around these visions. I think it is possible that all of this could drive someone crazy. But I cannot remember any time when I did not have racing thoughts, so the visions are not troubling, at least now."

"I do not know how you deal with these so well. I know Aunt Maria has told me she has racing thoughts all of the time as well. Just thinking about this too much could make me crazy." Lizzy smiled.

They finished with dinner. Angie helped her mother clean up then she went to sit in the Arizona room for a bit before she went to bed. She knew she would have trouble getting to sleep because of the visions and watching the stars always helped her to relax a bit.

20

In the following weeks the business license had been amended and work on the back storage building began. The contractor had already added the new doorway between the two buildings and the electrician had been busy adding lighting to what was going to be the new fabrication shop.

As before, Joseph arraigned a business loan for Dominic, and Dominic put Angie in charge of supervising the work to transform the storage building into a shop and to purchase the equipment necessary. Dominic also reminded Joseph that this did not need to be a gift as the business was doing very well.

Angie was excited when the equipment began to be delivered. The new lift was installed, and she and Eric began to place each piece of equipment in the places that they felt would be best. Some of it required bolting to the floor and the contractor took care of that as well. Angie and Eric planned where the benches should be and began to order the steel required to build these.

One thing Dominic did that surprised Angie was he had a painter come in and prep and paint the inside walls white. This made the new shop look very bright and clean.

There was much work to do before they would be ready to begin business. Angie and Eric worked preparing the new shop a few hours after work on Mondays, Wednesday's, some Saturday nights and on Sundays when they did not go racing. Usually, at least once each of these times Angie would have an image flash in her mind's eye. As these generally are, she saw a glimpse of what appeared as someone with a cloth bag over their head. She also saw what appeared to be someone sitting on a chair and she thought she saw this person's legs tied to the legs of the chair, but she couldn't be certain. Angie could not work late on Tuesday's and Thursday's because those were the nights that she trained.

The steel for the benches was delivered and they began to cut and weld the angle to make bench frames. Once they finished framing all of the benches, they took measurements and ordered 12-gauge steel sheet cut to size for the bench tops. When these were delivered, they fitted each and welded them onto the frames. Then they painted the frames.

While they were discussing building the rack for raw materials. She saw what appeared to be a room with quite a few people filled with what she thought was fog. She thought it was odd for a room to be filled with fog. She wondered if it was smoke from a fire, but no one was running out of the room. Another image flashed in her mind. She saw someone pointing a gun and she thought it was aimed at her. She couldn't determine what any of these meant.

They built the rack to hold the steel angle; bars; tubing and sheet steel they would normally stock. By the time they were finished building the benches and racks Angie's stick welding was looking professional. They still had many things to do before they could officially open the fabrication shop.

Angie and Eric discussed what they would require to begin to build frames. Eric said that they would need a very heavy duty cross braced bench or rack large enough to hold a whole frame and it needed to be completely square and plumb. They then would use this to mock-up and build the frames. For the basis of this, they would need 2-16 foot long 8" x 12" I beams and the extra material for bracing and height adjustment.

Angie made the decision to fabricate this bench/rack right away. Angie sketched this out and she and Eric determined how much of each type of steel would be needed. Then Jack placed the order for the steel. The basic frame would be two 8" x 12" I beams 16 feet long and the bracing would be made out of 4" x 6" x .250" tubing with crossmembers using 3" x 3" x .250 angle. They would need to make 8 legs with heavy duty height adjustment bolts. They also ordered 8 locking casters with a 1500-pound capacity each. They wanted this to be sturdy enough to support building integrated frames with the OEM body attached. And the wheels would make it possible to move it around easily and to store it against a wall.

The steel arrived and they needed to use the engine hoist to lift most of the cut pieces of steel and put them on jack stands to tack weld everything together. Then they would verify that everything was square and plumb before final welding. Afterwards they painted this as well.

Angie met her friends at the Bum Steer. "Gina, those pants look great! Are they real leather?" Janet asked. Gina had worn her new black leather pants with the chain belt her mother had bought for her. She thought she looked a lot more like Joan Jet now.

"Yes, they are leather. My mom just bought them for me today. Our relationship has been so close since I talked to her. She turned to Angie and hugged her. "If it wasn't for you, I never would have talked to my mom and our relationship wouldn't have become so close. I mean, everything with my family is so much better. I feel like I am closer to my dad too. You're amazing, Angie, I want to thank you again!"

"I am happy to hear that, Gina. But I still do not understand how I had such an effect on you."

"What's important is that you did!" Gina said. "And my mom and dad told me that after I graduate and get a job, they are going to help me buy a car! Do you believe that! That's so great!"

"That's cool!" Paula said.

It was the usual Saturday night of dancing and karaoke. They all ordered burgers and ate.

When they finished eating Gina and Angie sang Karaoke. As usual, Gina went first. She went up to the stage and the guys started screaming and whistling. One screamed, "You look hot like Joan Jett!" Gina loved it.

She asked for "Venus." She sang better that she had before. It seems that the more she sings the better she is getting. However, she still doesn't sing like Angie. The song ended and the crowd roared!

Angie went up. She asked for "Haven't got time for the Pain." The place got quiet. They were waiting to find out what she was going to sing. The song began and she began to sing. The crowd got wild screaming and whistling. She finished and somebody screamed, "Another, another."

She turned and asked if he had "Nobody Does It Better." She knew it had just been released for the James Bond movie "The Spy Who Loved Me."

He had it. When the into played, everyone knew what it was. Everyone went wild again. This time the cook and the manager came out to see who was singing. They thought it sounded just like the movie. "Who is that?" the manager asked one of the people sitting at the bar.

"That's Angie Tucci! She sings all the time and she is great! Isn't she?"

"She is amazing!" he said.

She finished and the crowd roared! She handed the mike back and went to sit. Gina looked at Angie and said, "Angie, I think that was your best yet! It was amazing!"

"Thank you for your complement, Gina." Angie replied.

Just then, the manager came to the table. "Angie, would you ever consider singing songs all night? You could be the live entertainment. I would pay you."

"Really? You think my singing is good?"

"You are kidding me, right?"

"No. I am serious. You would want me to sing all night? I do not know. I do this for fun. I do not know that I would want to sing all night. But thank you for the offer, sir."

"Sir? Just call me Jake. Well, if you change your mind the offer is still good. You were amazing. I think if I advertised that you would be singing some night the place would only have standing room. Think about it, OK?"

"I will think about it, but I still do not believe I would want to sing all night. Thank you for the offer." Angie said.

The manager walked away. "He asked you to sing? What an offer! See, we told you that your singing is awesome!" Janet said.

The disk jockey played some music. He does this to break up the karaoke.

Between songs a guy came up to Denise and asked her to dance. She said OK. When the song was done, the disk jockey played a slow song and this guy still wanted to dance with her. As she danced, she put her arms around his neck. She thought he was cute. When the song was done, he asked her out and she said yes. He told her his name was Mario.

He made a date to go out with her the following night, Sunday night. She was very excited. She gave him her address and phone number. She went back to the table and told everyone. "Did you see the guy I was dancing with?"

Paula said, "Yeah, what about him?"

"Like, He asked me out on a date for tomorrow night. His name is Mario." Denise said with a bit of excitement. She was almost giddy.

"Mario? Do you know anything else about him?" Paula asked.

"No. We didn't talk much but he is really cute."

Gina asked, "Which guy? I didn't see."

"See that guy over there with the brown shirt?" She pointed to where a bunch of guys were talking. "Like, he was sweet and said he would like to take me out."

Gina looked. "Those guys look like gang bangers. They look scary. You think this guy is OK?"

"I don't know. Like, he danced good and all and he was nice to me. He said I was the cutest girl he ever saw!"

"I guess you will find out. I need to go to the bathroom. Anyone else need to?" Gina said.

Angie said she did and went with her. They had to pass these guys to get there. Angie and Gina both looked them over as they passed them. When they were in the bathroom Angie said, "They look like gang bangers."

"That's what I thought. Maybe they just look like that. But I think we should watch them. Denise is giddy and she has had a couple of beers. I just don't want her to get involved with a bad group." Gina said.

"I agree Gina. But there is not much we can do."

"Yeah, I know. She is our friend, and I don't want to see anything bad happen."

"We will just have to wait to see what happens." Angie said.

An image flashed in Angie's head as she and Gina walked past them again going back to the table. She thought she saw Mario with a bloody nose. She had to glance back at him to check. He looked at her with a strange look. He didn't have a bloody nose. She thought that was strange. "Gina, this may sound strange, but I just had an image of Mario flash in my head, and he had a bloody nose."

"That is strange." Gina looked over at Mario again. "He looks fine now."

"I know."

When they got back to the table Janet and Karen were talking about those guys too. They thought Denise should know more about the guy first. But she told them he is taking her out tomorrow already. She wasn't going to change her mind about this.

They danced more and a few more people sang karaoke. When they finished their beers, they paid and went home.

22

The following night Mario picked up Denise. He took her to this bar in South Tucson that looked shady. But Denise was too infatuated with Mario to notice. Paula and Gina had been worried and had decided to follow them. Gina borrowed her mother's car. She had a difficult time following because she didn't want to look like she was following.

"I want to stop at a bar where my friends hang out for a while. OK Denise?" Mario said.

"I guess that's OK." Denise was infatuated with Mario. She didn't notice that he had taken her to a bar in South Tucson.

He parked and got out. Then he opened the door for Denise and reached to help her out. He was getting very excited. Almost to the point of laughing but he held it in. "Hey, look, there are some of my friends. I'll introduce them to you." They walked over to the table where they were sitting.

"Hey Mario. Who's this lovely girl?" One guy asked.

"This is Denise. We met at the Steer last night. Isn't she cute?"

"Yeah. Really cute!" He moved over to make room for the two to sit.

Mario moved to let Denise sit first then he sat. "These are some of my friends. This is Tony, Ricardo but we call him Ricky, and that is Freddy."

"It's nice to meet you." Denise said.

The bar tender came over with two mugs of beer and set them on the table Tony, the guy next to her, started talking to her. Mario dropped something into one beer and it fizzed then stopped. He pushed it over. "Here Denise."

"Thanks." Denise took a big gulp of it. They all talked and by the time she drank most of it she looked as though she was going to pass out.

"See, that stuff works good." Tony said.

"This is going to be fun." Mario said. "Better than last time. She is so cute the other girl was homely."

"We had fun though and she didn't remember anything." Tony said.

Gina and Paula were a little afraid because of the neighborhood. They watched Mario open the door and reach to help Denise got out of the car. Then they went into the bar. "Maybe we should have asked Angie to come with us. I am a little worried to be here by ourselves." Gina told Paula.

"Maybe we should call her. Maybe she could meet us here." Paula said.

"Her car would stick out. You think that's a good idea?" Gina said.

"I don't know, I am afraid for Denise. What is something happens?"

"I don't know. They just went into that bar. We don't know that anything will happen." Gina said.

"Should we maybe go in there and check it out?" Paula said.

"I'd be afraid, but maybe we should. There is a pay phone right outside of the place so if we need to, we could call Angie." Gina said.

"I think we are going to stick out. We don't look like anyone around here." Paula said.

"We need to do it for Denise. We can't let anything happen to her. She's our friend. I don't have a good feeling about this. What do you think? Gina said.

"I guess." They sat there for a while deciding whether to go or not. They just saw lots of guys that didn't look safe going in. A few had women with them and they even looked dangerous.

After about 5 minutes Gina said, "I think we should try to call Angie first and tell her what is going on."

"What are you going to tell her, we followed them and maybe something is happening? Paula said.

"Well, we could look quickly and then call her if something looks bad. I will keep some change in my pocket in case."

"OK. I still don't like this." Paula said.

Gina took some change and put it in her pocket, and they got out of the car and locked it. They walked on the sidewalk to the bar and as they passed the phone booth she glanced inside and it appeared to be in working condition. They went into the bar. The door was propped open. Mexican music was playing loud.

There was quite a bit of cigarette smoke hanging in the air, so much it looked like fog. It was kind of hanging there across the whole bar. They looked around and saw Denise at a table in the back of the bar. Gina and Paula sat at the end of the bar close to the door and watched. The bar tender walked up and said, "What'll it be ladies?"

Paula said, "Ah, two beers." He turned and walked to get the beers. He came back with two bottles of some kind of Mexican beer they never heard of.

"That's a dollar and a half each." He said.

Paula took out a five-dollar bill and gave it to him and he walked away. "I guess he figured the change was a tip."

They each took a sip. "Look Paula. Denise is sitting with a table full of guys and she looks like she is about to pass out. She couldn't have had that much to drink yet. I think they put something in her beer."

"Yeah, she looks really drunk. The guys are all laughing and touching her. This doesn't look good, I'm going to call Angie. Maybe you should wait here so it doesn't look suspicious." Gina gave her the change she had put in her pocket. Paula stood and said as a diversion in case anyone was watching them, "I left it in the car. I'll get it." Loud enough for the bar tender to hear. He didn't even look. Paula walked out normally hoping no one would notice her. As she left Denise passed out and laid over the table.

Paula went to the phone booth and went in. She put in change and dialed Angie's number. It was ringing, "Angie, please be there. It rang a few more times. C'mon Angie, pick-up." She thought.

"Hello?"

"Angie," Paula sounded almost frantic. "Gina and I followed Denise and that guy to this bar, and it looks like they drugged her. She looks like she is ready to pass out. She is sitting with a group of guys and they are all laughing and touching her."

"What?" Where are you?"

"We are at this bar on 29th street in South Tucson. It's on the corner of 4th Avenue."

"I'll be there as fast as I can. Don't let them take her anywhere." Angie hung up. She was worried because she had just seen an image of Denise with a bunch of guys, and she had a strong feeling that they were going to rape her.

Paula left the phone booth and went back into the bar. There was a Mexican guy hitting on Gina and he was being very pushy and touchy. It was obvious she didn't like this. She walked up and sat on the stool.

"You got a friend too? We can have lots of fun, all of us."

Gina was pulling his hands of her. "Take your hands off of me asshole!"

"Oh c'mon, you like it." He kept touching her.

"Stop it!" She slapped him.

"Angie is on her way Gina." Paula said sounding a little relieved.

"Good." She turned to the guy. "Our friend is coming and she'll kick your ass."

"Oh, I'm scared. A girl is going to kick my ass. That'll be the day. So, there are three of you. Even better. Ha Ha. We're gonna have lots of fun tonight. Me and my boys. We already have one bitch over there. When is you friend commin?"

"She will be here in about 15 minutes now."

"Great! I tell my boys." He turned and walked away.

Gina turned to Paula, "he said they already have one. I think he meant Denise. This is bad. Don't drink anything more. I don't want us to get drugged too."

Paula was about to drink some of her beer and put it down. "I guess it's a good thing we only drank a little. Did you see the guy open these?" She was referring to their beer bottles.

"No, I wasn't really paying attention. He could have put something in them."

"If he did, I hope we didn't drink enough. Now I am really scared."

It took Angie about twenty minutes to get there. Gina and Paula knew when she arrived because they heard a loud car engine and a car skidding to a stop right in front of the place.

Angie got out of the CUDA and put her Eskrima sticks in the bag she had tied to her waist before she left home. She walked into the bar ready to fight. She saw Gina and Paula and walked up to them.

"Hello Gina and Paula." She reached out and hugged each of them. "Where is she?"

"She is over there." Paula pointed. "But this place is trouble. That guy there was giving Gina trouble when I got back from calling you. He said they were going to have fun with us and the girl they got already."

"You are not drinking, are you? I see two beer bottles." Angie was a little worried.

"Before we knew anything was wrong, we ordered beers because we wanted to look at least a little like we fit in. We each only took one sip and we haven't had any more." Paula said.

"Don't drink any more. Both of you wait here." Angie turned and walked towards the table that Denise was laying over. As she walked past the guy Gina and Paula pointed out he looked at her and went and grabbed her. He started to say, "Hey you're pretty." and she grabbed his hand and immediately broke his wrist with the Nikyo wrist lock like it was nothing. He fell over and screamed.

"You broke my fucking wrist bitch. He laid there holding it. A few other guys noticed that. They thought she just hit him and laughed.

She continued walking. When she got to the table she asked, "What did you do to my friend?" She pointed to Denise.

"What are you going to do about it bitch?" A guy beside her reached to grab her arm and she put him in a Nikyo wrist lock, and he went down on his knees and screamed. Another guy went to grab her, and she hit him with two fast punches with her other hand and he fell on the floor with his nose bleeding. The first guy was still screaming.

"I will only ask one more time, what did you do to my friend?"

"Fuck you!" he said.

Angie immediately broke the wrist of the guy she was holding and tossed his hand away. Then she punched Mario so hard Gina thought she heard his nose break from across the bar. He sat back screaming and was in a daze. Now all the other guys were noticing what was happening and began walking over to the table. One guy went to grab her, and Angie pulled out her sticks and began hitting him and the other guys so fast they couldn't even put their hands up fast enough. You couldn't see the sticks. She spun and hit one guy then another. Then she turned and hit two more guys. Now they were starting to back off. The bartender walked up with a 45 automatic and pointed it right at Angie. The gun was about one foot away from her. She stopped and put her sticks in the bag, turned and looked at him. She immediately took the gun away. He looked at her in shock. She then spun and hit him with a 360 deg roundhouse. He fell over and his head crashed onto the edge of another table and knocked it over. He fell on the floor and didn't move.

Angie held the gun pointing it at some of the guys. She called Gina, "Gina, come here!" Gina quickly walked over, and she said, "Here take this." She handed her the gun and said, "If anyone moves, shoot them."

Gina had a shocked look for a few seconds then screamed, "Don't move assholes, I am trained in the use of this kind of gun, and I am not afraid to use it!" In reality, she never held a gun before, but they didn't know that. But she sounded as if she was dead serious.

Angie turned looked at Mario and said, "Move now or they will take you out in a body bag!"

He stared at her in disbelief then got up from the bench holding his nose as it was still bleeding. The blood was dripping on his shirt.

Angie grabbed Denise's arm and pulled her to the edge of the bench. "Leave me alone I want to sleep mom."

Angie said sternly, "Denise, stand up now." She helped her stand then put her arm around her waist. "Get back! Now!" One guy moved towards her, and she kicked him in the face with a forward roundhouse. He went down and didn't move. Everyone else moved back. The bartender was still laying on the floor unconscious. She helped Denise walk towards the door. Gina followed walking backwards pointing the gun back and forth at the guys.

Other guys were watching, and they began to move towards her. Angie said, "Stay back or you will get what the bartender got. Get back! Paula, come here." She kind of ran over. Take Gina's keys and go start the car and pull it up behind mine.

Paula took the keys from Gina and ran out to Gina's mother's car. She started it and drove to the door.

As Angie got Denise out of the door Angie reached into her pocket with the hand she wasn't holding Denise with and grabbed her keys. "Gina, open the door but keep the gun pointed at the doorway."

Gina grabbed the keys and opened the door. Angie got Denise into the car and closed the door. She took her keys from Gina and said, "Get in the car with Paula and follow me. I am going to take Denise to St. Mary's emergency." She ran around the car, pulled out her sticks and tossed them the back seat, got in, started the CUDA. She blasted away smoking the tires. Paula followed.

The guys in the bar were stunned. They couldn't believe a girl did this. Some went to the bartender to help him. Others went to help the guys with the broken wrists. Another was looking scared and said, "I know who she is."

"Mario said, "Who? Who is she?""

"Remember in the news a while back there was a girl that killed everyone in the child sex ring? She's her."

"That's her? Really? I don't believe it!" Mario said.

"Look what she just did. Who else could she be?"

Mario said, "No way! She just messed with the wrong guys."

"Are you crazy? She killed 15 guys that night! And they were all armed! She has a reputation around that she is deadly. I heard she scared the shit out of one of the Tucson cops."

"She scared a cop? Right." Mario said.

"My cousin knows a cop that told him she fights like Joe Singso. He said one of the guys from the child sex ring grabbed her around the neck with a rope and she ran up the wall to get out of it. He said she killed him right after. He said a lieutenant saw the whole thing."

"I don't believe all that karate crap." Mario said.

"There is more. She also killed three guys that attacked her at her dad's shop one night. And two guys had guns and one had a big knife. You saw what she did to Jimmy didn't you?" (Jimmy is the bartender)

"Yeah, I saw." Mario said. "She took the gun away from him and knocked him out with some kind of kick in like a second! I wouldn't mess with her."

Maybe yer right." Mario said.

23

"What should I do with this?" Gina asked Paula. She still had the 45 automatic.

"I don't know. We can ask Angie when we get to the hospital."

When Angie got to the emergency room she stopped and shut off the CUDA. She ran around and opened the door and helped Denise out and into the emergency room. A nurse came to help. "What happened to her?" The nurse asked.

"She was at a bar and someone put something in her drink. She was passed out when I got there."

The nurse helped Angie take Denise to a bay and helped her into a gurney. She started asking Angie questions. By then Gina and Paula arrived. They ran into the ER and found them. "Gina and Paula, could you help the nurse with her questions please? I need to call Lieutenant Edwards."

"OK" Gina said.

Angie asked where there was a pay phone and the nurse pointed one out. She dialed Lieutenant Edwards, "Hello Lieutenant Edwards?"

"Hello Angie, how are you?"

"Not very well sir. I just picked up one of my friends from a bar where they drugged her. I am at St. Mary's ER now. The Bar is at 29th St and 4th Ave. You will find the bartender knocked out and a couple of broken wrists and noses. They wanted to drug my friends and me as well."

"Angie, that's South Tucson. Why would you go there?"

"My friend Denise went on a date with a guy that took her there and two of my other friends followed because they did not trust this guy. They called me when they found Denise passed out laying over a table shortly after they went in."

"I see. I will need to talk to the South Tucson Police. That is out of my jurisdiction. I will come to St. Mary's to talk to all of you. The South Tucson police may want to talk to you, too."

"I understand, sir. I just wanted to get Denise out of there before they did anything to her.

"I will come right now. Please wait there for me."

"We will sir, thank you. I believe we will be here for a while." Angie hung up and went back to see how Denise was doing.

A few minutes after Angie's call to Lieutenant Edwards, the South Tucson police showed up at the bar. It was just as Lieutenant Edwards described. Two guys had broken wrists, the bartender was still out cold on the floor, and another had a broken nose. They ended-up arresting Mario and Tony because they had a bottles of Quaaludes in their pockets and the possibility that they were using them to have nonconsensual sexual relations with girls.

Denise was awake but very groggy. She sat up a little and put her elbow down to hold herself. She didn't understand what happened. She was shocked that she was in the Emergency Room.

"Where am I? What happened?" she said sounding out of it.

Gina said, "You're at St. Mary's Emergency Room. We brought you here."

"Wha.." Her eyes were dilated and moving around. "I feel terrible." She moved her arm and fell back down onto the pillow.

Gina and Paula tried to tell her what happened, but she was not coherent enough to understand. Angie walked over and told them the Lieutenant was on his way. "Gina, what did you do with that gun?"

"It's in the car. I didn't know what to do with it, so I put it under the seat."

"We can give it to the Lieutenant when he gets here." Angie said.

It wasn't long before the Lieutenant arrived and met them in the Emergency Room. "Hello sir. These are my friends, Gina and Paula, and this is Denise." She was still lying down mostly out of it. "Lieutenant, Gina has a gun to give you that I took from the bartender. He pointed it at me, so I took it away."

"A gun?"

"Yes sir. When I got involved, a few guys tried to do something to me and I broke their wrists. Then the guy that took Denise out would not tell me what happened, and I broke his nose. Then a few other guys tried to hit me and I used my sticks. I just bloodied them and they backed off. At this point the bartender came up to me and pointed a gun at me and I immediately took it from him and knocked him out. It is likely he also has a broken finger. When I take a gun from someone, if their finger is on the trigger, it will break it. I gave the gun to Gina because she was not panicking like Paula was. Then we left. The gun was never fired. At least when we were there sir."

Angie, just as I have stated before, you should have called me right away. You could have been killed."

"Sir, when I arrived, I did not have time to call before things began happening. I called as soon as I could. I was more worried about Denise at that time. I had no idea what they gave her, and she is one of my very best friends. I needed to get her here to the ER as soon as I could."

"I understand Angie. But you can't keep getting into these situations. One day you won't be so lucky."

"I understand Lieutenant. I do not want to get into these situations at all."

Lieutenant Edwards went with Gina to her car to pick up the gun. She gave it to him, and he left. Gina went back into the Emergency Room.

Paula had called Denise's parents and they came to the hospital. When they walked up, they said hello to everyone. Denise's mother said, "Angie you are a hero again. You saved Denise from who knows what." She reached out and hugged her.

"Ma'am, I don't feel as though I am a hero, I just did what I had to do to get Denise away from those guys."

"Angie you are such a sweet young woman. You don't give yourself the credit you deserve. But thank you for what you did."

"You are welcome, ma'am. We should be going. It is becoming very late, and I am certain all of our parents may begin to worry. It was nice to see you both. I hope Denise will be OK."

The three girls walked away. They kept Denise for a few more hours and then released her to her parents.

As Angie drove home, she thought about a few images that had flashed in her head. The room filled with fog, Mario with a broken nose someone pointing a gun at her. She realized she had seen this before it happened. But there was not enough to determine what was going to happen. She thought to herself, "I wish these visions were more detailed. Then possibly I could use them to help me when the situation comes."

Denise was finally completely recovered by Tuesday night. She was worried about her job at the Doctors office. She had never even been late before much less missed a day. But when the doctor heard what had happened to her, he was very sympathetic. He even offered her help if she needed it. He had been told that it was a Quaalude that was used and since these are highly addictive, he said he would help her if she needed it. Fortunately, she didn't have any problems related to the incident.

The next day Angie went to work as usual. She didn't say anything to anyone about the night before. The day went without any problems and Angie and Eric worked on the new shop.

Tuesday, after work, she went to the Dojo. She told her sensei's about what happened the previous night and they asked if her friend was OK. She said yes. So, they went to work.

They explained that she will need to be certain to do all of the isometric exercises during her daily workouts. She will need to do these at home every day now. They explained again that these will increase her stamina and speed. They went over the complete regimen of exercises. Angie was already fast but they wanted her to become even faster. "Angie, you be fast that no one block." Sensei Akio told her.

"You ask how we so fast. This from isometric. It not build big muscle, just lean strong and fast. Soon you see." Sensei Kotomi said.

They worked the entire time with teaching Angie complete isometric regimen. She left somewhat sore. This was a completely different workout.

The next day after work she and Eric were working on a few things for the new fabrication shop when she stopped and rubbed her arms. "What's wrong?"

"I am a bit sore."

"You, sore? I never saw you sore before." Eric said.

"My Sensei's are teaching me isometric exercises, and these made some of my muscles sore. You do not need to worry."

"What are isometrics? I never heard of that."

"It is a way of strengthening the muscles without movement." Angie said.

"What do you mean, without movement? How do you work out without movement?"

"You work on certain muscle groups, and you tighten them and hold them in one position. They have a frame they use that is made from two channels with holes every inch and a doll rod that you put through the holes. And you adjust it to different heights to work on different muscle groups. Then they have this other piece of equipment that has a bar attached to the base with a chain and a spring that stretches when you pull up in it. This creates the resistance. Between these two you can work on most of your muscles."

"Do you need to make any specific equipment for this? We could make it here."

"Thank you for the offer, Eric. Remember when my father and I were making something out of wood?"

"That was the equipment? I wondered what you were making. So, this will make you stronger? I can't imagine you much stronger. I think you are already stronger than I am."

"I don't know about that. You are very strong."

"We can stop for today, you know. If I know you, you're going to go home and work out. You could give your muscles some extra time before you work on them again."

"Yes, that is a good idea, Eric." They cleaned up and left for the day.

Angie went home and went over all the exercises. She didn't do them using much strength. She just wanted to go over all of them again to commit them to memory.

25

Angie had Sherri, Gina and Janet over on Sunday. Everyone else had other things they had to do. They sat in Angie's room and listened to the radio and talked. About a half hour later Angie's mother knocked on the door. "Angie, I have iced tea for everyone."

"You may come in mother." They were talking about singing karaoke at the Bum Steer.

"Angie, you sing so well it is amazing. I wish I could sing like you." Gina said.

Lizzy opened the door and rolled the cart into Angie's room. There was a pitcher of iced tea, a container of ice and 4 tumblers. "I thought you may like a refreshment."

"Thank you, mother, you are very thoughtful!"

"If I may ask, what singing are you talking about?" Lizzy asked.

"Some of us sing Karaoke at the Bum Steer." Gina said.

"Please excuse me, what is karaoke? I have heard the term, but I do not know what it means?"

Sherri said, "Don't feel bad Mrs. Tucci. Karaoke is where they have a machine that plays popular songs without the singing part, and they display the lyrics on a screen so you can sing along. It is usually just one person singing at a time though."

"Angie is amazing at it!" Janet said. "You should hear her."

Angie blushed. This was one of the few times she showed embarrassment.

"Really? I did not know you sang Angie." Lizzy said.

Angie struggled for words for a minute. "Yes Mother, I sing. You stand on the stage in front of everyone."

"You should hear her Mrs. Tucci. Angie sings just like the actual singers. She is fantastic! Everyone always screams when she goes up." Sherri said.

"Maybe you should come sometime to hear her, you and Mr. Tucci." Gina said.

"Oh, possibly your father and I could come sometime. I would love to hear you, Angie. Unless you would be embarrassed." Lizzy said. "I would love to hear you, however."

"I am fine with that mother. Gina and I sing in front the whole place so I would not be embarrassed."

"Well, sometime you could let your father and me know when you will be singing. You said they have food there. Possibly your father and I could have a date night. We could sit somewhere not too close to all of you. This way you may talk without feeling self-conscious. And your father and I could have a date night. I could be something like we did before we were married." She smiled and turned to leave. "I will let you be."

"Thank you, mother." Lizzy left the room closing the door behind her.

Gina said, "Angie, your parents are amazing! They would go to hear you sing and treat it like a date. That is so cool! And she was worried that we might feel uncomfortable if they sat with us. Your parents are so great!"

"Thank you for the complement, Gina. And I agree, my parents are wonderful and thoughtful."

Since it was Sunday, they hung out most of the day.

26

The following weekend they planned to go to the Bum Steer for karaoke and a night of fun. Angie told her mother that they would be going on Saturday night. Lizzy said that she didn't know if they would be going or not that night since she hadn't talked to Dominic yet.

Saturday night came and Lizzy went to talk to Dominic. "Dom?" Lizzy said after he got out of the shower. He had been home from work for about 30 minutes.

"Yes Lizzy?"

"Did you know that Angie and some of her friends sing karaoke at the Bum Steer?"

"No, I did not. They told you that?"

"Yes, when they were here last Sunday, I brought them some iced tea and they were talking about it. Gina suggested we go and hear Angie sing."

"They invited us?"

"Well, it was informal." I suggested that possibly we could go and eat there but sit away from her and her friends. This way it would not make them feel uncomfortable. We could hear her sing. I believe it was Janet that said that Angie is amazing."

"That sounds interesting."

"I suggested this could be something like a date night for us. I thought it could be fun. And we could hear Angie sing at the same time. Angie said they would be going tonight. Would you care to go tonight?"

"It sounds as if it would be fun. Let us get ready then."

Dominic dressed in nice jeans, a sweater and cowboy boots. Lizzy put on jeans, and she wore a very nice long sleeve print cowgirl shirt. She also put on cowboy boots. They decided to leave about 7:00. They took Lizzy's car because it did not stick out like the truck. Dominic thought that they could get there before Angie and her friends. This way they wouldn't know that they were there.

They arrived about 7:30 and parked. They didn't see Angie's car. They went in and found it already becoming somewhat crowded. They found a small table across the room from the stage and sat. A waitress brought them menus and Dominic ordered two glasses of beer. "This place is interesting. Look at all the things hanging from the ceiling and on the walls. I believe it would take days to see everything." Dominic said.

"I can see why Angie and her friends like this place. It has a warm feel, and it has crazy things everywhere."

They looked at the menus. "They have quite a bit. I think I will order a bacon cheeseburger and fries." Dominic said.

"I think I will have the same, Dom. This almost feels like one of our early dates, remember?"

"Yes, I remember. This does feel that way. Maybe we should do things such as this more often."

"I would like that, Dom."

They were served the beers and they decided to order salads as an appetizer. "Ma'am, we would each like to have a salad with house dressing to start. Then a little later we each would like to have a bacon cheeseburger cooked medium with the works and fries."

"Thank you, sir." She walked away.

"These menus are cute. Everything is drawn. I like this place." Lizzy said. She drank some beer.

Dominic said, "Lizzy look over towards the door, Angie and her friends are here."

"I see. They are sitting right in front of the stage."

Soon the disc jockey began playing music. Angie and her friends were already dancing. As he played more songs Dominic and Lizzy finished their salads. The waitress told them their food would be up shortly. They enjoyed watching Angie and her friends dancing and having fun.

"And we were worried that she would not make any friends." Dominic said to Lizzy.

Angie and everyone sat down and ordered food. Denise said, "I don't want to dance with any guys. I don't think I even want to go out with any either. At least for a while. How am I going to trust guys now?"

"Denise," Karen said, "Just don't think about it. You will meet someone nice. You will see."

"How do you know? I always choose bad people. Like that guy in high school." She looked sad.

Gina rolled her eyes and looked at her, "C'mon Denise. One guy? One guy and you are going to give up? There's lots of guys. They are not all like that creep Mario. And wasn't that guy in high school just really shy and timid? He wasn't bad, was he?"

Denise said, "I guess not, you're right."

Paula looked at Denise. She felt bad about what happened, but she didn't want her to feel bad all night. "C'mon Denise, let's go dance." She grabbed her arm and pulled a little. Denise got up and everyone else followed. They danced for a couple of songs then sat down.

Lizzy and Dominic's cheeseburgers and fries came. "The aroma is wonderful Dom."

They began eating. The disc jockey set up for karaoke and right away Gina went up. They thought she sang OK. However, they did not know the song. She finished and handed the mike back. Then they were surprised when they heard someone scream, "Hey, it's Angie!"

She took the mike. The music began. Lizzy said, "this is Masquerade."

The intro played and she began to sing. The crowd was screaming.

Dominic said, "Are they playing a recording?"

"Dom that is Angie!"

"It is?" He looked at the stage. "I cannot believe it. She sounds like the original recording on the radio! She even has vibrato in her voice! I did not know she could sing like this."

She finished. Everyone was screaming and whistling. Someone screamed, "Another." Someone else said, "Do You're So Vain!"

"She can sing You're so Vain?" Lizzy said.

The intro for "You're So Vain" began. Lizzy and Dominic sat there almost in shock. It sounded as if was the original recording. The crowd was screaming just as if they were at a real concert. It got so loud that it was beginning to drown out the music. But they could still barely hear the singing. Lizzy got tears in her eyes. She could not believe it was Angie singing. She was so choked up she had to stop eating.

Dominic felt Lizzy's hand grab his and she squeezed. It made him smile. He looked at Lizzy and thought how blessed they had been. He thought that he would never have guessed that Angie would be so talented. He thought again that anything she tried she excelled in.

The song ended and the screaming was unbelievable. They watched Angie go and sit down. "Janet said that Angie was amazing, but I never thought she would sing as she did, Dom."

"I would not have believed it if I was not hearing it myself. She is something is she not?"

Lizzy just smiled at him. She picked up her napkin and carefully blotted her eyes. The waitress came to ask if they needed anything. Lizzy just looked and said, "That was our daughter that just sang."

"Angie is your daughter?" the waitress asked, then she looked at Lizzy and said, "I see the resemblance. She is fantastic, isn't she?"

"She is. I am beside myself." Lizzy said.

"She sings a lot and every time is crazy like this. She is so good she should sing in a band. Would you like another beer?"

Dominic said, yes please, for both of us."

She turned and walked away.

There was an older couple sitting at the table next to them. The lady turned towards Lizzy and said, "Excuse me, I could not help but overhear. That girl is your daughter?"

"Yes, ma'am, she is. We came tonight to hear her sing." Lizzy said.

"You should be proud. She is incredible!" the lady said.

Her husband had turned to Lizzy and Dominic. "Pardon me, but aren't you Dominic? From Dom's Auto?"

"Yes sir. I am." Dominic said.

"I bring our car there for repairs. I thought you looked familiar. And that was Angie the mechanic singing?"

Lizzy said, "Yes, that was her."

"Amazing." He said. They turned back.

Other people sang and then Gina did again. They didn't have the same impact on the crowd as Angie, however.

Lizzy and Dominic were enjoying the night. They never thought listening people singing karaoke would be this entertaining. And the burgers were the best they had had in some time. As they sat there Angie went back up. She took the mike, and everyone was already screaming. She sang, Angie Baby.

"I know this song." Lizzy thought for a minute. It's Angie Baby. It's amazing, she sounds like the original recorded song now!" Everyone was screaming and whistling. Lizzy squeezed Dominic's hand again. Dominic smiled.

Angie stayed up on stage and sang another. This time it was one Dominic and Lizzy knew well. It was White Rabbit. The into started then Angie began to sing. They couldn't believe it. She sounded like it sounds on the radio! They were shocked. They couldn't believe she sang this well. "Dom, she changes her voice to sound like the actual singers. I am astounded!"

The crowd roared. "I am enjoying this very much." Dominic said. We should do this again Lizzy. What a fun night!" This had the feel of when they were dating except at that time Dominic didn't have much money. He had to watch what he spent.

They stayed until about 10:00. They paid their bill and left. When they got home, they went and sat in the Arizona room for a while. They talked about Angie singing. They talked about the Bum Steer. Dominic had his arm around her and she was leaning against him. They just took in the stars. Around 11:00 they went to bed.

27

The following week Angie and her friends went to the bum steer again. Mario and his friends came in and Angie and her friends saw them. Angie noticed that they were staring at them as they walked past. They appeared angry. So, Angie went to talk to the bouncer. "See those guys over there? They drugged one of my friends recently and were going to rape her. I stepped in and saved her but some of them got hurt. They have been staring at us since they came in, so I wanted to let you know in case they try to start something. I do not want to fight in here."

"You think they would try to fight with you? A girl?" the bouncer asked.

"There are some things that you may not know about me. Yes, I can fight. Likely much better than you may think. I do not want anything to happen in here, sir. My friends and I like this place quite a bit and we do not want to have anything happen that would get us kicked out."

"I don't think you need to worry."

"Thank you, sir." She went back to her friends and sat down.

Paula asked her, "What did you say to him?"

"I told him that those guys drugged one of my friends and a few of them were hurt because of it. I said I did not want any trouble in here from them. He said not to worry."

"I don't think they will do anything in here Angie."

"I hope you are correct."

They spent the night eating, drinking and singing.

They left and when they walked outside and were crossing the parking lot, Mario and some of his friends came up to them. "You caused us to get arrested. Now we are going to teach you a lesson. I don't care that you are a girl." He went to punch her, and she blocked it, and leaned towards him and hit him with 4 punches so fast now one knew how many times she hit him. Then she spun and hit him on the side of the head with her elbow. He went down.

Another went to kick her, and she grabbed his leg under her arm, twisted it and hit his leg muscle with her elbow maybe 4 or 5 times. He screamed and backed off hopping on his other leg.

As this was happening Gina ran into the Bum Steer and got the bouncer.

Another guy grabbed her from behind and she used him to hold her so she could kick another in the face. That guy fell back, and his head crashed on the asphalt. That knocked him out.

The bouncer came running out with Gina just as Angie pushed one arm under one of the guy's arms that was holding her and wrapped it around his arm and pulled down. She grabbed his hand with her other hand and twisted it around further and leaned to the side. It broke his arm and he flipped over onto his side. The bouncer was shocked! His eyes were open wide in disbelief! If it would have taken him a few more seconds to get outside, he would have missed all of it.

Angie turned to the guy whose leg she hit with her elbow, and he was trying to run away but was limping hard. She turned back to the guy that she just threw down and saw he had gotten up was running away while holding his arm. Angie backed down. This all took maybe 15 or 20 seconds.

Someone had called the police and they had just pulled up. They got out and saw two guys laying on the ground and Angie and her friends standing there. They looked in disbelief. One cop asked, "What happened to these guys? We were just called and told four guys were attacking a girl. We were just down the street."

Angie answered, "Sir, we were leaving, and four guys jumped me."

"Where are the other two?"

"They ran away as soon as injured one guy's leg muscle and broke another's arm. Then I kicked another guy."

"You kicked another guy? What do you mean, kicked another guy?"

"Sir, these guys drugged one of my friends and they were going to rape her a few weeks ago. I came and stopped it and a few of them got hurt. They said they were going to teach me a lesson because I got them arrested."

"So, what happened to them?"

"Sir, I can see that you do not know me. I am the girl that caught the guys that kidnapped all the young ladies for the sex ring."

"Angie Tucci? You're her?"

"Yes sir. I am."

But you aren't big. I mean, I thought you would be someone big."

"Sir, I am a 4th degree blackbelt in Muay Thay, Taekwondo, Karate, Aikido and Shaolin Kung Fu. I do not need to be big."

"You knocked these guys out?"

"Yes sir. After they attacked me."

The other cop had called for a shift supervisor, and he just arrived. It was Lieutenant Edwards. "Angie, what happened?"

"Hello sir, these are two of the guys that drugged my friend. They came here to teach me a lesson. Two others ran away."

"I would have thought by now most people would know about you. We'll take it from here. You and your friends can go."

"Thank you, sir." She turned and walked to her car and everyone else followed.

"Sir?" One officer asked. "That's the girl that killed all of those guys that kidnapped all of the kids?"

"Yes, officer."

"Her? She looks like a model, not a fighter."

"Looks can be deceiving. That is why I always tell everyone not to assume. That's an easy way to get killed. I have seen her fight. You don't want her after you. When she was fighting those guys that abducted all those girls, I got shot and saw her fight. The only way I can describe it is she looks like Joe Singso with her head. And I am dead serious. And she can disarm anyone. Trust me you do not want her after you. She is a very sweet person otherwise and just talking to her you would never know."

By this time the two guys were conscious. They looked beat up. The officers pulled them up, hand cuffed them and arrested them. They put them in the back seat of their squad car and they both got in and drove away.

"Do you believe what the lieutenant said?" one officer said to the other.

"I kind of don't believe it but I have heard lots of things about her from other officers and other people that witnessed her fighting. I don't know what to believe. You know she messed up those guys that tried to rob the Arizona Bank a while back. She broke one guy's arm, knee and some ribs. The other guy couldn't walk by himself. And she disarmed both of them. I saw the reports, and the reports said that too. I don't know. Sargent Hernandez told me he walked in as she was in midair then kicked one guy. And he said the guy flew over a desk."

The other officer said, "And there's that child sex ring she supposedly ended. They say she killed 15 armed guys. I still think that sounds like movie stuff. It's in the reports and I can't believe anyone would falsify them."

"If she really can do that, I wouldn't want her mad at me. That's for sure."

"But if she can really fight like that, maybe sometime I could see it." They drove back to the station.

Angie and her friends were walking back to their cars and the guy that tried to kiss her walked up. "Angie, now I am glad you didn't do anything more to me. You know, I am really sorry I did that. I guess us college guys can be pretty stupid sometimes." He turned and walked away.

"Angie," Gina said, "You are bad ass! I can't believe what you did. I ran to get the bouncer and by the time we ran out it was over!"

"Like, you really do look like Joe Singso with your head like everyone says." Denise said. "Like, you look like a completely different person when you are fighting."

Janet added, "And when you started to fight it was so obvious you tensed up. We could see your muscles. When you fought, I couldn't see your arms. You moved so fast and that kick, I don't know, it was almost scary."

"Thank you everyone. But when I am threatened, I just react. It is almost as though everything else turns off and I am solely focused on the danger. I do not think about what to do. I just do it."

Paula said, "This was an interesting end to the night. I never expected anything to happen just leaving."

Everyone hugged then got into their cars and went home.

28

When Johnny got home, he called his friends. He invited them over to go over his plan. He had devised a plan to kidnap Angie's mother to get Angie to come so all of them can fight her together to prove to her that she is shit then kill her. Since one of the guys that she killed at her father's shop was the brother of Johnny's friend Andy, Andy was ready without any thought. Anything to get back at that bitch for killing his brother.

They all went to Johnny's apartment to discuss everything. Johnny looked at Lenny, "I want you to drive up to her house in your Western Gas truck. This way, if she looks outside, she won't know we are up to something. I'll follow in my mom's boyfriends white panel van. He thinks I am helping a friend move. Lenny, you go to the door and ring the bell. You need to be wearing your uniform and badge. Andy and I will wait on each side of the door just out of sight. We will be wearing the masks and gloves I am going to buy. When she opens the door, we will push it open and Andy will use the sleeper move. I'll tape the note to the wall then we will drag her and put her in the back of the van. Then we go to my aunt's place. Everyone got it?"

They all said yes. "We will do this on Monday October 4th late morning, so Angie and her dad are at work."

Then Lenny went to buy beer and Johnny ordered pizza. They sat around and drank beer and ate pizza. The were watching some TV and talking about how great the plan was.

The next day Johnny went and bought latex gloves, a couple of Devil Halloween masks, and heavy rope.

Late Monday morning Lenny drove up to Angie's house in his Western Gas truck with Johnny following in the van. They parked in front of Angie's house. They knew Angie's mother will not know what they are up to and think they are legitimate. Lenny rang the doorbell. Lizzy was talking to Lilly on the phone and told her, "Hold on Lilly, someone just rang the doorbell." She put the receiver on the counter.

Lizzy answered the door and it was a Western Gas man. He said, "Hello Ma'am, we have a gas leak in the area and we are checking every house. Is it OK if I come in and take some readings?"

Lizzy didn't see a problem because he was a Western Gas man with an ID and she saw the Western Gas truck. She told him, "You may come in and check." She stepped aside to let him in.

Immediately Johnny came in from around the doorway and grabbed her. He was wearing a devil Halloween mask and latex gloves. Lizzy started screaming as loud as she could. Andy followed also wearing a devil mask and latex gloves. Andy put a sleeper hold on her. Her scream became garbled and, in a few seconds, it stopped and she was out cold. They carried her to the van and put her in the back. Johnny ran back and taped a note on the wall next to the door, left the door open, ran back to the van and they both sped away.

Lilly heard Lizzy answer the door in the background and talk to someone for a minute then start screaming. It was a terrible scream, and she knew someone was doing something to her. Lilly was horrified and frantically hung up and called the sheriff's office. Lilly told them what just happened, and they said they would send a car there right away.

Meantime Angie was working on a customer's car and kind of jumped like she just got an electric shock. She screamed, "They have her, oh my God! They have her!" She dropped the tools she is using on her bench. "Oh my God!"

The guys asked her, "What's wrong! Who has who?" They looked around as if she was talking about someone there. Angie took off her gloves and hat and threw them down on her bench, ran and grabbed her purse and ran out the door. She got into the Cuda, started it, and sped out of the lot behind the shop. They watched her tires smoke as she sped and fishtailed around the corner onto Stone.

Eric was shocked and ran to the office and told Dominic what just happened. "Dominic, Angie just jumped like she got an electric shock then screamed, 'They have her, oh my God!' and ran out, got into her car and sped away down Stone. It was almost like she had a vision of something bad. I never saw anything like that." He was visibly agitated.

Dominic knew what it meant when she jumped like she was shocked. He knew she saw something in her head. He thought, "What could she have seen to cause her to run out?" He looked at Eric and said, "Thanks Eric." Now he was trying to think of what she could have seen. All he could think to do was to call Lieutenant Edwards.

Lieutenant Edwards answered the phone, "Hello, how can I help you?"

"Lieutenant, Angie just saw something, I mean like she saw the things about those two guys then screamed, 'they have her' and ran out and sped away." I do not know what to think. Something must have happened, but I do not know what."

Lieutenant Edwards could hear the concern in Dominic's voice, "Dominic, I was just listening to the police radio, and I heard the Pima County sheriff call one of his guys and tell them to get over to your house right away. Someone called in that something happened to Lizzy."

"What!" He slammed down the phone and ran to his truck and sped away just as Angie did.

The guys in the shop and Jack ran to the overhead door and saw Dominic blast out of the lot and go north onto Stone. They were now wondering if something happened at their house. Now they were all concerned.

Angie drove as fast as she could. She skidded into the driveway before the sheriff's deputy got there. She saw that the door was open and jumped out of the Cuda leaving it running with the door open. She ran into the house screaming, "Mother! Mother! Mother! She looked all over the house then saw a note taped on the wall just inside of the door. By now she was sobbing. She looked at the note and it said, "We have your mother, Angie. We will contact you soon to tell you what we want."

Just then she heard the squad car pull up and a deputy came running into the house and saw Angie reading a note. "Angie, what happened?" It was Deputy Moody. He saw Angie sobbing and deduced that her mother was kidnapped.

Through her tears she said, "They took her! They took her!"

"Who took her?" the deputy asked.

"I do not know. It does not say." She held the note out.

Another vehicle skidded to a stop. It was Dominic. He got out of the truck and ran to the house and saw Deputy Moody and Angie. And she was almost hysterical. "Father, they took her!" She showed him the note. "They took mother!"

"Who took her?"

"I don't know. Why would someone take mother?"

Dominic looked at the note. It just said they would contact Angie. "What? Contact Angie?" He shrieked! "What does this have to do with you?" he asked Angie.

"I have no idea. What did I ever do to anyone for them want to take mother?" She was still crying.

Dominic went and took her into his arms. "We will get her back."

Deputy Moody called this in, and the sheriff told him he was on his way. He also had the forensic team come as well. He told Deputy Moody to get Dominic and Angie out of the house, so they don't destroy any evidence.

Deputy Moody went back into the house. "Dominic and Angie, you both need to come outside now. Don't touch anything. The forensic team is on their way to investigate."

Dominic handed him the note and they went outside. It didn't take long for the sheriff and the forensic team to arrive, and they began to investigate. They were looking for anything. They dusted for fingerprints and pulled plenty of them. They told Dominic and Angie to go with Deputy Moody to the station. They needed to try to determine why Lizzy was kidnapped.

As they walked to the truck Dominic reached in and shut off the CUDA, took the keys and Angie's purse and closed and locked the door.

The sheriff spent hours talking with Dominic and Angie and did not come up with anything. The only thing Angie thought of was the fight with Johnny. But she thought it was difficult to believe he would kidnap her mother because of that. And that was in November of last year. The sheriff's office takes every lead seriously, so they were going to investigate this.

Dominic and Angie went home to an empty house. They both felt lost. They felt as if their hearts had been ripped out of them, they both cried. They hugged. Angie told Dominic, "I saw mother kidnapped. She struggled and they used a move on her to make her lose consciousness, but I did not see anything else. It makes me angry. Why can I not see everything father, what is wrong with me, I should be able to see this." She cried more. "I feel the same as I did when I was trying to see where all those young ladies were last year. This is frustrating."

Dominic hugged her and said, "Remember Aunt Maria said that you cannot control what you see. And what you do see may be just bits and pieces."

"I understand but I feel as though I should see everything. I am so very sorry father. I feel that I caused this." Angie cried more.

"You did not cause this Angie. It is not about you, it is about them, whoever they are."

"They wrote the note to me, so it has to be my fault."

"Angie, you cannot take responsibility for this. It will tear you apart. Somehow this must be connected to you because they wrote the note to you. But that does not mean you caused it. Remember, they are the criminals not you. They did this, not you. And it is likely they wrote the note to you to make you upset." Dominic was trying to be strong because he felt if he showed his true feelings, that would destroy Angie.

Angie was calming down somewhat. "I understand father. Now I understand what you and Aunt Maria went through when Grandmother died. How did you both cope? I feel lost as if there is a huge void."

"We cried just as you have been, and we did not have a choice. We had to cope to survive. I do not know how we survived. We were just kids. But it is the same feeling."

They hugged for quite a while then went to bed. They didn't feel hungry at all. They both tossed and turned but finally slept.

The next day, Tuesday, they both went to work but it was obvious that they were upset. Neither were their normal jovial selves. The other mechanics were worried about Angie. She was so down. They never saw Angie this down. She didn't talk at all. She barely even said good morning. Nothing they said cheered her up. None of them knew much about what happened since neither Angie; Dominic nor Jack discussed it. All they knew was what was on the news. Everyone worked and just went home.

By the third day the sheriff still had no information or leads. None of the fingerprints were any different from fingerprints from all over the house. All they could do was wait to be contacted.

However, Angie did remember to call her sensei to tell him why she had not been there tonight and likely not on Thursday either. He told her, "Angie, you be careful. You easy kill now. No want anger drive fighting. That not good."

"I understand sensei. I have been beating my punching bags to work through my frustrations, sir. Thank you." She hung up.

Angie's friends were sad as well. They heard about it on the news, and Sherri told them what little more she knew from what she has seen. It was on every news station. They came over the next evening, Wednesday, hoping try to cheer her up, at least a little. They met at Angie's house and went to the door. Dominic opened the door. They all said, "Hello Mr. Tucci."

"Hello ladies, Angie is in the big garage working out." He pointed to the garage. He looked sad.

Angie was working out with her punching bags. She had two 100-pound bags hung in the garage about six feet apart to act as if she is fighting two people at the same time. She was punching and doing reverse 360-degree roundhouses.

As they walked to the garage, they heard Angie kicking and punching her punching bags. At first, they just stood and watched Angie work out for a while. They were in awe at the speed and intense force she had. Then she saw them and stopped. Sweat was dripping off of her head and her cloths were soaked. She grabbed a towel and wiped her face.

"Hi Angie, Gina said. "You are amazing! I wouldn't want to come up against you anywhere."

Angie forced a slight smile; it was obviously forced. Even with the forced smile it was obvious she was despondent.

"We heard what happened and we are so sorry. I can't even begin to understand how you must feel." Janet said. Everyone else said the same. They all looked very concerned and worried about Angie.

"Like, is there anything we can do?" Denise asked.

"Thank you for coming everyone." Angie sat down. "I do not think there is anything any of you can do. But I really appreciate your sentiments." She looked as though she was lost in thought, sad and about to cry.

"What were you just doing?" Janet asked.

"I exercise this way every day and sometimes I use this to get my mind off of everything. But it is not helping. And I am frustrated that I have not seen where she is." She had her head low and tears were falling from her eyes. "I work out like this every day." Her voice was quivering as she spoke.

Sherri was with them and she didn't look very happy either. She knew exactly how Angie was feeling. She went and put her arms around Angie. "I told everyone that we are trying to find your mother and have seen some things but not much. I hope you don't mind."

"That is alright Sherri."

"I wish there was something we could do for you." Janet said. "I feel so helpless." She sat down across from Angie and took one of Angie's hands in hers.

Angie saw that she was teary-eyed and half smiled. "I feel so lost and I am disappointed that I cannot see where she is."

"Oh Angie, I know this won't help but I wish there was something I could say or do to help. I feel so bad." Paula said.

"I understand your sentiments Paula, and thank you, I appreciate you visiting, all of you. I do not feel so alone now." Her chin was trembling. "This is all my fault. If anything happens to her, I will never be able to forgive myself." She was full on crying now.

"How can this be your fault? What would make you think that, Angie?" Karen asked.

"They wrote the note to me. It said, 'We have your mother, Angie.' Something I did made them do this."

"How does that make it you fault? They did this not you." Karen said.

"That is what my father told me but I still feel as though I caused it." She continued crying.

Karen went over to Angie and bent down and hugged her. All she could think of to say was "I'm so sorry Angie."

Angie turned and hugged her back. She still had tears rolling down her cheeks.

"We are all here to support you, Angie." Gina said. "We will do whatever we can. If you need help with anything, cleaning or doing laundry, cooking, whatever. We will be here."

Angie sniffled and cleared her throat, "You are all laudable. I cannot believe you are such good friends."

Gina said, "Laudable?"

"Sorry, praiseworthy or commendable." Angie said. "I do not mean to use words you will not know."

"It's not a problem. We understand you are very upset. Who wouldn't be?" Gina said.

They all sat there for a while and didn't say much. It was a difficult situation.

"I am feeling very tired now. You guys helped me calm down. Thank you. I have not slept much since this happened."

"We can go. I'm happy we helped you calm down, at least a little." Karen said.

"Like, if there is anything, I mean anything we can do please ask. You saved me from being gang raped from those guys and I want to do something for you, anything." Denise said.

"You are very sweet Denise. I cannot think of anything at the moment, thank you for offering everyone."

Each of them gave Angie a hug and told her good bye.

Sherri stayed after the others left so she could talk to Angie in private. "Angie, have you seen anything since they took her?"

"No, nothing. I feel as if there is something wrong with me."

"Angie, remember what you told me? You said that when you are emotional or you have yourself immersed in something that the visions stop. You have been upset and rightfully so. You aren't going to see anything while you are like this." Sherri told her. "I have seen something and I need to tell you."

"What did you see?"

"I saw an old run-down shack where they are holding your mother. But that's all. I can see she is alright, well, I don't think she is hurt. I see that she is very upset, worried distraught and she is crying."

"Do you see anything else?"

"Just the shack. I saw a window but I can't see anything through it. It looks like the sun is shining on it, it is very dirty and it is all glair."

They sat for a while but neither saw anything more. Sherri just hugged Angie and went home.

Angie turned off the lights, closed and locked the garage door. As she walked into the house, she thought of the image she saw a while back of an old shack. And for some reason the thought of the cholla cactus that appeared driven over came to her as well. She thought, "Is this where they took mother? Sherri said an old run-down shack." She laid on her bed and thought about this until she dozed off.

The next day, Thursday, Angie and Dominic went to work and it was an uneventful day. That evening Sherri went to Angie's house to see her. Angie said, "You saw a shack? Tell me about it. Maybe it will stimulate something. A while back I had the image of an old shack flash in my head. Maybe it was this one?" Angie looked as though she pushed her feelings aside. This is something she was able to do at times in a tense situation just as her father could. She just put everything out of her mind and concentrated on the shack.

"Well, I see a shack, no it looks like an old farm house but has been abandoned for some time. It's dirty, dusty and dilapidated. Your mother is locked in one room. As I said last night there is one small window." Sherri explained.

"Can you see anything out the window?"

"Um, I am trying. The sun moved and the glare is gone. But the window is so dirty it is hard to see much. I see the same things that grow around here. Cholla cactus, lots of bursage, a mesquite tree."

"Why are you saying the same as here? Do you feel she is far away?"

"I don't know. I feel like it isn't that far away but not around here. I don't know how far. It could be very close but I can't tell. I can't see anything else." Sherri said. "Wait!" Sherri was concentrating on the house, "I see the corner of an old barn! And the back of a white van outside. But this one doesn't have windows on the side. Nothing is on the sides. You know like a name of a store. It's like those custom vans that guys custom paint but it is just white."

Angie sat back on the couch she was sitting on. "Maybe if I concentrate on what you have said." She sat and put her arms on her lap and closed her eyes and concentrated on the old house. She was trying to picture an old abandoned farm house. After about ten minutes she said, "I see an old farm house in a field with a barn next to it. There is a white Ford van next to the barn and a white pick-up truck."

"The pick-up truck has something on the doors. Some kind of logo. But I cannot make it out. There are Cholla cactus all over where they drove in. There are also many scrubby trees and bursage. Past all of the trees I see a fence, a split rail fence. The type you see around a ranch. It is made from sliced trees with two pieces between each post in a zigzag pattern."

"You see all that? You can't see the logo on the pick-up truck?"

"I cannot. It is not clear, as if I am too far away."

They both sat there for some time but did not see anything else. Sherri went home.

30

Then on the fourth day, Friday, Dominic and Angie went to work. Again, they were not their usual selves. The guys didn't talk to Angie much during the whole day. At lunch she came into the break room and sat away from everyone. She ate and didn't even look at any of them or say anything. She had her head low. She cleaned up her things and went directly back to work.

As the other mechanics finished their lunch Migel said, "Angie is really messed up about this. She didn't even say anything."

"Yeah, I hope they find her mother and I hope she is ok. I can't even imagine how she would be if her mother was killed." Scott said. It looked as though he had tears in his eyes.

"Man, don't even say that." Johnny said.

Eric said, "I'm sure he didn't mean anything Johnny. I don't want that to happen but you never know with kidnappings. They don't even know why they did this."

"Why would anyone do something like this? Man." Scott said shaking his head back and forth. "I almost feel like it is my mom. Geeze. I never felt so close to anyone that isn't my own family. Angie just makes it so easy to feel close to her."

"You can say that again." Hector said.

Scott said, "You know, she feels like a sister to me. It's crazy, but I feel like I would do just about anything for her. I feel so bad."

The guys cleaned up and went back to work.

Shortly after lunch, the mail was delivered and Angie received a small package. It was addressed to her but didn't have a return address on it. Dominic walked to the back and called Angie. "Angie, you got a package."

Angie looked up tossed the tool she had in her hand on her bench, took off her gloves and threw them down and ran up front to Dominic. She hoped it was from the kidnappers. They went into the office and Angie quickly tore open the box. It was a small box about 2 1/2" square and about 1" thick. Inside was a gold watch that looked like the one her grandparents gave her mother for high school graduation. She always wore it. There was also a short note. She purposely didn't touch the watch because she thought maybe there would be fingerprints on it. She turned the box so she could see the back of the watch. Inscribed on the back it said "Elizabeth, Love Mother and Father." Her Aunt Lilly had an identical one so it definitely was her mother's.

The note said, "Angie, here is you mother's watch so you know we have her. We will contact you again with further instructions."

"That's it? Why are they doing this father?" She was in tears again. It is obvious this has something to do with me. What did I do to get mother taken from us? It is my fault. If they kill her, it is my fault. I will never be able to forgive myself." She was crying hard now. Dominic stood and took her into his arms.

"Angie, this is not about you. It is about them. They took her from us. What could you have possible done? Whoever did this is sick and twisted."

"Father, I killed the three guys that broke into the shop. Maybe it is about that. Or maybe the guys I killed that abducted those little ladies. Or maybe Johnny felt humiliated because I beat him and broke his arm. Or maybe it is the guys from Tucson Burger on Oracle and Wetmore or the guys from the bar."

"Guys from Tucson Burger on Oracle and Wetmore? Guys at the bar? I do not recall anything about Tucson Burger or guys at a bar. What bar?"

"It is possible I did not tell you about those. A while back I was at Tucson Burger on Oracle and Wetmore with my friends eating and these four guys came in. While they were in line to order, they became obnoxious. They were saying things they would like to do to us loud enough that everyone could hear. There were a few mothers there with little kids. Gina got up and went over and asked them to quiet down because there were little kids there. One of the guys grabbed her arm and was saying he was going to take her and they would show her a good time. She tried to get away but this guy would not let go. I went over and asked him to let go and he just laughed and he asked what I was going to do about it. He raised his other arm and I grabbed his wrist and put it in a wrist lock and he let go of Gina and went down on his knees. I asked him if he was done because I could easily break his wrist and he said, 'Yes.' So, I let him go. I did not think he was finished and he tried to punch me and I blocked it and put him back into the wrist lock, only harder, and he went back down on his knees and screamed. One of his friends was going to help him but Gina told them that I was the one that killed the three-armed guys that broke into my father's shop that was on the news recently. And if he continued, they would need to call an ambulance, so he stopped. He told the guy that I was holding to stop. The guy said alright. I let him go and he stood up and threw another punch and I broke his arm. Then they left. Remember the Sunday before last? Paula called me and said Denise might be in trouble. Remember I left in the early evening? Denise met a guy at the Bum Steer the night before and he asked her out. He picked her up that Sunday and took her to a dive bar in South Tucson. Evidently Gina and Paula followed them. They didn't trust this guy. The guy got her a mug of beer and spiked it with a Quaalude. Paula called me and told me Denise was passed out laying over the table and the guys were touching her. When I got there, I went to see what was going on. One guy grabbed me and I broke his wrist. Then I asked the guy that took her out what was going on, he said, "what are you gona do about it?" I punched him hard in the nose and broke it. Another guy went to grab me and I broke his wrist. And when the others started to grab at me, I took out my sticks and beat them back. Then the bartender ran up with a 45 automatic and pointed it at me. I took it away from him and then kicked him with a 360 degree reverse roundhouse and he went down. Then everyone backed off. I gave Gina the gun and helped Denise out to the car and we brought her to the emergency room. At that time, I had no idea what they had given her. Then I called Lieutenant Edwards."

"Then last week outside of the Bum Steer four of them came and said they were going to teach me a lesson. I knocked two of them out and hurt the other two and they ran away. When the police came, they arrested the two I knocked out. It could be them."

"You think any of those that would cause them to kidnap your mother?"

"Well, I suppose not but these are the only things I can think of." She grabbed a tissue and blotted her eyes.

"I need to call the sheriff about this package and you can tell him about Tucson Burger and the bar. He picked up the phone and dialed the sheriff's office. He told them who he was and that he had information for the sheriff. While he waited, Jack stopped at the office.

"Everything OK?"

"Yes, thank you, Jack."

He glanced at Angie with a concerned look. He turned and went back to the counter.

The sheriff came on the phone, "Sheriff Smith, how can I help you?"

"Sheriff, it's Dominic. We received a small package from the kidnappers with Lizzy's watch and a note that says, here is you mother's watch so you know we have her. We will contact you again with further instructions."

"Have you touched the watch?"

"No sir. We purposely did not. Just the note."

"You are positive it is her watch?"

"Yes. We can see the inscription on the back. It is definitely her's. Also, Angie thought of a couple of other incident's she had that possibly could have led to this."

"Where are you now, Dominic?"

"We are at the shop, why?"

"I will come to pick up the watch to see if we can find any prints on it and Angie can tell me about the other incident's then."

"Alright sir, we will be here. See you soon." He hung up.

"Angie the sheriff is coming now to pick up the watch and hear about those incidents."

"OK father. While we wait, I will go finish the car I was working on. It is about complete. It should only take a short time." She got up, blotted her eyes again and went into the shop.

About twenty-five minutes later the sheriff arrived. He walked into the front of the shop and said to Jack, "I am here to see Dominic and Angie."

"OK, follow me." Jack brought him to the office. Angie saw him and walked up front.

"Uncle Jack, this car is finished, here is the invoice and the keys."

"Thank you, Angie."

She went to the office.

"Hello Angie, how are you holding out?" The sheriff asked.

"I am managing."

"Well, you don't sound too convincing. Can you tell me about those two incidents?"

Angie sat down on the other chair. "Sir, I just remembered two other incidents immediately after I opened the package. A while back I was at the Tucson Burger on Oracle and Wetmore with my friends eating and these four guys came in. While they were in line to order, they became obnoxious. They were saying things they would like to do to us loud enough that everyone could hear. There were a few mothers there with little kids. Gina, one of my friends, got up and went over and asked them to quiet down because there were little kids there. One of the guys grabbed her arm and said he was going to take her and they would show her a good time. She tried to get away but this guy would not let go. I went over and asked him to let go and he just laughed and he asked what I was going to do about it. He raised his other arm and I grabbed his wrist and put it in a wrist lock and he let go of Gina and went down on his knees. I asked him if he was done because I could easily break his wrist and he said, 'Yes.' So, I let him go. I did not think he was finished and he tried to punch me and I blocked it and put him back into the wrist lock, only harder, and he went back down on his knees and screamed. One of his friends was going to help him but Gina told them that I was the one that killed the three-armed guys that broke into my father's shop that was on the news recently. And if he continued, they would need to call an ambulance, so he stopped. He told the guy that I was holding to stop. The guy said alright. I let him go and he stood up and threw another punch and I broke his arm. Then they left. Then the Sunday before last my friend Paula called me and said one of my other friends, Denise, might be in trouble. Denise had met a guy at the Bum Steer and he asked her out. He picked her up that Sunday and took her to a dive bar in South Tucson. The place is on 29th street and fourth Avenue. Evidently Gina and Paula followed them. They did not trust this guy. He brought her into this bar and got her a mug of beer and spiked it with a Quaalude. Paula called me and told me Denise was passed out laying over the table and the guys were touching her. When I got there, I went to see what was going on. One guy grabbed me and I broke his wrist. Then I asked the guy that took her out what was going on, he said, "what are you gona do about it? And swore at me." I punched him hard in the nose and broke it. Another guy went to grab me and I broke his wrist. And when the others started to grab at me, I took out my sticks and beat them back. Then the bartender ran up with a 45 automatic and pointed it at me and I just took it away from him and kicked him with a 360 degree reverse roundhouse and he went down. Then everyone backed off. I gave Gina the gun and helped Denise out to the car and we brought her to the St. Mary's Emergency Room. At that time, I had no idea what they had given her. Then I called my father's friend, Lieutenant Edwards and told him about it and he came to the emergency room to talk to us. Gina gave him the gun as well. He had said he needed to call the South Tucson police."

"Then last week outside of the Bum Steer, four of them from that bar came and said they were going to teach me a lesson. I knocked two of them out and hurt the other two and they ran. When the police came, they arrested the two I knocked out. Possibly it could be one of these."

"That is an interesting story, Angie. How did you defend against these guys? And you said something about sticks?"

"Sir, I do not believe you know about me as of yet. I am a fourth-degree black belt in Tai Kwando; Muay Thai; Karate; Aikido and Shaolin Kung Foo. The sticks I mentioned are Escrima sticks. These are bamboo and about 24" long. I use these fighting at times."

"That is some list. Really? All of those?"

"Sir, I was the person that killed the fifteen guys that had kidnapped all of those girls."

"You? You did that yourself? That is hard to believe."

"Yes sir. That was me. You can ask Lieutenant Edwards if you like. He saw me fight the last few guys after he was shot."

"If you say so. I will see if we can find these guys. We don't have any other leads. Thank you for the information, Angie. And Dominic, I will get the watch dusted. Maybe we will get lucky and get a print."

"Thank you, sir." They stood, shook hands and the sheriff left.

As he drove back to the station, he thought about what Angie told him about her martial arts. He smiled and thought this was farfetched. He thought, "Fourth degree black belt in all of those martial arts? Yeah, right" He chuckled as he drove as he didn't believe that.

Dominic said to Angie, "Why do you not go home now. Possibly you can relax somewhat. There is not anything pressing we cannot handle for the rest of the day."

"Alright father. She hugged him and turned and walked out of the office. She saw Uncle Jack and walked over and hugged him and told him she was leaving for the day. She grabbed her purse and left. She said bye to the guys as she walked out.

Angie drove home and thought about everything that happened this week. It brought tears to her eyes. When she got home, she took a shower and went into her room, laid down and tried to relax. She closed her eyes. As usual, thoughts raced through her head. She thought about the old farm house and barn and finally drifted off to sleep.

Later, Dominic came home. He looked for Angie and found her asleep on her bed. He closed the door quietly and let her sleep. He knew she hadn't slept much since Monday. He went into the kitchen, made himself a sandwich and poured a glass of iced tea. He went out to the deck and sat and ate. As he ate, he thought about how upset Angie has been. He thought about when his mother died and how he and Maria felt. He couldn't believe he could be in the same place again. Tears began running down his cheeks. He closed his eyes and tried to put that out of his mind. He prayed for the safe return of Lizzy and that they would be together again.

After a while he got up, picked up his plate and glass and went into the house. He put them in the sink and went to bed.

31

Dominic woke, got up and went and took a shower. When he came out of the shower, he smelled bacon cooking. He put on his robe and went to the kitchen. "Angie, you did not need to cook."

"Good morning father. I needed to do something to keep me occupied." She had just finished the bacon. "I made bacon, eggs and English muffins." She took the plates and put them on the table. Then she opened the refrigerator and took out the orange juice. She poured two glasses and returned the pitcher to the refrigerator. Then she picked up the glasses and put them on the table. "Sit down and eat father."

He sat and Angie did as well. They both ate without talking. As they were eating Dominic had tears running down his cheeks. He picked up a napkin and blotted them. "Father, are you alright?"

He looked at her and said, "I was just thinking how much you look like your mother standing there cooking." He put his head down in his hands.

Angie got up and walked around the table and hugged him from behind. "Father, I love you."

He reached with one hand and squeezed her arm. As she was hugging him, she said, "We will get her back, father." Then she thought about what she just said. "Father, that just came to me and came out. I was not thinking that. But now I feel that we will."

"I hope you are correct."

"I believe so. I still do not understand how things come to me." She let go of Dominic and took the plates, silverware and glasses and brought them to the sink and began washing them. She rinsed them and put them in the dish rack to dry. "I am going to get ready for work, father." And she left the kitchen.

Dominic got up and did the same. When he came back into the kitchen, he saw his and Angie's lunchboxes on the table. He opened his and saw that Angie had made lunch for him. She had also put in a thermos full of coffee in it. He thought, "She still amazes me."

Angie came in to grab her lunchbox and said, "I made lunch for us father. I put a thermos of coffee in yours as well."

"I cannot believe you Angie." He went and hugged her.

"Thank you."

"You are welcome. I am leaving for work now. See you soon. I love you!" She turned and walked away.

Dominic smiled. He couldn't believe Angie. He thought, "Even with all of this going on she has been taking care of me." He picked up his lunch box and left for work.

Work passed without anything major. It was just a normal day. Angie finished, said goodbye to everyone and went home. She was upset that she hadn't seen anything more. She changed and went outside to work out.

Later, when Angie finished working out, she went into the house and took a shower. She dressed and went into the Arizona room and sat and looked at the mountains. As she was sitting there the doorbell rang. She got up and went to the door. She opened it and it was Sherri.

"Hi Angie. I saw some things and thought I would come over to tell you."

Angie reached out and hugged her. "Hello Sherri. I have not seen anything else." She stood aside to let her in. She closed the door and they went into the Arizona room and sat down.

"Angie, I think I saw 5 guys talking and walking to the barn. I saw the van and the pick-up truck. I think it says Western Gas on the side, but I am not sure."

"Possibly if we both concentrate, we will see more. Let us try holding hands." Angie reached and took Sherri's hands. They closed their eyes and concentrated on the old farmhouse and the barn.

After a few minutes Angie said, "Now I see someone is going into a room that has a padlock on it. He unlocked it and is going in. My mother is there. She is terrified. She thinks they are going to kill her. She is looking at someone and she sat up."

"What do you see now? Angie."

"I am seeing through the guy's eyes. He is looking at my mother and raising his arm. Oh my god! He has a gun in his hand!" Angie screams terrified, "No! No! My god he is putting a gun to her head." She started to cry. "No! Mother! He pulled the trigger. Aahhh!" Angie jumped and fell off of the couch. "Nothing? He is laughing. The gun wasn't loaded. He did that on purpose to frighten her. That bastard. He is going to pay." Angie was crying. She opened her eyes, stood and sat back on the couch.

Sherri sat next to her and put her arms around her. She was crying as well. "Angie" was all she got out. She hugged her tight. "We will find her. I know we will find her. I feel it in my heart."

By this time, it was late. After a few minutes they both fell asleep while hugging each other. Dominic came home and saw them there in the Arizona room sleeping. All he kept thinking was, "Angie could lose her mother just as I did." Now tears were rolling down his cheeks. He was feeling like he did when his mother died and all of that grief came back at once. He had a lump in his throat and his stomach felt like it had butterflies in it.

Then the doorbell rang and kind of snapped him out of it. He walked to the door and opened it. It was Maria. She was in tears and walked in and hugged Dominic. "Big Brother, I feel so sad for you and Angie. All I can think about is how I felt when mother died. This cannot happen. We have to find her."

As they walked into the house Angie awoke. "Aunt Maria." And she jumped up and ran to her. She was crying as well. Angie hugged her.

Sherri awoke and walked up. "Hello Mrs. Bertini." Her eyes were red from crying.

"Hello Sherri." Maria said. "I came because I saw some things. Maybe we can figure out where they are. I thought that possibly if the three of us got together we could stimulate each other."

"Ma'am, Angie and I were just doing that. Angie saw some things I didn't." They all went into the Arizona room and sat.

"Could we face each other? Do you think that would help Aunt Maria? It felt like we were bonded when you came and talked to me a while back."

Maria said, "Maybe." She stood up and walked to the dining room and grabbed a chair. She brought it back and placed it in front of the couch and sat so she was facing Angie and Sherri.

Dominic was standing in the hallway watching.

"Let us hold hands. Close your eyes and concentrate on Elizabeth." They all held each other's hands almost in a circle. Maria said, "I see her opening the door. It is a Western Gas man.

In a low tone Maria said, "Hello Ma'am, we have a gas leak in the area and we're checking every house. Is it OK if I come in and take some readings?"

"You may come in and check." Maria was repeating what each of them said. Her voice was high now.

Dominic stood there shocked.

Angie said, "Then two guys rushed in and grabbed her. One put his arm around her neck and it caused her to pass out. They carried her out and put her in the back of a white Ford van. The van has no side windows. They slammed the doors and left. Now they are laughing."

"They are wearing Halloween masks, except for the gas man." Sherri said. "Devil masks. How fitting."

"I cannot see the license plate number. They backed and drove so fast." Angie screamed, "His eyes!"

"What about his eyes Angie?" Aunt Maria asked?

"I see his eyes and they are familiar. I know those eyes." She opened her eyes and let go of the others hands. "I know those eyes. How do I know his eyes?" She was thinking. "I cannot think of who it is dam it."

"Relax Angie." Sherri said. "You will not see anything if you are angry or tense."

Maria was shocked! She didn't know that. "I never identified that in the past. You will not see anything if you are angry or tense! All of these years I never identified that."

They reached and held hands again. Dominic was standing there looking shocked. He couldn't believe what he was hearing. He thought to himself, "They saw when Lizzy was abducted!"

Angie said abruptly, "Turn onto I10 east." She opened her eyes. "That was strange. It just popped into my head as if someone just said it to me." She closed her eyes again.

Dominic was beginning to feel as though they would find Lizzy. He still didn't understand why they kidnapped her. He walked quietly to his office and grabbed a pad of paper and a pen to begin writing this down. He walked back and continued to stand in the hallway.

After another 20 minutes they didn't see anything else. They decided that was all they would see at this time.

Dominic went into the Arizona room. "I want to keep track of everything each of you have seen so far. I overheard you saw them abduct... Liz," he swallowed, "Lizzy." He almost couldn't say her name. He held back the tears. "And they drove onto I10 east. Have you seen anything else?"

Sherri said, "They have her in an old, abandoned farmhouse and she is locked in a room."

"Angie said, "Father, I saw the farmhouse. It is the same old shack I saw in a flash image in my head a while back before this happened. At the time I did not know what it was. There is also an old barn close to the farmhouse. There is quite a bit of Cholla cactus, bursage, there are mesquite trees on one side and an old split rail fence like ranchers have around their property. The kind that has two long chopped pieces of wood between posts and is kind of zig zagged. There are also lots of scrubby tree like bushes. Sherri thought she saw 5 guys walking to the barn.”

“What did you see when you were at the shop? The guys said you screamed, “They got her!”

“I saw two guys, each one holding one of her arms dragging her out of the house.”

“If all of you see enough, we may be able to determine where she is.” Dominic said. “Maria, what did you see initially?”

“Dom, all I saw was Lizzy screaming. Then Lilly called me and told me that she was on the phone with Lizzy when she went to answer the door. She said she heard Lizzy screaming something like, ‘What are you doing? Why are you doing this?’ She said that was all she heard over the phone and it was in the background since the phone is so far from the door.” Maria said. “But now that I know being angry or tense blocks our ability, I will try to stay relaxed if I can.”

“That goes for us as well Aunt Maria. It will be difficult to relax.” Sherri agreed.

Dominic wrote everything down on his pad of paper.

Angie, Sherri and Aunt Maria sat for a while longer and didn’t see anything else. Aunt Maria and Sherri decided to go home.

32

It was already six days now since Lizzy was abducted and the Sheriff still did not have any good leads. The next day both he and Lieutenant Edwards worked together to check out the leads they had. The lieutenant checked on the guys at the bar in South Tucson. Since he had arrested two of them outside of the Bum Steer he had their contact information. He also found the guys from the Tucson Burger on Oracle and Wetmore. He had driven there to talk to the manager hoping to get information about them and it so happened that these guys were there. And one guy had a cast on his arm which made the lieutenant positive these were the guys. The store manager then verified that these were the guys. After talking to these guys, he was convinced that they were not involved. They were punks but he did not believe they were capable of kidnapping someone.

The sheriff checked out Johnny but he had an alibi, although not solid, that checked out. And so far, these guys haven't called or contacted Dominic or Angie outside of the box with Lizzy's watch.

On Monday, Angie and Dominic went back to work. Dominic called Lieutenant Edwards, "Good morning, Lieutenant."

"Good morning, Dominic. You sound a little better today. What can I do for you?"

"Sir, Maria, Angie and Sherri sat together and they saw when Lizzy was abducted. Maria repeated what the guy at the door and Lizzy said almost as if she was in a trance. She said the doorbell rang and Lizzy answered and they guy said he was from Western Gas and said there was a leak and wanted to take readings. Then Lizzy said it was OK and two other guys in devil masks ran in and took her. She said they drove away in a Western Gas truck and a white van. And since the sheriff didn't believe what Angie said about her martial arts training, I do not believe he would believe me if I told him this."

"He didn't believe her? Maybe I should set him straight. I need to tell him about this. I will think of something."

"Thank you, sir." He hung up.

The day went by and Angie didn't see anything. She went to the Dojo and worked with her sensei's. She told them that she was distraught and needed to work out with them. She usually went on Tuesdays but they were OK with this since it was just working out. She also asked if they were OK with her coming on Wednesday for the same this week. They agreed. They reminded Angie that she should not fight with anger. It will cloud her thinking and she might hurt the wrong person.

She went home and prepared dinner for Dominic and herself. They ate and she cleaned up. She took a shower and went to bed.

As was beginning to be common for the last week, they both tossed and turned before finally getting to sleep.

Tuesday, Dominic and Angie went to work again and it was a normal day without any incidents. The guys haven't been talking much during this time because Angie wasn't saying anything outside of what was necessary for work.

After work Angie drove over to Sherri's house to see if she saw anything else.

While stopped at a stoplight she saw a cowboy riding a horse. He stopped then got off and walked over to a big tractor. He got into it and started it. Then he drove away. Angie thought to herself, "What does this have to do with mother? Then she had a vision of a white van turning off of I10. But she couldn't see the exit sign."

She arrived at Sherri's house and rang the doorbell.

"Hello Angie, it is nice to see you. I feel so sad for you. I cannot imagine what you must be feeling."

"Thank you, Mrs. Winston. I came to see Sherri. Is she here? I saw her car outside."

"Yes. She is in her room. You may go back."

"Thank you, Ma'am." Angie walked to Sherri's room. She was going to say hello but Sherri was sitting still with her eyes closed and she felt that Sherri was seeing something right then. She stood there for a few minutes.

Sherri opened her eyes and said, "Hello Angie."

Right away Angie said, Hello Sherri, "On the way over here I was stopped at a light and I saw a cowboy riding a horse. Then he got off and got into a large tractor, started it and drove away. I don't understand this. I wonder if it is connected. Then I saw a white van turn off of I10 but I could not see the exit sign."

Sherri said, "A cowboy? I haven't seen anything like that. But I just saw them take the exit for SR80."

Angie wasn't certain what she meant. "SR80? What is that?"

"State Route 80. They took that exit."

"That is exceptional. Now we need to find out where they went on SR80."

They sat together and concentrated on the farm house and SR80 but did not see anything more. They talked for a while then Angie went home frustrated.

Angie and Dominic went to work the next day, Wednesday. It was just a normal day of work. Again, Angie did not talk about anything except for what was necessary to work. After work she went to the Dojo and worked out again. Just as on Monday, she went home and made dinner. She sat with Dominic and they didn't talk again. When they finished Angie got up and cleaned up.

Dominic hugged her and told her, "Thank you, Angie." And went to bed.

Thursday, Dominic and Angie went to work and it was another day like Monday, Tuesday and Wednesday. Angie did not see anything.

Afterwords, she decided to go to Sherri's house again.

When she arrived, she went to the door and rang the doorbell. Sherri answered. "Hi Angie." She reached out to hug her.

Angie hugged her back. "Hello Sherri. I thought we could sit and try to see anything again."

"Let's go to my room." They walked to Sherri's room and Sherri sat on her bed and Angie pulled over her desk chair.

They talked a little and then Angie got a shock. "I am seeing through someone's eyes. He is walking into the farm house. Now to the room my mother is in. He went inside." She began to say what this person was saying in a low voice, "I guess you aren't very important to them. We only asked for $10,000 and they refused to pay. I am glad I'm not you. You're not even worth $10,000. You aren't much use to us anymore. Poor you. Ha, Ha." Angie was seeing this as it is happening. He pulled out a gun. "He's going to shoot her in the head. My god! NO! Bastard. CLICK. Angie jumped and fell off of the chair. The gun was not loaded again. He is tormenting her. He thinks it is funny. He is laughing hard. Mother!" She was crying. She had been positive her mother was going to die this time. "Bastard! I am going to break his neck!" Then Angie started crying harder. Through her tears she said, "I cannot believe I said that. I never thought like this about anybody. I feel as though I am going to go to hell now." and she continued crying.

Sherri stood and went and helped Angie up and onto the chair. Sherri and hugged her. "Angie, I can understand how you feel. I don't blame you for thinking that. I think I would think the same if I was in your place. You are under terrible stress and not always thinking straight. I am sure you will be forgiven."

Angie turned and stood and hugged Sherri back. "I do not know what I would do if I did not have you and the others. All of you have given me something I did not know I needed." She cried more.

Mrs. Winston came to the doorway with two glasses of iced tea. Now she was teary eyed. "I am so sorry Angie." Her voice was trembling somewhat. "I brought you some iced tea. Here I will put the glasses here." She set them on Sherri's nightstand. She looked at Angie and placed her hand on her shoulder for a second and turned to leave.

Angie said through her tears, "You are so considerate ma'am. Thank you."

"Always so polite." Mrs. Winston said as she left.

"We will find them Angie. I feel it very strongly. I wish I knew how I feel this, but I am more positive about this that anything I have felt." Sherri told her.

After some time, Angie calmed down. They sat and drank some iced tea. "I still can't place those eyes. I know I have seen them but it is just out of my grasp."

They sat in silence and after she was there about an hour, Angie decided to go home. She was sure they would not see anything more.

Lieutenant Edwards called Western gas and found out that a pick-up truck assigned to Lenny Anderson was missing and he has been out of work and hasn't called in. Lieutenant Edwards called the Sheriff and gave him this information.

When the Sheriff asked him how he knew to call Western gas, he told him that he had stopped to see how Dominic and Angie were holding out and a neighbor stopped him and told him that they saw a Western gas truck and white panel van pull away from their driveway the day it happened. He said the neighbor had not thought it was odd until he read about it in the newspaper.

Angie got home and couldn't find her father. She looked in all of the rooms. She began to think that he was kidnapped as well. She was beginning to get frantic and was beginning to panic. Then she saw that he was sitting on a chair on the patio facing the Santa Catalina's. She opened the sliding door and walked over to him. She found him crying.

"I don't know what to do. I cannot live without her. I do not know how I will survive. Angie, I am so afraid."

Angie stood there for a minute trying to take in what he said. "Father, she is everything to me as well. I do not know what to say." She was in tears again. "All that comes to mind is you must have felt much like I do now when Grandmother died. Only you were younger. I feel lost father. I am afraid as well. I feel like they pulled out my heart."

He reached out and pulled her onto his lap. "I have been remembering our whole life. I remember when your mother told me she was pregnant. I could not believe it because they said she could not conceive. Now you are all grown up. It feels almost as if it was yesterday. You are all I have. I would die if I lost you too."

"Father, do not think like that. She is not lost. She is still alive and ok, I feel it. I will get her back. That is all that keeps going through my mind. I feel as though I will get her back but I do not know how. I do not know where she is other than Cochise County. She will be back with us father. I do not know how but the feeling that she will be back with us is incredibly strong. But I also feel that somehow, I will get her back and it will not be the police. I do not know why I feel that."

"Angie, I do not want you to do anything stupid. I cannot lose you. I just cannot."

"Whatever happens father, I will be fine. I see it. I see us all together here celebrating. I am just afraid that something could change everything. Aunt Maria told me that the medium said she will see what is coming in the immediate future if nothing changes. I am worried that something will change." She was crying hard again.

After a few minutes Angie said, "I need to calm down. I cannot see anything if I am angry or distressed. I have to calm down. I need to see where she is. I do not know if we can wait for them to notify us of what they want. I feel that time is of the essence." Then she looked like she didn't understand what she just said. "Father, I never used that phrase, 'time is of the essence.' I am not certain I have even heard it. It just came out."

"Angie, my mother used to say that quite a bit. I wonder if she had this ability. Do you think she is helping you somehow?"

"I do not know father. But I will take all the help I can get. Let us go in and get something to eat. I have not eaten since this morning. For the first time since this happened, I actually feel hungry."

They both went into the house and to the kitchen. Dominic almost couldn't go into the kitchen. All he could think was Lizzy wasn't there. Angie looked at Dominic, "Father, please go sit down in the dining room. I will make something and bring it to you. Please go and sit down."

"I cannot believe how strong you can be sometimes. I love you." He kissed her on the forehead and went into the dining room and sat.

Angie looked around the kitchen and found French bread, mayonnaise, cheese, lettuce and cold cuts. She cut the bread and made-up sandwiches just as her mother usually made. She put them on plates and made iced tea. Then she put everything on the serving cart along with the pitcher of iced tea she had made. She rolled it into the dining room up to the table. "Here father." She handed him a plate, then poured a glass of iced tea. She took the other plate then poured herself iced tea and sat down across from him.

He looked at her as if he was going to say something. "What were you going to say father?"

He was teary eyed again. "When you walked in here, I almost thought you were your mother. I never saw or realized this before. You move and act very much as your mother does. And you have the same pure heart."

Angie did not know how to respond to that. She just sat and said, "Let us pray father." They folded their hands. "We pray to you our father to help bring back my loving mother and my father's loving wife. We pray that she will be returned unharmed. Please give us the strength to endure this hardship. And please watch over her so that she will remain unharmed. Please bless us and everyone in the world. AMEN."

"Angie that was very nice, thank you."

"You are very welcome father." They ate and afterwards Angie cleaned up. They talked a bit more then decided to go to bed.

Friday came and work was as it had been all week. After work they went home. Angie sat in the Arizona room and Dominic went to take a shower. Then the doorbell rang. Angie got up to answer.

"Hi Angie, we came over to give you some company. We thought you might need someone to talk to." It was Gina, Paula, Denise, Karen and Janet.

"Please come in ladies." Angie stood aside and closed the door afterwords.

"We called Sherri but there was no answer. We don't know where she is." Paula said.

"She is shopping with her mother tonight. She told me last night." Angie said.

"How are you managing? Is there anything we can do for you?" Karen asked.

"I do not know. I have not been thinking well. I am too preoccupied. I am trying not to be but it is difficult not to be. I do not see things when I am preoccupied and that is causing me to be upset."

"Like, maybe we can help you do something. Maybe that will make you feel less upset." Denise said.

"Did you and you father eat dinner yet?" Janet asked. "We could help you cook. Or maybe we could cook and you could relax."

"We have not had dinner yet. I have been cooking for us and making us breakfast and lunch for work since this happened."

"Come on, let's go make dinner then." Gina said. Before Angie could say anything they all had gone into the kitchen and looked in the refrigerator and through the kitchen to find something to make.

Angie followed. "You do not need to do this. I can make dinner."

Gina said, "I know we don't need to do this. We are just going to. Sit down, we will handle everything."

Angie sat down at the table. She felt somewhat uneasy as no one besides she or her mother usually cooked or prepared food in their kitchen.

They looked in the refrigerator and found lettuce, tomatoes, cucumbers, carrots, green peppers and some shredded cheddar cheese. They also found some Italian dressing. Gina, Janet and Karen began cutting these up to make a salad. Paula and Denise found green beans and cream of chicken soup. They used these to make a bean casserole. They combined these in a casserole dish and put it in the oven. Gina then looked for something for a main course. She found a package of chicken breasts just about thawed in the refrigerator. She grabbed these and put them in a baking pan and seasoned it with some garlic salt, black pepper and oregano. Then she put it in the oven with the bean casserole.

Angie sat there watching and said, "I cannot believe you. You did not need to do so much. This is whole dinner."

Angie, like, we want to do this for you. You're our friend. And you're sad. We want to make you feel better." Denise said.

"You do so much for everybody. It's our turn to do something for you." Janet said.

"You are making quite a bit. All of you should eat as well. It may also make my father feel better as well."

"We can do that. I didn't think of your father." Gina said. "Um, I'm sorry Angie."

"Do not worry about that Gina. You guys are great!"

Dominic was walking to the kitchen and said, "Angie, what are you making? It smells goo." He was shocked when he got to the kitchen. "What is going on?"

"Father, my friends came over and insisted they make dinner for us. They are attempting to cheer us up."

"Hello Mr. Tucci. I hope you're not angry at us." Gina said.

"What would make you say that? I am just surprised. I was not expecting this. Angie, you have very kind friends. Thank you, all of you." Dominic said.

"They all said about the same time, "It is our pleasure."

Denise said, "Mr. Tucci, Angie has done so much for us and we wanted to do something. She saved me from getting raped and who knows what from those creeps. I feel like I owe it to her."

"You are all sweet. You are all going to stay and eat with us, are you not?"

"Yeah, of course we are." Karen said. "And we will clean up everything too. We don't want you to need to do anything. It's the least we can do."

Dominic sat down. He still couldn't believe they were doing this. He thought, "What a break for Angie. She has been doing so much." As he sat there, he worked hard to hold back tears. He could not believe Angie's friends.

Paula got out dishes and silverware and set the table. As she did that Karen found serving utensils and hot pads and put them on the table. Denise picked up the bowl of salad and put that on the table.

Soon the chicken was done. Gina took it out of the oven and put the pan on one of the hot pads. Then she grabbed the bean casserole and put that on the table. Janet said, "we forgot something to drink."

Angie said, "There is a large pitcher of iced tea in the refrigerator."

Janet went to the refrigerator and took it out. Karen looked in the cabinets and found glasses.

They all sat down. Angie said, "Let us pray." Everyone bowed their heads. "We pray to you father for bringing us all together tonight. May this feast we are about to partake nourish our bodies. Thank you for my wonderful friends that have just prepared this feast. And please bring my loving mother and my father's loving wife back to us unharmed.

Give us the strength to endure this hardship and I pray that you watch over my mother. Please bless those to whom are less fortunate than all of us. In your name I pray, Amen."

Everyone said, "Amen."

"Angie, that was very nice, thank you." Dominic said.

Gina reached for the salad bowl and passed it to Angie. She took some and passed it to her father. Gina then put a serving spoon into the bean casserole. "Maybe I should hold it for everyone. She put on the oven mitt and picked up the casserole and held it out for Angie. Then she held it for Dominic. Then she held it for everyone else. When everyone had some, she put it down and grabbed the pan with the chicken and held it out for Angie, then for Dominic. Then she held it out for everyone else. She put it back down and sat.

Everyone began eating. Dominic said, "This is all very tasty. This bean casserole is amazing! I never had anything quite like this."

"It's really easy to make. It is my mom's recipe." Denise said. "You just put green beans in a dish and pour in Cream of Chicken soup right from the can and mix it up and bake it."

"That does sound easy." Dominic said. "This was extremely caring of all of you to do. You are all wonderful friends to Angie."

"Angie is an amazing friend to all of us Mr. Tucci." Paula said.

Angie said, "I believe this is something the both of us have needed. A true act of kindness. I do not know," Angie got choked up and teary eyed. She cleared her throat and finished, "I want to thank all of you. I was feeling uncomfortable with all of you preparing this in our kitchen. My mother and I have been the only people cooking here until now with the exception of the server heating things up at our parties. But now I am grateful. I feel much better now."

Denise said, "I am so happy Angie. Like, I have been wanting to do something for you so much since you saved me."

"Us too." Everyone agreed.

They all finished and Gina said, "We will clean all of this up. Why don't you maybe go sit in the Arizona room. I know you really like it there Angie. And Mr. Tucci, please go and do whatever you usually do. We will take care of everything."

"Thank you, all of you. This was a nice surprise." Dominic said. He went to his office.

Angie said, "Thank you all so much." She turned and went to the Arizona room and sat.

Everyone worked and cleaned up, washed the dishes and put them all away. Then cleaned up the kitchen. They shut off the lights and went to the Arizona room to see Angie. They walked into the Arzona room and found Angie crying.

"Are you OK, Angie?" Denise asked. "What's wrong?"

"Angie turned and blotted her eyes with a tissue, "Nothing, I am so moved at what you guys did. I just cannot believe it. You are all so wonderful." She stood and hugged each one of them.

"Angie, we are so happy that you liked it. As we said before, if you need anything, please ask." Janet said.

Gina said, "We should go. It is getting late and maybe Angie will be able to sleep tonight."

They all said bye and hugged Angie. Angie opened the door for them to leave and said good bye again.

They all squeezed into Denise's mother's car and left.

Angie closed the door and went to look for her father. He was in his office. Father, everyone left. They cleaned up everything. I cannot believe them."

"You have such caring friends, Angie."

"I know. I cannot believe it. I feel tired now. I think this is the first time I have been relaxed enough to feel like this. I am going to go to bed. I love you father." She kissed him on the cheek and hugged him.

Dominic kissed her on the head and hugged back. He decided to go to bed as well.

36

The next day, Saturday, they went to work. Angie felt fairly good for once. She said, "Good morning." to all of the guys. This is the first time since her mother was kidnapped. The guys thought it was amazing. They wondered what changed. She wasn't her joyful self but she said "Good morning." She still didn't talk much during the day.

At lunch everyone was in the breakroom and Angie said, "You guys will not believe what happened last night."

Eric said, "What happened?" He was showing concern.

"My friends came over to my house and insisted on making dinner for my father and me. They made a nice salad, a bean casserole and baked chicken. It was such a nice gesture."

"Really? That was nice of them." Hector said.

"It somewhat filled the hole I have had since my mother was taken. It calmed me and I believe I slept fairly well for once since this happened."

"You have nice friends." Miguel said.

"Thank you, Miguel. I am sorry I have been so closed to everyone. I have been deeply preoccupied." She sat through the rest of lunch without saying anything else.

After work, Angie went and picked up Sherri. They were driving and Angie screamed, "Johnny! Those are Johnny's eyes! Bastard!"

"Are you sure Angie?" Sherri asked.

"I am positive. I do not recognize any of the others however. We need to tell Lt. Edwards. Look for a phone booth."

They found a phone booth and Angie called Lieutenant Edwards. "Hello sir. I need to tell you what I just saw."

"What was that, Angie?"

"His eyes, I saw his eyes sir."

"Whose eyes?"

"Johnny's eyes. I saw them last Sunday when I was with my aunt and Sherri. We saw the abduction. They were wearing devil masks and I saw his eyes. But I could not place them. But a few minutes ago, I saw Johnny with some other guys in the old house where they have my mother and they were his eyes."

"OK, I will do more investigating on Johnny's alibi. Thank you, Angie. "You said something about an old house."

"They are in an old farm house somewhere in Cochise County. I know they took I10 to SR80 but that is all."

"Maybe someone in his family owns this house. I will look into that too and then talk to the sheriff. Thank you, Angie."

"You are welcome, sir."

37

Sherri and Angie talked more trying to figure out where the abandoned house and barn were. They were sitting in the Cuda on the side of the road. Neither saw anything else so Angie drove Sherri home.

Angie then drove home, went into the house and sat down in the Arizona room. She ended up laying down and she fell asleep. Dominic came home and saw her sleeping. He went and got a blanket and put it over her and left her to sleep. He felt that maybe she would get some sound sleep for once. He went to bed.

Later that night Angie woke up very excited although still worried. She went to look for her father. She said, "Father, father, I need to tell you something. Father?"

Dominic got up and walked out of the bedroom, "What is it, Angie?"

"Father, I saw Grandmother!"

"Grandmother Kristina?"

"No Grandmother Caroline! She came to me in my dream."

"She did? Did she say anything?"

"She came and lightly caressed my face and woke me. Then she smiled and said, 'Angelina, sweet Angelina, do not worry. You will find your mother off of Cowboy Trail. You already know that which you need, but time is of the essence my dear. I love you and am proud of you my dear. I am also proud of your father for taking charge when I died and taking care of your Aunt Maria. And tell your father and Aunt Maria that they make me proud as well. And your wonderful mother is your father's savior. She is very much like me.' Then she faded away.

Then I woke up. She was more beautiful than in any of the pictures I have, and it appeared as if she was glowing. Her Aura was glowing white, red and green."

Dominic had tears in his eyes. He truly believed she saw her. What Angie said was exactly how she spoke.

Angie saw his tears. She reached and hugged him. "I could feel her heart; it was so pure father. I wish I could have known her."

"She was an amazing lady."

"I need to find Cowboy Trail. I need to see the map." Then she thought for a second, "Oh, Sherri has the map, it is her fathers. She looked at her watch. It is 2 AM, I cannot call her now; it is too late."

"Angie, maybe if you lay down and think about your Grandmother Caroline you will relax enough to fall asleep."

"I will try father. I love you." She hugged him again and went to her room and laid down. She thought about her grandmother and fell asleep.

38

She dreamt about her mother and her captures. In the dream she saw Johnny and his guys taunting her mother. They had put a noose around her neck and she was standing. The rope was thrown over a beam and they had her wrists tied together behind her back and duct tape over her mouth.

They don't really hurt her but they make her think they are going to hurt her.

Lizzy was petrified! She could barely stand because her legs were shaking.

"We are going to hang you whether or not Angie shows up." Johnny said. He pulled on the rope and it tightened around her neck. He pulled a little harder and her feet came off of the floor.

Her eyes were big and opened wide. She tried to scream but nothing came out. The rope was choking her. She was certain this was the end. She kicked her legs and they all laughed.

He let her down on her feet. She tried to cough but the tape was tight. Her coughs went through her nose and mucus ran down over the tape and over her chin and dripped off. Her face was red. She was trying to catch her breath. She felt as if she was going to pass out.

Johnny let her almost catch her breath and he did it again. He pulled her off of the floor. Her reaction was exactly the same.

"You deserve this." Johnny said. "For having that bitch!" He let the rope go and they walked away.

Lizzy was finally catching her breath. She stood there with tears running down her face and prayed, "Heavenly father, please spare Angie from dying. If someone needs to die, please take me. Angie has her whole life in front of her. Please, please take me and not her."

They walked back. "We were going to kill you now but we decided that we want to do it in front of Angie so she can see what her actions caused. I want her to see you die just before we kill her." Johnny laughed a sinister laugh. It was almost giddy.

Lizzy's eyes were red and bloodshot. She had the worst pounding headache ever and she was worried that her legs would give out and she would hang herself. She was shaking uncontrollably.

"Angie has no chance against us. All six of us are Karate champions. No way she can fight us all at once." He told her. "We are going to beat her to death so she can feel her own medicine. Ha, Ha, Ha." He laughed.

Andy said, "Let's do it again. I liked seeing her choke."

"OK." Johnny said and pulled the rope. Lizzy's feet were off of the floor and she was kicking. Her face was bright red. He held her there for what she thought was an eternity. Then he let her down. She tried to cough as before and more mucus came out of her nose. She thought, "Why do they not just do it." She was hysterical but couldn't really show it with tape over her mouth and her hands tied behind her back.

They all stood there laughing. They thought it was funny seeing her choke and struggle. Johnny didn't think about her suffering. He just thought this would bring Angie there. He was laughing as they walked away from her.

Just before Angie woke, she saw a vision of her mother's headstone. Everyone was there and they were all crying. It was her mother's funeral and she heard a voice, "Angelina my dear, do not wait for the police. It will be too late and this is what you will then see. Remember, you already have that which you need and you will handle them with ease. Remember, time is of the essence. Your mother is counting on you." She knew it is her grandmother Caroline talking. She continued, "As I said Angelina, you will find her off of Cowboy Trail in Cochise County. Angelina, I am proud of you and will always be with you."

It was Sunday morning and Angie woke up and knew what she must do. But first she needed to get to Sherri's house to see the map. She needed to find Cowboy Trail. "I hope that is good information." She thought.

Angie called Sherri and there is no answer. She tried again then remembered that Sherri and her family were going to be at her cousin's house all day. What is she going to do all day?

Dominic got up and said, "Good morning, Angie. Are you going to go to shop to work on the fabrication shop?"

"Yes. I just remembered Sherri was going to her cousin's house all day. I will not be able to see her until later. I need her to help me to find and determine if this Cowboy Trail exists and where it is. And possibly she will see something else to help find mother. I will need to keep myself occupied until later."

"Ok Angie. I am going to stop at Tucson Burger to pick up coffee and something to eat. I will see you soon." He hugged her and left.

Angie changed into her uniform, ate a bagel with cream cheese and left for the shop. It was a bit humid as being Monsoon season it had rained. She found it difficult to keep her mind on what she was doing. But she made it through the day by painting some of the new benches and the chassis table. Later in the afternoon she quit for the day. She went and said goodbye to her father and drove directly to Sherri's house. It had been raining in bursts around the city and some areas in the mountains there was fog. It was late afternoon so the sun was low. When she drove west the sun reflected of the pavement. It was blinding as if the pavement was a dark mirror. She was squinting trying to see as she drove.

After teasing Lizzy for a while today they got the idea to rig the rope with something heavy so they don't actually need to pull it when Angie got there. They looked around the barn and found some old rusty metal thing that looked as though it was part of the power take off from an old tractor. They put a wood stand together strong enough to hold it. They used old pieces of wood that were around the barn. It took all of them to drag this thing over and lift it up onto the top of it. They tied the other end of the rope that was around Lizzy's neck to this so it is tight but not enough to choke her much. Then they tied another piece of rope to this thing and pulled it to a support for the barn and tied it tight to keep it from falling off. Then they carefully tapped out one leg of the stand. This caused the stand to tip slightly. They took a piece of wood and wedged it under to support the wood frame that was holding the tractor part. Then they took off the rope they had tied to the support. Now all that kept this tractor part from falling off and hanging Lizzy was this one piece of wood. Now all they will need to do is shoot at the piece of wood and it will break and the heavy metal thing will fall and pull the rope hanging her. They figured they will just let her stand there and if she falls asleep, she will hang herself. "She deserves this for having that bitch for a daughter," Johnny thought. They stepped back and admired their work laughing. "All any of us will need to do is shoot at that piece of wood and it will break and hang her mother. Perfect. When that bitch gets in here and sees her mother, we can shoot the piece of wood and all she will think of is saving her mother and we can all attack her together. That bitch will finally get what is coming to her. Ha Ha! Now we can send the letter to get Angie here." Johnny said.

At the end of the day Dominic called Lieutenant Edwards and updated him on the new information he had about the location of the shack. Little did he know that Angie was about to go rouge. She was about to avenge her mother. Grandmother Caroline told her again in her dream not to wait for the police so Angie was determined follow what she had told her.

Angie arrived at Sherri's house and they went to her room. As Angie was telling Sherri about the dream and seeing her grandmother, she got a shock again and saw more. She was in a trance like state and began speaking. "Turn onto SR80. Now drive about 2 ¼ miles. There is a street called Cowboy Way. You need to turn there. See, it's coming up. Yea, turn there. OK, now in about ½ mile turn right at the Tee, see it up there. OK now go to the trees and turn in where the jumping cactus is."

Angie had said this out loud.

"Angie? Were you just saying what Johnny said?" Angie looked like she was in a trance. "Angie, Angie?"

Angie snapped out of it. "What, huh?"

"Angie you were talking like you were telling someone directions."

Angie thought for a minute and said, "Turn onto SR80 and go about 2 ¼ miles on SR80 to Cowboy Way. Then in about ½ mile turn right at the Tee and go to the trees. It looked like it was about 1000 feet. My grandmother said it was Cowboy Trail. Maybe they changed the name or maybe she did not see it clearly."

Sherri wrote this down. "This is where they are?"

"Yes. I know where they are now. I saw the shack and barn. Sherri, I am going home to get ready. There is no time to waste."

"We are going to get you father and Lieutenant Edwards, right?"

"I am sorry Sherri. I cannot wait. I will see you later. You will always be my best friend." Angie ran out of the house, got into the Cuda and sped away. She raced home.

When she got home, she dressed all in black. A black stretch long sleeve shirt, black stretch pants, black socks, black gym shoes. She did not wear her cross because after rescuing the kids and losing it she didn't want to chance it again. She wore a black headband around her forehead and tied her hair into a pony tail with a black ribbon. Her shirt had a hood and she tucked her hair down her back and she pulled hood over her head. Then she grabbed a black covering something like a cloak and put that on. She had seen it at a store and felt she needed to buy it. She then grabbed her Eskrima sticks and the bag that tied around her waist. She wanted to inflict the most pain on Johnny as possible. And last thing she grabbed was the pair of thin black leather gloves she had recently bought on impulse. She was preparing for a fight to the death if necessary and it was the guys that kidnapped her mother were going to suffer. She left immediately. It was 5:30 PM. It would be getting dark soon but not before she arrived. When she had looked at the distance on the map at Sherri's house, she expected to be there in maybe 35 minutes at the speed she would be driving. She intended to drive as fast as the Cuda would go.

Sherri was scared. She called Dominic frantically, "Mr. Tucci, we just figured out where they have Mrs. Tucci and Angie left saying she was going to get ready. She is going herself. We have to stop her sir. I am worried that she is going to be hurt or worse."

"Where are you, Sherri?"

"I am at home."

"I am going to call Lieutenant Edwards and have him meet me at our house. Can you drive there now? We need you for directions and maybe we can catch Angie before she leaves."

"OK Sir. I will leave as soon as I hang up." She hung up and ran out to her car and drove to the Tucci's house. Angie's Cuda was not there. A few minutes later Lieutenant Edwards and Dominic pulled into the driveway in the Lieutenant's squad car. Sherri ran up to them.

Lieutenant Edwards screamed, "Get in!"

Sherri got in and as soon as she closed the door, he sped up the driveway. "Where is this place you saw Sherri?"

"Well, it is in Cochise County. We need to take I10 to SR 80, then drive about 2 ¼ miles to Cowboy Way. It's a dirt road that goes to the right. Then we need to go about ½ mile and then right at the tee in the road. It is about 1000 feet in a group of trees. I'm worried. Angie said she going to do whatever it takes. I'm worried that they will kill her." Sherri was now crying. "Why did she have to go herself? I'm going to lose my best friend."

Lieutenant Edwards said, "I just learned that Johnny's aunt owns a piece of property with an old farm house and barn on it. And it is just off of Cowboy Way." He got on his radio, "This is Lieutenant Edwards, patch me through to Sherriff Daniels, fast."

In a minute or so they heard, "This is Sheriff Daniels, what is the problem?"

"Jim, this is John. I have information on the location of Elizabeth Tucci. We are in route now. Can you and whoever you have available to meet me there as soon as you can."

"Why are you in such a hurry?"

"Angie Tucci already left and if we don't get there soon all we will be dealing with will be bodies."

"What do you mean? You think she's going to shoot them?"

"Absolutely not. Angie is, how do I say this, ah, just picture Joe Singso with a young woman's head. I believe this whole thing is about getting her there they can try to beat her to death. But they don't understand how deadly she is. I fear that if she engages them, she will kill them all."

"If you say so. I find that hard to believe. I'll get who I can and meet you there. Where are they?"

"There is a dirt road about 2 ¼ miles down SR80 called Cowboy way."

"I know where that is. I know the guy with a ranch down there."

"Well, there is an abandoned farm house and barn."

"I know right where that is. We will meet you there."

"Thanks Jim."

Angie drove as fast as the Cuda would go. She couldn't get there fast enough. The speedometer is pegged most of the way there. The HEMI was screaming. She passed a squad car on I10 with two deputies in it taking radar in Cochise County. She went by so fast they couldn't identify the car and when they looked at the screen it said 144 MPH. "What the hell was that? Did you see that?"

"I'm not sure, I saw a pink blur. You going to chase?"

"You kiddin? Whoever that was is probably in New Mexico by now. We couldn't catch that!"

Angie slowed as she saw the SR80 exit sign. She turned onto SR80. Now she needed to drive about 2 ¼ miles to a dirt road and turn right. She made note of the odometer and as it got to 2 miles, she began watching for the dirt road. She remembered that she saw a street sign but it was off the highway a bit which made it difficult to see. This dirt road is Cowboy Way. She saw it and turned. It was a bumpy sand road. In about ½ mile there was a Tee in the road to the right that she needed to turn on. In about 1000 feet the drive would be to the right in the middle of a large group of trees. She saw it and turned in. She could only drive about 30 feet because of the Cholla Cactus. She figured if she tried to drive through, she would get the Cuda scraped up and possible alert the guys at the house. She stopped and got out. She could still see where they drove through. She slipped her Eskrima sticks in the bag she had tied to her waist and put on the leather gloves. She looked as though she was a black ghost.

They were driving with the siren on I10 and they heard chatter over the radio about a pink car that they clocked at 144 miles per hour about 20 minutes ago going east on I10. Dominic said, "That had to be Angie."

Lieutenant Edwards said, "Who else could have a pink car capable of that kind of speed? I hope we aren't too late."

Angie began walking carefully because there were so many Cholla cacti there. She started to follow a typical split rail wood fence. As she was getting closer to the old farm house and barn, she ran into a young cowboy. "Hey Li'll Lady what ya doin here?" She jumped into her stance and asked angrily, "Who the hell are you?"

"Woah there, I'm not here to hurt ya Ma'am. Name's Dalton, Ash Dalton I work at the ranch here. Just fixin the fence.

"You are not one of the guys holding my mother over there?" She pointed at the shack and barn in the distance.

"The place is abandoned, no one lives there. Been abandoned for years." He glanced over and saw the van and pick-up truck. He wondered why he hadn't seen them before Angie arrived.

"There are guys hiding out there that abducted my mother. I may need to kill them to get my mother back."

"Kill um with what? Ya don't have a gun."

"I do not need a gun. I use my hands and feet."

"I never saw nothin like that. They got your mother?"

"Yes sir."

He was a little surprised by the "sir." You have a plan? To go in there, I mean."

"I will figure out as I go."

"Good way to get killed Ma'am. Ya know how many of um are there?"

"No need to use Ma'am. Call me Angie. There are 6 guys."

"OK Miss Angie."

"Just Angie, Ash, just Angie."

"Ok Angie. Do you think you need any help? See, I have a revolver holstered on each side like in the movies, I have a 9MM auto here" he showed her it was in his belt in the small of his back, "And I got this little one here." He showed her a derringer in his boot, "and I have this rifle." He picked it up. It was an AR15 with 4 extra clips attached to the side of it.

"You look like you are ready for a war."

"You never know what you will come up against out here. I like to be prepared."

Angie mumbled, "Sounds familiar."

"What was that, Angie?"

"Nothing. Maybe I could use some help. I am going to retrieve my mother and if these guys resist, they will not live past tonight. These guys kidnapped her because the leader forced me to fight one day outside of a store. In less than a minute I broke his nose, his right arm, gave him 2 black eyes, cracked ribs and a limp. This caused him to be kicked out of his Dojo permanently. His Sensei said he was a disgrace for attacking me. Evidently that was enough to make him kidnap my mother. I believe he kidnapped her to draw me here. He has five guys with him, most of which are likely trained in some form of martial arts."

"How are ya goin to go against five guys?'

"I did not tell you I am a 4th degree black belt in Karate; Taekwondo; Aikido; Maui Thai and Shaolin Kung fu and I have learned how to kill. They do not know what I am capable of Ash, but they will learn quickly."

"That is an impressive list, Angie. And you learned to kill, why?"

"I have been unfortunate to have been put in a position that I needed to fight for my life 3 instances and my Sensei told me that sometime, I may face someone that can fight as I do and that would not be good. He and his brother taught me these additional skills."

"What do you plan to do?"

"My plan is to assess the situation from a closer point and then decide my exact plan of attack. I will take a few minutes to meditate and clear my mind. Then I will be as stealth as possible as I do not want my mother hurt. I will be making my way to the trees just outside of the barn and hopefully some of them come outside. Then I will take them out before I go inside. How about when I go inside you get to the trees and wait for my signal."

"What would that signal be?"

"If I need you, it will be obvious. Thank you in advance Ash. You have been a gentleman."

"Thank you, Angie."

Angie began to make her way to the barn. By now it was about 6:00. She had called for a weather report, before she left her house, to find out when sunset would be, and they said 6:05 PM. They were correct, it was about twilight which she thought would help her cover.

Ash thought her story about being taught to kill was stretched at best. He couldn't believe anyone could fight like that. He felt he will need to be watching what is going on in the barn if he was going to save her. He followed her to the trees outside of the barn. Then he noticed what appeared to be her sitting on the ground meditating. She sat down, crossed her legs and put her hands on her legs palms up. She sat there until it was full dark, with the exception on the moon light which only took a few minutes.

Angie stood and began to walk out from the trees and had an encounter with the first guy as he was doing his rounds to check for anyone. He saw her and went up and put his gun to her back—wrong thing to do. In seconds he was dead. She spun and expertly took the gun out of his hand then took him down with the v of her hand in the throat. He was down on his back and she dropped to her knees, and punched him in his neck full power and it crushed his throat. He couldn't make a sound other than soft gurgling for the few minutes it took for him to die.

Ash saw this and was completely shocked. If he would have blinked, he would have missed this. "Maybe she can fight like she said," he thought.

Another guy came out looking for the first guy. This guy had a rifle strapped over his shoulder. He called to him in a loud whisper, "Jake? Jake? Where the hell are you?" he didn't get an answer. As he investigated, he found him lying on the ground. He checked and found that he was dead. He jumped up full of adrenalin and pulled out his pistol. Before he could run and tell everyone Angie dropped down quietly behind him from the tree above. She had climbed into the tree right after she crushed the first guy's throat. Ash was shocked because he didn't see her do that. Then she wrapped an arm around his neck from behind and pulled him backwards over her back. He dropped the pistol, frantically grabbed at his neck and began to choke. She grabbed his forehead with her other hand then did a quick pull that broke his neck. He went limp. She just threw him aside. "Two down, four to go." Angie thought. From there she ran to one corner of the barn.

Ash heard Johnny scream from inside the barn to another guy, "Where did those two assholes go to. Go check Lenny." Lenny went to the door and pulled out his 9 MM automatic, looked out and saw nothing then he went outside and began walking around the barn. When he got to the corner of the barn he was hit with a kick in his face. It broke his nose. Angie stepped around the corner and got into her stance. The guy grabbed his nose and his eyes were watering he said, "So you want to fight?" He got into his stance and in an instant, she kicked him with her right leg in his ribs then a punch to the face then to his neck. He stood there choking grabbed at his neck and she did a 360-degree reverse roundhouse to the side of his head and his head slammed into the side of the barn and he bounced off and fell limp.

Ash was watching all of this and was even more shocked and somewhat horrified. The second guy had a rifle strapped over his shoulder and a pistol and never got a chance to use them. He figured the third must have had a gun in his hand but he didn't have the time to use it. Ash remained in the group of trees.

Johnny, Rick and Andy began to realize the other three were not around anymore because they called them, and they were not answering. Then they heard a bang on the barn wall.

Johnny looked around and said fairly loud, "She's here."

Andy said, "Who's here?"

"That Angie girl. She's here. The others are dead. Dam it. I wasn't ready."

"You're sayin she killed Donny, Jake and Lenny?"

"Yea." Johnny said.

"Bullshit. There're probably at the house drinking beer. You know them." Andy said.

Rick looked scared. "You think this girl killed three guys that were karate champions? You said she was shit and this would be easy. You didn't say we were going to be up against someone like that. I'm not going to die for this shit." And he turned and ran out the barn door. He was still holding his gun pointed in front of him. And just as he turned towards the house, he saw Angie dressed all in black in her stance. He said, "Oh shit! Look, I didn't want..." Was all he got out before she began kicking him. She was using all her force. She first kicked the gun out of his hand then kicked him in the face and broke his nose. Then he tried to punch her and she grabbed his arm and pulled him to her and used her knee on the side of his rib's multiple times. He was wheezing and gasping for air. She spun and used her elbow and broke his jaw. He was bloody and in shock. His eyes were bulging and could not believe what was happening. She turned and took some steps away from him. He thought she spared him. She turned and ran at him. He screamed only for an instant. She did a running side kick to his throat and he flew back into the barn wall then fell forward. He was dead.

Johnny and Andy heard Rick scream and then it was cut off then they heard a loud bang on the barn wall. They knew for sure it was Angie and she just killed Rick. They ran and hid.

Ash was watching all of this from the trees and was shocked!

Angie stepped into the barn and saw her mother with a noose around her neck, tape over her mouth and her hands were bound behind her back. Her eyes were bloodshot and she was crying and looked petrified. When Angie stepped into her view, Lizzy only saw a dark figure. Angie turned and the moonlight shining through the doorway showed the silhouette of her face. She put a finger over her mouth to say ssshhh. Her mother's eyes were big like she thought Angie was in grave danger. Angie pulled out the Eskrima sticks and took one in each hand.

Andy ran out screaming AAHHHH getting ready to punch and kick. Lizzy thought, "Oh my lord, Angie!" She thought Angie was done for. Angie turned around and started on him with the sticks. He didn't know what to do to defend against those. He never learned about fighting with weapons. He had learned Karate for competition. Lizzy was watching this and thought her daughter was the female Joe Singso.

In seconds Johnny jumped out and engaged Angie. Andy was in shock and trying to recover from the sticks. He was stepping back away from Angie and he was bloodied all over. Johnny started kicking as Angie backed off. She blocked his kicks. She wanted to see how he was going to fight. She told him in a deep angry tone while staring into his eyes with looking up at him with her head tipped down, "I am going to kill you last! And I never break a promise!"

Johnny had a shocked look of fear in his eyes as she started on him with the sticks. He kicked and she hit his leg 4 or 5 times with the sticks. He tried a roundhouse with the other leg and she hit that leg 4 or 5 times. Both his legs were very sore now. By this time, he was angry. This wasn't how he planned this. They all were going to attack her together. He wanted to kill her. She gave him a few seconds to recover. Then she unleashed with the sticks again. Arms, ribs, legs. She was so fast he could not do anything but take the hits. He was putting out his arms trying to block but couldn't. She didn't use the sticks full force. She wanted him to hurt. When he was just holding his arms over his face she stopped. She looked at this pathetic piece of trash and said in a low tone, "I don't need these anymore." And threw the sticks down. She wanted to be closer and inflict real damage now. She was in her stance moving her arms and hands around staring directly into his eyes. He looked at her confused not knowing what to expect.

"These were movements from movies, not real martial arts." Johnny thought.

Ash had figured out that Angie wasn't going to give him a signal and went to the barn door and saw her fighting. He saw Angie beating the hell out of Andy and he could see that he couldn't defend against her.

Andy had gained some strength from adrenalin and ran out to help Johnny. He picked up a piece of rope that was laying in the floor and threw it over her head. It was wrapped around Angie's neck and he pulled her away back towards the wall. She tried to hit him with her elbow but couldn't. Then she turned and pulled him close to the wall of the barn and ran up the wall using him to stabilize herself and flipped over Andy getting out of his hold.

Johnny watched this and couldn't believe it was real. He never saw anyone run up a wall before, even in movies.

Angie turned and swung her right arm back and hit him in the side of the head with her fist then did the same with her left arm. This whole thing took about 6 seconds. Ash watched this and stood there with his mouth open in complete disbelief.

This whole time Lizzy was watching this from across the barn. She was in shock seeing her daughter fighting these guys.

Andy kicked at Angie but she grabbed his leg, twisted it and pounded on the side with her knee multiple times. He screamed with pure agony. She let go of his leg and did some kicks using her shin to his ribs again. Andy was now gasping for air, wheezing hard because she broke the ribs on his other side and knocked the wind out of him. "You terrorized my mother with an unloaded gun. I saw it through your eyes." Andy looked at her confused wondering how she could know that.

"How could you know that?" Andy struggled to stand up. He was bent over now with his arms over his stomach.

"I see things and I saw through your eyes." She said in a deep voice.

Angie turned and looked back at Johnny to see where he was. He stepped towards her and tried a punch and she immediately grabbed his wrist and hit the side of his elbow with her arm it broke his arm. Johnny screamed out loud.

Ash grimaced as he saw Johnny's arm bend the wrong way.

Johnny stepped back. Angie turned to Andy, as he was still partly bent over holding his ribs and stomach wheezing hard. She ran and did a jumping side kick to his head. He looked up and screamed just as she hit him and his head snapped back and it broke his neck. He fell backwards dead.

Ash saw her kick him in the head and it snapped back farther that it should have and knew she broke his neck.

She turned back to Johnny. She stepped towards him and used eye gouging. He was screaming again trying to block her with one hand. He couldn't put the other arm up because of the broken elbow. She stepped away and did a running side kick to his chest and he flew back onto his back. He didn't get up. She knew he wasn't dead yet but thought he was knocked out.

She could only think of her mother and ran towards her but Johnny sat up and had picked up one of the rifles that he had placed around the barn. He was supporting it with the arm with the broken elbow and screamed, "I'm going to kill you but first I'm going to hang your mother while you watch. All I have to do is shoot out that support and the weight will pull you mother up."

Angie stopped and turned around. She was beyond furious now. Angie tipped her head down and looked at him with her eyes turned up and said in a low tone, "You are already dead. You just do not know it." He laughed. He shot the wood block holding the rope that kept the heavy metal thing from falling. It fell pulling Lizzy up by her neck. Ash aimed his AR15 and shot the rope just above Lizzy's head. Lizzy fell onto her side. Her arms were still tied behind her and the tape was still over her mouth. She laid there.

After the shot from Ash, Johnny looked to the side to see where the shot came from. Angie ran to Johnny. She pulled the rifle from him and threw it across the barn. When she turned to throw it, he got up. She turned back and kicked him in the face and started to punch. He tried to defend himself, but she is far too fast and he was too hurt. She continued punching his face and kicking him in each side. He kept backing up trying to get away. She kept it up. She kicked him in the ribs on both sides and he was now in bad shape gasping for air. He could barely stand he had no energy to even defend himself. Angie said through her teeth, "This is for my mother asshole. She ran back about ten feet then turned and ran at him. He screamed as she did a running side kick to his chest so intense, he broke through the rotted barn wall and fell back onto the broken wood and got impaled on one of the boards. He raised his head in shock for a few seconds and went limp.

Angie turned and ran to her mother and removed the noose from her neck, untied her wrists and carefully pealed the tape off of her mouth. Then she helped her up and they hugged. Angie started crying and said, "I am so sorry mother. This was all my fault. I almost got you killed. If I had not engaged Johnny that day this would not have happened. Will you ever be able to forgive me?"

Lizzy reached and pulled Angie to her and hugged her tight. Her voice was raspy and weak and she was shaking. She said, "Angie, you have nothing to be sorry for. You did what you had to do." She was crying now. "Now you are my hero, honey." She coughed a few times. "I could not have a more loving, caring and amazing daughter. Now I understand why those young girls called you Saving Angelina."

"Mother, I came here today to avenge you. That name does not fit."

Ash had walked over to them and chimed in, "If I may make a suggestion ma'am, how does Avenging Angelina sound? That would be more fitting. After I saw you fight, I don't know what else to call it but pure vengeance little lady."

"Mother, may I present Ash. Ash, this is my mother, Elisabeth."

"Pleasure to meet you ma'am." He reached for her hand and kissed the back of it. "You have an amazing daughter. I only met her maybe 10 minutes ago, but in that time, I have gained an enormous amount of respect for her, ma'am."

"Thank you, Ash. It is a pleasure to meet you as well." Her voice was raspy and labored and she coughed. "I want to thank you for coming when you did. You saved both of us." Lizzy said.

Angie said, "I am sorry I did not signal you Ash. I was a little busy. Thank you for showing up when you did. You saved both my mother and me."

"Little lady, it was a pleasure, I never saw anyone fight like that. I am shocked. I must admit, I didn't believe you earlier but now I do."

Angie let go of her mother and turned to Ash and hugged him. "You saved my mother and me, Ash. "I need to thank you. I cannot think of how at the moment, but I will do something." The three of them turned and left the barn Angie had an arm around Lizzy's waist to help her and Ash was on her other side doing the same. Lizzy was having a difficult time walking. Her legs were weak and shaky. As they walked out Angie reached down and picked up her Eskrima sticks and slipped them into the bag tied to her waist and put her arm back around her mother's waist again to help her walk.

Just then Dominic, Sherri, Lt. Edwards, Sheriff Daniels, and the deputies showed up. Lieutenant Edwards had told the Sheriff that if he knows Angie, they will just have bodies to deal with. The sheriff still didn't believe him. They walked towards Angie, Lizzy and Ash.

Dominic ran up to them and took Lizzy into his arms and hugged her. He couldn't believe she was alive. "I thought I had lost you. Then when Angie left without us, I thought I was going to lose her as well. I would not be able to keep living." Then he let go of Lizzy and hugged Angie.

"I cannot believe both of you survived. You are my life." He was in tears. Then he realized Ash was standing there. "Who is this?"

Sherri had just come up to them.

Angie said, "Father, may I present Ash, a sweet cowboy from the ranch next to here. He came at the right time and shot the rope from the noose that was around mother's neck just as Johnny was hanging her. Johnny was going to shoot me but when Ash fired, he looked for where the shot came from, and I took care of Johnny for good. He's lying in the wall over there. She pointed to the hole in the barn wall. Dominic looked and saw Johnny's body laying backwards impaled with a board from the wall. There was just enough moon light to see. And the storm was getting closer. The flashing of the lightening lit the hole in the side of side of the barn and it appeared as if it was a scene in a horror movie.

Lieutenant Edwards and Sheriff Daniels walked up to Angie. "I need to ask Angie?" Lieutenant Edwards asked.

"Six, there were six and they were all armed. It was Johnny sir. He told me a week after the fight with him that you told him next time he would be in jail or dead. You were correct, sir."

"Sir," Ash looked at Lieutenant Edwards, "I don't know how to describe Angie. She fought like no one I have ever seen."

Lieutenant Edwards nodded then he and Sheriff Daniels walked to the barn. "She did this? By herself?" Sheriff Daniels asked. He was shocked.

"As I told you Jim, Angie is like no one I ever have met."

"She told me she was a 4th degree blackbelt in I think 5 different martial arts. I didn't believe her. I still can't believe it. She killed 6 guys that were armed? Without a gun herself?"

"As I said before, she can disarm anyone and based on how I have seen her fight, I don't believe there is anyone that she cannot defeat."

"She must be something to see." The Sheriff said.

"It is shocking, Jim. I watched her fight after I was shot at that child slavery thing. One guy threw a rope over her head and pulled it around her neck trying to choke her. He was behind her. She pulled him close to a wall and used him to stabilize herself and she ran up the wall and flipped over him. She instantly got out of the rope hold. I saw it, and I still don't believe it."

"She ran up the wall? That sounds impossible."

"Everything about her seems impossible. The first time I saw her fight, 3 guys broke into her father's shop when she was there alone late one night. Just as I ran in, I saw her lick the last guy. He was a fairly big guy and it looked like he was hit by a truck. Then she turned towards me. She was tensed up and ready to kill. It took a minute for her to recognize me. All I can say is she scared the shit out of me. She was all tensed and I could see her muscles and she was in this position, much like Joe Singso is in when he fights. She was growling. I kept screaming that it was me and she finally recognized me and stood down. She told me she was surprised when she saw that last guy and didn't know if there were any more. I can just imagine what these guys think when she fights them.”

“I don’t know what to say John.” They were walking around the barn. Then they saw Johnny. It was shocking to them seeing him impaled on wood in the wall. “Just imagine the force she had to generate to do this!” He couldn’t believe it. “That beautiful young girl did this? Alone? Unbelievable.” She sheriff was shaking his head back and forth.

Just then one of the deputies came to them. “Sir?” he said to the sheriff. “There are two guys over by the trees to the south. Both had guns with them and one had a rifle slung over his shoulder. There are two guys just outside of the barn that are dead and they both had hand guns and one still has a rifle strung over his shoulder too. There’s one guy just inside the door. I don’t know where the sixed one is yet.”

The sheriff pointed to Johnny impaled in the wall.

“Holy Shit! Who did that?”

“That beautiful blond girl outside.” The sheriff told him.

He shook his head in disbelief. As he walked away.

Angie pulled her hood back exposing her face and hair and pulled out her pony tail.

Ash took a double take. He had a shocked look on his face. “What is wrong Ash?” Angie asked. His jaw had dropped.

“Ah, I’m sorry, that was not polite ma’am. I, I can’t believe it,” he was shocked, “If I saw you on the street, I would think you were a model. You are beautiful! Seeing you dressed in black with the hood I couldn’t see your face. I never would have guessed.”

“Thank you for the complement, Ash.” Angie said. She was blushing. “You have made me blush.” For the first time she actually believed someone that told her that she was beautiful.

“It brings out the blue in your eyes.” Ash said.

Dominic looked at Lizzy and they both remembered when they went out for coffee the night after they first met. “I remember you blushed when I said those exact words.”

"Yes, you said it brought the blue out in my eyes. I love you." She hugged him. She was sore all over and her voice was still raspy. She coughed after she spoke.

The deputies had all run to the barn and house. There was only a crime scene to preserve along with six dead bodies. The worst was Johnny to whom was impaled on a board in the wall of the old barn.

Of course, the Sherriff wanted everyone to stay until they finished the investigation. During this time, he had called the coroner. The news came as usual, and Angie was in the spotlight again. When the news came to talk to Angie, she grabbed Sherri and made certain she got credit for finding her mother as well.

"Angelina, how did you find your mother here?" the news guy asked.

"Sir, this is my best friend Sherri, and the two of us kept going over the bits and pieces information we had received and between the two of us we were able to find this location."

"Really? We had been told that you were clairvoyant."

"Who told you that? That sounds like something from movie. If we were clairvoyant, why would it have taken us so long to find this place? We spent hours looking at a map and going over notes we took from anybody that had any information. We ended up talking to the gentleman over there," She pointed to Ash. "He told us about suspicious activity at this property that had been vacant for years. We finally put everything together. That is how we found her."

The news guy looked at the camera, "There you have it. It was just plain hard work and investigation." He signaled to cut.

Angie saw two deputies looking at her car. She walked over. "Is this your car ma'am?"

"Yes sir." Angie replied.

"You wouldn't have been driving on I10 not too long ago at 144 miles per hour, would you?" One asked her.

"Are you kidding? 144 in this car? Maybe I was breaking the limit by a few miles per hour because I was in a hurry to find my mother."

"Lieutenant Edwards walked up. "What's the problem guys?"

"Um, nothing sir. We were just admiring her car." One officer said.

"You weren't going to accuse her of speeding, were you?"

"Ah, No sir."

"Because we all know that Angie would not break the speed limit. But if you would like to see her race, she runs at Tucson Dragway on Sundays."

"Really? You drag race?"

"Yes, I do sir. Most Sunday's"

"I need to get her back. There are a lot more questions for her." The lieutenant walked back with Angie. "You know they got you driving 144 miles per hour?"

"I was not looking sir. I just had the pedal to the floor."

"I understand. However, I don't want to hear anything like that again Angie."

"Yes sir. You know I do not normally speed."

"I know. This was an exception. Let's keep this between us, OK"

"Yes sir. And thank you sir."

While everyone was waiting to be excused Angie went over to Ash and said, "Ash, when I said I would pay you back, I meant it. I feel that I need to pay you back somehow for saving my mother and my lives."

Ash thought for a minute, "How about you allow me to take you to dinner sometime soon? That would be more than enough to pay me back Angie."

Angie thought about this. "I will agree under one condition. You may take me to dinner, but I need to pay for it. I would not feel comfortable otherwise. This would allow me to feel as though I am doing something for you."

Ash looked at her, "It would not be gallant of me to allow you to pay but I will agree as long as you let me pay if we were to go out another time."

"Are you asking me out on a date Ash?" Angie was somewhat uncomfortable, but she was attracted to his manors and gallantry.

"Yes ma'am. I would be a fool to pass up the opportunity to spend some time with such a well-spoken, confident, resourceful and beautiful woman."

"You are making me blush again Ash. I do not know what to say besides yes."

"Could I get you phone number so I can call to make arrangements?"

"Of course." Angie went back to the Cuda to get her purse. She came back and gave Ash a piece of paper with the house phone number. She did not want to give him her private bedroom number. She couldn't believe she said yes particularly since she had been discussing this with her friends lately. But she felt it was only two dinners. That would not interfere with her plans.

The following Saturday night Angie met her friends at the Bum Steer. They sat down and immediately Paula asked Angie how she got her mother back. They all knew very little about it because the news didn't say much. They all liked hearing about how Angie kicked butt and they wanted to know how her mother was doing.

Sherri said, "Angie left without the police. That really upset me. I thought they were going to kill her." She had tears in her eyes.

Karen was sitting next to her and slid her chair close and put her arm around Sherri. "She is OK Sherri."

"I know, but when she ran out, I was so scared. I know how she fights but I thought they would have guns and they would shoot her."

Angie said, "I was fine Sherri. You know I am always extremely careful."

"I know, but I was still scared."

"Sherri, I need to explain to you, I had help. My Grandmother Caroline came to me in a dream and told me I should not wait for the police, or I would see my mother's headstone. She told me I knew that which I needed and would handle them with ease. I have not told you this yet."

"You saw your grandmother? Really?" Gina said.

"She came to me in a dream and told me the name of the road that went to the farmhouse and barn."

"I thought you saw that!" Sherri said.

"No, my grandmother came to me and told me." Now Angie had tears in her eyes. "She was so beautiful, and she told me she was proud of me." Now she had tears running down her cheeks. She picked up a napkin and blotted the tears.

Karen said, "Wow! If my grandmother came to me in a dream, I don't think I could function afterwards. I miss her so much."

Angie reached and put her arm around her and squeezed a little. "After that I could not wait. I had to leave as soon as I could. She also said she would always be with me. Because of that I felt that I somehow had support of sort from her."

"I can understand that. But I was so scared." Sherri said.

"So, what happened?" Gina asked.

I arrived and walked towards the farmhouse and ran into a cowboy fixing a fence. I thought he may have been one of them. He was very polite. Something I did not expect. When I told him my name, he called me Miss Angie. I told him I was going to get my mother back from the guys that kidnapped her. He did not believe I could do it myself. He ended up following me. Before I got to the barn, I took out two of them. A third I ran into walking around the barn, and I took him out. A fourth ran out of the barn and I took him out as well. All of them had guns. I met one of them shortly after I walked into the barn and began fighting. I used my sticks and as I was beating him, Johnny came out and began fighting. After a bit I broke one of his arms. The other guy threw a piece of rope around my neck and I pulled him towards the wall and ran up the wall and flipped over him to get free."

"You ran up the wall? What? How could you do that?" Janet asked.

"I used the guy as a support and ran up the wall and flipped over. Then I took him out. Johnny came back and continued using my sticks until he could not block anymore. Then I used eye gouging. That is a move where you go at your opponent's face like this." She put her hands up with her fingers bent and motioned one had after the other.

"Karen went "Eehhh, Yikes!" She looked shocked.

"I kicked him a few more times then ran back and kicked him hard and he fell back onto his back. I had thought he was knocked out as he did not move. I turned and ran towards my mother and I heard a shot.

Johnny shot out something he had rigged to hang my mother and the rope pulled her up by her neck and an instant later there was another shot and the rope broke and my mother fell. The cowboy had followed and shot the rope just as my mother was hanged. When Johnny turned to see where the shot came from, I took care of him. He had stood. I ran and pulled the rifle from him and threw it away. I ran back about 10 feet then ran at him and kicked he so hard he broke through the barn wall and got impaled on a board. Then all the police arrived.

"He got impaled in the wall? EEEHH!" Paula reacted with a shocked look on her face.

"What did you do then? What happened to the cowboy?" Gina asked.

"First, I ran to my mother and took off the noose, took the tape off of her mouth and untied her hands. Then I told the cowboy I needed to pay him back somehow for saving my and my mother's lives."

"What did you do? Did you kiss him? Did you?" Gina was excited because Angie had been saying she didn't want to date.

"No, Gina. I did not kiss him. I hugged him and told him he could take me out for dinner provided I pay."

"Provided you pay? How is that taking you out?" Gina asked.

"Gina, I need to do something for him and paying would allow me to do something for him. He is going to call me."

"Like, what's his name?" Denise asked.

"His name is Ash. Ash Dalton. And he was as polite as my father always is."

"So, you are going on a date, a real date?" Gina was excited. She was so worried about Angie not wanting to date.

"Well, it is not officially a date. I am not ready to date as of yet. But he asked that if he took me out again could he pay and I told him yes."

"Not officially a date? Really? What does that mean?" Gina asked.

"I like him but I do not know much about him. I cannot make any decisions as of yet."

"That is so cool! Oh, you didn't say how your mother is. Is she OK? How is she doing?" Gina asked.

"Yea, how's your mother?" Karen asked.

"She is basically fine. They did not hurt her too much physically. Her neck is red and chafed from the rope and her wrists have ligature marks and are sore from being tied behind her back and she is hoarse. She is weak from the whole thing. They did not give her much to eat or drink. I think she lost some weight. But I suspect she is traumatized from this. I can see that she is attempting to cover it up. I do not think she wants to burden me with her problems. But I expect it to come out in time anyway."

"I'm glad they didn't physically hurt her." Karen said.

"Let us order now. I do not want to take the night down. We are here to have fun." Angie said. "I want to put all of this behind me."

The waitress came and they ordered burgers and fries again then went up to dance.

Gina and Angie sang a few times each. As they ate, they all continued to talk about what happened. Then Angie remembered. "I almost forgot. I drove to this place as fast as my car would go. It turns out there were Cochise County sheriff's taking radar and they clocked me at 144 miles per hour."

Karen said, "144 miles per hour? Your car goes that fast?" She was shocked. "Did you get in trouble?"

"No, I did not get in trouble. After everything was over, two deputies were looking at my car and I went over. They asked me if I was driving 144 miles per hour not long ago. I told them I may have been breaking the speed limit a little but not that much. Then Lieutenant Edwards asked if they were going to accuse me of speeding and they said no, they were just admiring my car."

"Like, you didn't get in trouble? Wow, were you lucky." Denise said.

They finished eating and drank some more beer. Angie and Gina sang again. Afterwards, they finished their beers and left.

Ash called Angie a few days later and they decided on the following Saturday evening to meet for dinner. Angie gave him directions on how to get to her house. He said he would pick her up at 7 PM. But he told her that he needed her help to decide where to go. He didn't live in Tucson and didn't go out at all where he lived. He had no idea where to go.

Saturday evening Angie got ready. She had bought a pair of beige suede pants with short fringe up the outside seams and a horse's head embroidered on each of the back pockets. She put on a black long sleeve light knit sweater and wore her cowgirl jacket. The jacket was also beige suede with fringe up the sleeves, across the back and front. She put on her nicest cowboy boots and wore her black cowboy hat. She had painted her nails white as well and made up her eyes dark as she learned from the make-up artist they used for her 18th birthday. With her long straight blond hair flowing over the jacket, she looked stunning.

She walked out of her room and asked her mother, "How do I look mother?"

"I thought this was just a casual dinner? You look as if you want to impress him, honey." Lizzy said.

"Well, he saved our lives mother and I do like him. At least from what I know. I want to make a good impression. I do not want a boyfriend, at least right now, but I believe he will be a good friend. I want him to know I care about how I look."

"Be careful not to lead him on then. That would not be lady like."

"I will not mother. But since my 18th birthday I have felt as though I need to dress properly for any outing. And I expect he will be dressed differently as well."

Just then Dominic walked around the corner. "Angie, you look beautiful! You did not say this was a date."

"It is not father. I just want to look my best and want him to know I that I care about my appearance."

"Well, if this doesn't impress him, I do not know what would."

"Thank you, father.

Just then the doorbells rang. "I will answer the door and bring him into the Arizona room. You can make an entrance there. I will make this formal, so to speak." Dominic said.

"Thank you, father." She stayed there with her mother.

Dominic went to the door and opened it. Good evening, Ash. Please come in." He stepped aside to let him in.

He took off his hat. "Good evening, sir. It is a pleasure to meet you formally." Ash said.

"Please come into the Arizona room. You may wait here." They walked to the Arizona room. "Please excuse me, I will inform Angelina you have arrived." Dominic went to get Angie.

"Angie, he is waiting in the Arizona room. Have fun sweetheart." He gave her a hug.

"Thank you, father." She turned and hugged her mother. Look mother, I am nervous." Her hands were shaking.

"You will be fine." She hugged Angie.

Angie walked to the Arizona room and when she walked in Ash stood and the look on his face almost shocked her! "Good evening little lady. I don't believe I have ever seen anyone so beautiful! I never could have believed this." He took her hand and kissed the back of it.

"Ash, you look wonderful as well." Angie said.

He was dressed in deep blue jeans and a colorful cowboy shirt with a Bolo tie inset with a turquoise stone and of course, he wore cowboy boots. He was holding his cowboy hat to his side.

"Shall we go?" Angie asked.

"Of course, little lady." Ash replied. He let her go first then opened the door for her, followed her through and closed the door. Then he held out his arm for her to hold. She reached and held his arm. They walked to his truck. He opened the door and helped her in and closed the door. He was a perfect gentleman.

Dominic and Lizzy had run to the window to watch as Angie had not gone out with anyone other than her friends. Ash impressed the both of them with his gentleman like actions.

Angie and Ash ended up going to El Corral. They each had a few beers with dinner and talked.

"Angie, how did you get involved with martial arts?"

"I was seven years old. I had not made any friends in school but I always wanted to learn new things. I was already frustrated because I could not find things to learn. My father decided to take me to a karate class. I did not like it. But he insisted I continue. Then I learned to break boards with my feet and then with my hands. I thought that was cool! When I told some kids in school, I could break wood with my hands they did not believe me. I also had a teacher that did not believe me either. At that point, I wanted to learn more. And as with everything I do, I put every effort into learning and began to rise through the levels quickly. I was the first student my sensei had that excelled this quickly. Due to this he began teaching me Aikido. I excelled in this as well. Then he added Taekwondo. I studied these through grade school, middle school and high school. I achieved third dan black belt."

"I find that incredible. When and how did you begin the others? I believe you said Shaolin Kung Fu and Muay Thai?"

Angie didn't want to get into this now. It was too complicated she thought, and she was not comfortable to begin telling him about her fights. "How about we talk about you now. How did you come to work at that ranch?"

"Well," he thought, 'now isn't the time to tell her my life's story. I don't want to put her in the same position.' I came to Cochise County when I was young. I graduated high school there and looked for a job. Since I knew about taking care of horses and cattle, animals in general and I knew how to fix most things the ranch hand job was a good fit. I interviewed with the owner, and he hired me on the spot. I have been working there for almost four years now."

"You see your family at least on holidays, do you not?"

His expression changed. She thought she saw small tears in his eyes. She wondered what that meant.

"No, my family has passed. I spend a little time during the holidays with my employer and his wife."

"That makes me feel so sad, Ash. I find it difficult to think of not having family." She reached out and took one of his hands and squeezed.

"Is this what led to you moving to Cochise County in the first place?"

"Yes. I moved to live with relatives."

"What about the relatives you lived with when you came here? Do you see them?"

"They were very old when I came here and have since passed.

"I am so sorry Ash. I must be difficult for you. I did not know.

"You could not have known."

She could feel that he did not want to talk about this. "I see. Where did you live originally?"

"I am from Texas. Tell me more about your family. I perceived a closeness between you and your parents that night that I haven't felt in anyone for some time."

"Yes, my whole family is close. My parents always supported me, and they both taught me manors, how to speak properly and how to be a lady. In fact, my mother continues to teach me little things. What things do you like to do outside of work, Ash?"

He was not certain he wanted to discuss this yet. I do a few different things. But my work takes most of my time, so I don't do much."

They sat there for a few minutes without any discussion. Then Ash said, "Now that I am thinking about how you fought to free your mother, I remember an article in the newspaper from a year or two ago. I am wondering now if it was you. I don't read the paper often but one time when I was waiting for an appointment, I picked it up. It was something about a high school aged girl in Tucson and some kind of fight. I remember that the guy that started it was shot by the police. And the guy had killed his mother and father. That wasn't you, was it?"

Angie sat and thought for a moment. She didn't want to overwhelm Ash but had to tell him the truth. She would never lie. "Ash, it was me. It was a difficult situation that followed me through part of my senior year of high school. I do not wish to get into the whole story at this time. However, I will give you a brief description of what happened. I had just transferred to Canyon del Oro High school from Amphitheater High school for my senior year. I was a new student at the school. I am an over achiever and received straight A's throughout school. I drove a Panther Pink HEMI CUDA, and of course I still do, and many told me I was the most beautiful girl in the school. I did not believe that and continue not believing that. Due to these things, I was a target for the star football jock. I found out in the end, he only wanted sex with me but I was uninterested. This made him angry. He was a problem student with a father that was the Tucson city manager. Due to this, he was able to get away with most everything he did. He pulled a knife on me in school one day and I broke his nose while defending myself. He was expelled. Afterwards he did everything he could to get what he wanted. He ended up sneaking up behind me when I was alone in my father's shop and beat me until I was unconscious. He removed my shirt and jeans and tied me up laying on the floor. When I woke, he told me he was going to rape me and kill me. Another boy and the guy's father came in and distracted him long enough for me to break free. I fought with him for a brief time and when the police came there was an exchange of fire, and he was killed. There is quite a bit additional to this story, but I would rather wait for another time when it is more appropriate to tell you."

"A good thing came from all of this. I believe due to this situation I met my friends. They were the first friends I had made."

Ash sat for a while taking this in. He was completely shocked. "This happened in high school? How did you cope?"

"I had long discussions with my mother. Then I had my new friends. They showed me what great friends can do. I had a time of self-revelation. I learned much about myself and some of how my mind works. I grew significantly."

"Were you hurt much from this?

"Yes. I injured the hamstring in one leg. I did not perform a kick properly. I received a few fractured ribs; my jaw was sore enough that it was difficult to speak. I had split lips, black eyes, ligature marks on my wrists and ankles and a large gash on my cheek and a large bump on the back of my head. It took some time to heal. Due to this I had to stay home from school for a few weeks.

Ash sat and thought about this. "I would never guess you were hurt that bad. "You don't show it physically and I don't even see a mark on either cheek."

"I worked extremely hard to overcome the physical issues with my body. And after the gash healed, my mother took me to a dermatologist, and I had two chemical peels. That eliminated the small scaring I had."

"I don't know how to react to all of this, Angie. I feel bad that you had to suffer from that guy."

Angie thought he was sincere, and it made her feel better about telling him about this. She had not planned to tell him anything about her fights. "Ash?"

"Yes Angie?"

"I feel as though I need to explain where I am in my life. I am involved with many things, and I have plans for my life. Although I like you and I am attracted to you, I am not in the place to begin dating yet. I have significant goals I have set that I feel the need to accomplish first. I very much want to be friends, at least at this point.

Ash sat there for a few moments contemplating what she just said. "I don't know what to say. I don't know what I expected from this time with you. I feel attraction and I guess I thought we might possibly date from this. But I am a patient man. I also understand that we both need to be in the right place for anything to work out." Ash felt crushed. He was thinking that he may never see her again. He thought, this was the nicest, "I just want to be friends" let down he had heard.

Angie could see and feel his disappointment. "Ash, I do not want you to think I am rejecting you. I am sincere telling you that I want to be friends. I am not in the place in my life to have a romantic relationship now. I do not want you to think I am a typical girl letting you down. I do not want to do that. I do feel attraction to you. I very much wish to be friends. I feel that this could make a romantic relationship much closer if we had a friendship bond first."

"Are you sure? You are not trying to let me down nicely?"

"Ash, as you get to know me you will find out I am very direct and honest with everyone. I believe this was something my mother fought with when she was younger. She has told me that when she was younger, she tended to say what she thought without thinking. She said my grandmother told her she was too outspoken for a young woman. I believe I share this with her. Although I usually think before I speak. And as I stated earlier, I wish to be prepared for everything I do. I always attempt to plan everything in detail beforehand."

"I don't know what to say. I don't know whether or not to believe you as I don't know you well."

"Ash, all I can say is I promise you I want you as my friend. If you were to ask my family, friends or the guys I work with about me you will find out that I never break a promise. That is something you can always count on."

"I don't know how to respond to that either. I never met anyone that did not ever break a promise. It seems that everyone does at some point."

"I can assure you, I have never broken a promise, and I do not intend to in the future. People have told me that I am an extremely honest and complex person and I agree with that. But I want you in my life as a friend at this point. I am not prepared to date, and this has been the closest thing to a date I have been on."

"I will take your word for it."

"Do you remember what you told me after you showed me all of the guns you had with you when we first met?"

He thought for a minute, "No, why?"

"You said, "I like to be prepared because you never know what you could be up against out here."

"I remember now."

"I mumbled something, and you asked what I said. I told you it was nothing. What I said was "That sounds familiar." That was reference to how I always like to be prepared."

"I see."

"I rarely do anything without preparation. When I ran home to prepare to get my mother back, I had a plan already. I knew the cloths I would change into and I had an idea of what I would be up against and had scenarios running through my head beforehand. Even when I am confronted with a situation that I could not plan first, I am planning as I go and am usually ahead of myself in thought."

"I think I understand now. However, I never met anyone so open and honest. It seems everyone is always holding something in or keeping something from you. It had caused me to keep up a kind of shieled. I have always felt somewhat alone, and I have not been close to anyone since my family passed."

"That is sad Ash." Angie truly felt sad about this. "Ash, you need to let go of your pain and open yourself to others. There is so much to gain. Yes, there will be some hardship, but the rewards can be great. I learned to put down the shield I had built all my life when I met my friends. At first, I acted cross to them. But Sherri, she became my best friend, ended up immediately telling me that she felt she could trust me. I only knew her from my Physics class, and I had not talked to her. She ended up telling me something very personal. I could not believe she told me. I then sat with her and her two friends at lunch and opened up. This was at school. This began my first friendships."

"It sounds like you are giving me therapy." Ash said.

"No, I am not giving you therapy. I am just being open about what I believe."

"You are a very complex person. You constantly surprise me with the things you say, and I think how you say them as well."

Angie sat back and took a sip of her beer and thought, "There is so much he does not know about me. I hope when he learns it does not scare him away."

When they each finished their beer, Angie asked for the bill and paid as she said she would. They walked out and he offered his arm and she took it. He helped her into his truck. "Ash, I really enjoyed tonight. Sometime when we can both set up some time, I would like to do this again. I know you were uncomfortable with me paying the bill. But now I feel as if I have done something for you for your gallantry saving my mother and me."

"You are right, I did feel uncomfortable. But I understand and wanted to respect you wish. I enjoyed tonight as well. I will also respect your reasoning for not being ready to date. I hope we can stay in touch."

"We will Ash."

They arrived at her house and he got out and helped her out of the truck. He walked her to the door. "Angie I will wait until you are inside and safe."

"Thank you, Ash, you are a gentleman. We will talk soon. Good night." She turned, unlocked and went in.

Ash went to his truck and drove home.

Angie closed and locked the door. She turned to walk towards the kitchen. "Angie, how did it go, honey?" Lizzy asked. She was sitting in the Arizona room.

Angie turned and sat next to her. "I believe it went well. We had some small talk and he asked about how I got into martial arts. Then he told me that his family has all passed. I told him I thought that was sad and I could not imagine how that would feel. We talked more and then he said he was thinking about what happened and he remembered reading an article in the newspaper a while back about a guy that was killed by police and a fight with a high school aged girl in Tucson. He asked if that was me. I could not lie to him so I told him it was me. I told him a very condensed version generalizing about everything and told him this wasn't an appropriate time or place to get into the details. Then I told him about how the plans for my life did not include a romantic relationship at this time. He looked crushed. I assured him that I wanted to be friends and that I do have an attraction to him. He said it was the nicest 'I want to be friends' let down he ever heard. I ended up trying to reassure him that was not my intension and that I very much want to be friends and keep him in my life. I then told him that building a good friendship could make anything else that develops better. I believe he finally understood. He told me that I was the most complex woman he had ever met. I also assured him that I would like him to take me out for the dinner that he would pay for. He did feel uncomfortable with me paying."

Lizzy sat for a few minutes. "How do you feel about him?"

"Well mother, I like him from what I know. He is polite and a gentleman. I want to be friends and I can see that in time we could possibly have a relationship. But I am not prepared for that at this time. I wanted it to be clear to him and I believe he understands."

"Angie, you are a complex person and hopefully he doesn't turn away because of that. Some would. Some could feel threatened by that. I hope he does not."

Angie thought for a bit. "Mother, I do not believe he will be threatened by me. I feel that it will take some time for him to understand me. He told me that everyone lies at times but I assured him that I do not lie and I do not break promises. I do not believe he believed that. I think the thing that attracts me are his manors and that he acts like a gentle-man just as father does."

"We will see. One can be easily influenced by honesty."

"I am going to take a shower and go to bed mother." She leaned over and kissed her cheek and walked to her room.

41

Thanksgiving was at Grandfather Joseph and Grandmother Kristina's house this year.

Angie dressed in a gown again and everyone was again impressed. They had taken a family picture from each Thanksgiving and this one and last year were special to Angie because she dressed in a gown. Thanksgiving has been her favorite holiday and now it has more significance to her.

Everyone had arrived and were mingling in the solarium. Maria felt that Lizzy was not jovial as usual. Maria felt strong anxiety from Lizzy and a kind of foreboding in her. She felt that she should not ask her why so she let her be. Then she heard Lizzy sound as though she snapped at Dominic. It didn't seem to bother him however. But shortly afterwards, Lizzy looked as though she was going to cry.

Maria went over to Lilly and asked, "Lilly, is there something bothering Lizzy? It appeared that she snapped at Dom and then looked as though she was going to cry."

"I do not know if there is anything wrong. She does not seem to be herself today and feels a bit distant. I do not know why."

In reality, Lizzy has been suffering from PTSD. She had not slept much since the abduction. She had been reliving her captivity in her dreams. She didn't want to burden everyone with this. Finally, Lilly took Lizzy into another room and closed the door. "Lizzy, what is bothering you?"

"Oh, I am fine. I have just had a few poor night's sleep. I will be OK."

"Lizzy, it is me you are talking to. There is something wrong. I can feel it. You are not yourself. I can see that you are very upset. Please talk to me. We have always discussed everything. Lizzy, you are my sister and I love you. What is going on?"

Lizzy stood there for a minute or two just looking at Lilly. Lilly could see that she was struggling with something. She was trying to hold back her tears. Then they just erupted. Lilly reached out and pulled Lizzy to her. She put her arms around her and hugged her tight. "What is going on Lizzy? You are hurting, I know."

Lizzy grabbed a tissue from the box that was on the table next to her. "Lilly, I, I…" She cried more. "I, I cannot sleep. When I fall asleep, I dream of the abduction, about everything that happened. And it is so realistic I wake up choking. Just as if they were pulling me up with the noose. And the last few nights I feel that I am hanged, I cannot breathe, and I see them shooting and killing Angie. I do not know what to do. And the past week it has woken Dom. Now he is not sleeping well." She cried more.

"Lizzy, you should have told me. This makes me feel so sad. Now I understand why you have been looking sad today and why you have not sounded happy when we talk on the phone." She sat down and pulled Lizzy and got her to sit. She put her arms around Lizzy again. "Lizzy, we will figure this out. We will get through it. I will do whatever it takes. I do not like seeing you this way."

"I thought this would just go away but it is becoming worse. I feel that I do not want to burden anyone with this." Lizzy said.

"Lizzy, you are not burdening me. We have always talked to each other about out problems. That is what family is for. Remember how I acted when Shelly was born? Remember they said they did not expect her to make it and she was in the NICU for a few weeks? I was a wreck. I was able to get through that because of you. You helped me so much. And I will do the same for you. And remember how sad you were when the doctors said you could not conceive? We talked and cried every day. You cannot keep this away from everyone. We all love you."

Just then Maria knocked on the door. "Are you alright?" I am feeling as if there is something seriously wrong."

Lilly looked at Lizzy as if asking if she could let Maria in. Lizzy looked at her and shook her head yes. Lilly got up and opened the door. Maria came in and she closed the door. Maria had a look of concern. "Lizzy," she reached out to hug her. "I have been feeling turmoil from you. What is wrong?"

"Maria," Lizzy wiped her eyes again and cleared her throat. "I have been reliving the abduction every night. And some nights I feel as if I am actually hanged, and they shoot and kill Angie." Then she started crying again.

"Lizzy, we are all here for you. You know we will do whatever it takes to help you get past this. You know we are always here for you, do you not?" Maria said.

"I suppose. I did not want to burden anyone. I thought this would go away in time. It has been a month and it is becoming worse. And I am becoming short with everyone. I feel as though I am alienating everyone and hurting Angie and Dom. And I feel as if it is my fault" She cried again.

"Lizzy, you are not alienating everyone. You likely have post-traumatic stress disorder. You went through a frightening thing. We will do whatever is necessary to help you get past this." Maria just realized she had been hugging her the whole time she was speaking.

Lilly said, "Lizzy, maybe we should bring mother into the discussion as well. Maybe between all of us we can help you get passed this."

"I do not know why I did not tell you. You are both correct. We should include mother."

Lizzy had thought that she would not need to burden everyone. She had believed it would just go away. But now she was understanding that this was flawed thinking.

"I am going to go and have mother come here." Lilly left to get their mother.

"Mother?"

"Yes Lillian?"

"Could you please come with me for a minute?"

"Of course." Kristina followed Lilly.

Lilly knocked on the door. "You may come in." They walked into the room and closed the door.

"Oh, my lord, Elizabeth! What is wrong?" She saw that Lizzy had been crying and she went over to her and hugged her. "Elizabeth, whatever it is we will get through it."

Having her mother hug her as she did reminded her of when she was younger. Her mother always hugged her like this when she was sad. "Mother," tears came again. "Mother, I have been reliving the abduction every night since then. And it is so realistic that I wake choking. And in these dreams, I see Angelina shot and killed as I am hanging from the noose. I am a wreck! I am not getting much sleep and I am becoming short with Dominic and Angelina. I have been trying not to be short today but I snapped at Dominic in front of everyone. I feel so embarrassed now." She still had tears rolling down her cheeks.

"Elizabeth, we will figure this out. If necessary, we will find a psychotherapist to help you. You suffered through a horrifying situation. And frankly, I had been surprised that you did not look as though you were affected." Kristina said. "I should have asked you, dear."

Lilly said, "Maybe we should get back to everyone before they are all knocking on the door."

"That would be a good idea. Lillian, why do you not take Elizabeth into the bathroom to clean up? Maria and I will get back to everyone."

"Yes, mother. Come Elizabeth, let us get you cleaned up." They went into the bathroom and cleaned up Elizabeth's face. Her eyeliner had run down her cheeks and her eyes were a little puffy. Lilly carefully put more powder and eye liner on Lizzy. "This reminds me of when we began using eye liner. Remember, we put it on each other? And remember how shocked mother looked when she saw us?"

Lizzy was feeling a little better. "Yes, I remember. Mother was shocked. We thought we did a wonderful job but we looked like circus clowns." She giggled a little.

"See, the real you is still in there. We just have to unload the heavy baggage." They both smiled and went back to join everyone.

When they returned to the solarium Angie went and asked, "Mother, are you alright? I was feeling that you were extremely sad."

"I am fine Angie. I talked to Aunt Lilly."

"If you say so. They just announced that dinner is served. Let us go and sit." Angie led Lizzy to the dining room. Grandmother Kristina was already sitting and Grandfather Joseph walked over to push Angie's chair in. "Thank you, Grandfather."

"It was my pleasure, Angelina." He went and sat down.

One of the servers lit the candles and dimmed the lights. Then she turned on light music. As usual it was classical.

They had the usual turkey with all the trimmings.

The dinner went well and Lizzy did not show any other problems.

It was time for pie and the server cut and served everyone. The whipped cream was passed around for each to take what they wanted. "Angelina, your pecan pie is amazing again this year, my dear." Grandmother Kristina remarked.

"I agree." Grandfather Joseph said.

Most everyone agreed. "Thank you everyone, I appreciate the complements." Angie said.

Lizzy took a bite of the pumpkin pie and smiled and said, "Mother, you out did yourself. Your pumpkin pie is different and much better than previously."

Lilly said, "Yes, it is different. I am not certain what it is, but it is definitely much better."

"I was slightly concerned at the new recipe I made. I read about making the filling differently and wanted to try this. It does taste much different. In place of the white sugar, I used brown sugar and real maple syrup. I thought this would add to the flavor of the pumpkin." Kristina said.

"Mother, it is wonderful!" Lilly said.

"I agree, grandmother!" Angie said. "And Aunt Lillian, your apple pie is wonderful as usual. I fancy your apple pie because it is not quite as sweet as other's I have tasted. I believe it brings out the flavor of the apples."

"Thank you, Angelina for your complement. You are the first to remark about the sweetness."

"I have not identified that, Lillian. Angelina is correct. Your apple pies have always been slightly different that others I have tasted." Kristina said.

"Thank you, mother. I did not believe anyone had ever noticed."

They continued with their pie and one of the server's poured coffee for everyone that wished to have some. All the cousins were excused and went into the solarium to talk.

As would be expected, all the cousins wanted to hear about how Angie got Aunt Elizabeth back. "Cuz, are you going to tell us about what you did to get Aunt Elizabeth back? We have not heard much about it." Shelly asked.

"We wish to hear about it as well." Rosa said. "How about you Edward?"

"I like hearing about what Angelina has done. I think it is interesting." Edward said.

"If you wish to hear the details I will tell you." Angie said.

"Cool!" Edward said.

"Sherri and I had been seeing things a bit here and there and after some time we began to believe we would find my mother. Then Aunt Maria came over and the three of us sat together and we saw some additional things. We had determined the highway where that the place they were holding her was but we did not have the final road name. I was frustrated. Then one night my grandmother Caroline, this is my father and Aunt Maria's mother, came to me in a dream. She told me that she was proud of me," She got tears in her eyes and went for a tissue. "She said she was proud of my father for how he took charge and took care of Aunt Maria and she also said my mother was just like her and father's savior. After this she said I had everything I needed to find her and I would handle them with ease. But, she said, I should not wait for the police because otherwise I would see my mother's gravestone. And she told me the name of the road the place was on. It ended up not being the exact name, but close enough for us to find it. After this, I saw these guys driving and Johnny, the guy that started all of this, was giving directions on this road."

"At that point I rushed out of Sherri's house and drove home. I changed into all black cloths and I had purchased a light weight black cloak like coat that had a hood. I grabbed my sticks and drove there. Afterwards, I was told I was clocked driving 144 miles per hour on I10."

"Your car goes that fast?" Edward asked.

"Was not looking but there were two deputies taking radar that I passed."

"I found this place and parked and made my way towards this old dilapidated farm house and I ran into a cowboy fixing a fence. At first, I thought he was part of this. He introduced himself to me and told me he worked at the ranch near to this old farm house and barn. He said it had been abandoned for years. I told him why I was there and that I may need to kill some or all of them to get my mother back. I do not think he believed me. Then he said he would help me if I needed it.

I made my way to a group of trees near the barn and sat and meditated for a minute or two. I then stood and the first guy came up behind me and pushed a gun into my back. I turned, took away the gun and used my hand like this," she demonstrated, "And knocked him down. I dropped to my knees and punched him full force in his throat. That killed him. Am I boring you?"

Bella said, "No cuz. This is interesting."

"Alright, I will continue. After I killed this guy, I climbed into the tree above him to try to get a better look around. No sooner that I did that another guy came and found this guy dead and pulled out his gun. I quietly dropped down behind him, put one arm around his neck, turned and lifted him off of the ground. He was choking and grabbing at his neck. I reached for his forehead and I used a quick hard pull and it broke his neck. I tossed him aside."

"Then I ran up to the barn and another guy came out to look for the other two guys and he turned and I kicked him in the face and I believe it broke his nose. He dropped his gun and tried to fight but he was not fast enough. I hit him and kicked him and finished with a 360 degree reverse roundhouse and he flew into the barn and bounced off dead.

"I made my way to the open barn door and another guy came out with his gun pointed in front of him. He saw me and began to say something but I did not let him talk. I beat him and stepped back a few feet, ran and did a side kick to his neck and he flew into the side of the barn and bounced off dead."

"I went into the barn and saw my mother standing across the barn with her mouth tapped shut, her arms tied behind her back and a noose around her neck. I took out my sticks and another ran at me trying to engage me. I beat him with my sticks then kicked the sides of his ribcage and likely broke many ribs. This knocked the air out of him. I turned to find Johnny running up. He tried to engage me and I used my sticks on him as well. Just as the last guy, he did not know how to defend against these. As I was beating Johnny, the other guy came up behind me and threw a rope around my neck from behind and tried to choke me. I tried to hit him with my elbows but could not, so I pulled him close to the wall and used him to stabilize myself and I ran up the wall and flipped over him. This got me out of the rope. I turned and hit him a few times then did a side kick to his face and it broke his neck."

"You ran up the wall?" Bella asked. "How could you do that?"

"I used the guy to stabilize me and I ran up the wall and flipped over him. There was just Johnny left. I turned and used my sticks again until he could not defend anymore. I tossed my sticks down and he tried to punch me and I broke his arm. Then I stepped back and ran a few feet and hit him in the chest with a side kick and he flew back and down. Since he did not move, I thought this had knocked him out. I turned and ran to my mother and as I was running Johnny got up and picked up a riffle. He must have put a few around the barn. He said he was going to hang my mother before he killed me. He shot something he rigged and it fell and pulled my mother up with the noose and I heard another shot from the barn door. The cowboy I had just met, shot the rope and my mother fell down. I turned and grabbed the riffle from Johnny and tossed it away. Then I used eye gouging." Angie demonstrated with her hands.

Edward looked shocked and said "eehhh!"

Angie continued, "I then ran back about ten feet, turned and ran at him as fast as I could and did a running side kick to his chest and he flew into the barn wall breaking the rotted wood and was impaled by one of the boards. That is when all of the police came along with Sherri and my father."

Everyone sat quiet for a couple of minutes. Then Shelly said, "Cuz, maybe you should write these fights down and make a book about them. They could make a movie about you!"

"Would that not be cool! A movie about Angelina! What an idea." Edward said.

"Angelina," Rosa said, "It always sounds like you are telling us a story when you describe when happened. I picture it in my head. It is almost like watching a movie. Were you not scared?"

"When I fight, I just turn off all of my thoughts and concentrate in the fight. I do not think of anything else. To answer your question, no, I do not become scared. It does not come into my thoughts. I just fight."

"That is some story, cuz!" Bella said. "I love the way you explain your fights. It is as if we are watching an intense scene in a movie."

"Thank you for the complement, Bella. I just explain how I remember."

"You could be a story teller or writer." Shelly said.

"I do not know about that. I do not know where I would find the time."

They all talked about everything they each had been doing since they were together last.

Aunt Maria came over to them and said they were preparing for the family picture. They followed her into the living room. Grandfather Joseph set up his camera and the server took a couple of pictures.

Everybody talked more. As it became late, everyone began leaving. Kristina told Lizzy she would call her tomorrow to talk more.

42

Thanksgiving had passed and everyone was back to work and school. Angie was not seeing much in her head lately. Every so often she would see a kick or punch. Sometimes she would see a gun. But these images flashed in her head and did not feel important. She was becoming used to seeing images such as this and none appeared as though they were part of anything important.

She saw someone pointing a gun at someone and then this same person laying on the floor with a bloody nose. But since nothing had been happening, she tried to put them out of her head.

It was close to Christmas and the family was talking about what date to see the Nutcracker this year. As with the past two years, Angie invited Sherri. This year Sherri did not feel out of place. She already knew Angie's family. She liked all of them. She felt Angie was so fortunate to have such a caring and accepting family.

"Angie," Sherri said, "I want to pay for my ticket this year. I have been saving for this."

"Sherri, I know you would like to pay but I want to give this to you as my Christmas gift. You are continuing school and do not have a job. And this is quite a bit of money for you. I want to do this as an act of friendship and love. You are my very best friend. I will also be giving gifts to everyone this year as well. I have already purchased something for each of our friends."

"Alright, if you insist. But you know you may make everyone uncomfortable if you give them something. I know none of them have much spending money right now." Sherri said.

"I understand that. I want to give and I do not expect anything in return. All of you have given me an enormous amount of support. Particularly during the difficult times I have had dealing with my feelings from my confrontations. It is something I chose to do. And I have the means."

"Well, just expect everyone to be a little uncomfortable." Sherri said.

"I sincerely hope I do not make them feel uncomfortable. That is the last thing I want to do. You are all my friends and it means quite a bit to me to give to each of you."

The family chose a date, a Saturday of course. And they would do the usual, see the ballet and Grandfather Joseph will take the family out to dinner to the Palomino Restaurant afterwords.

Just as last year, Sherri rode with Angie and her parents. Her mother bought her a new gown so she would not have to wear the same one as last year.

When Sherri arrived at Angie's house she rang the doorbell. As usual, she thought, "Real Bells!" just as every time she rang their bell. Dominic came to the door.

"Hello Sherri, please come in." Dominic said as he stood aside. "You look beautiful."

"Thank you, Mr. Tucci." Sherri said.

"Please follow me." He led her to the master bedroom where Angie and Lizzy were getting ready. He knocked then opened the door for her then closed it again.

"Hello Mrs. Tucci. You look very beautiful Ma'am."

"Thank you, Sherri. You look beautiful as well Sherri. Is that a new gown?"

"Yes ma'am, it is. My mother did not want me to go in the same one as last year."

"That was thoughtful of you mother. But it was not necessary."

"Hello, Sherri, you look wonderful! I love your gown." Angie said as she walked out of the bathroom.

"Hello Angie. You look beautiful too." They hugged.

"Are you ready Angie?" Lizzy asked.

"Yes mother. We can leave now." She walked to the door and opened it. The three of them walked out.

"I am amazed, you must be the most beautiful ladies in Tucson!" Dominic said.

"Thank you, Dom."

"Thank you, father." Angie said.

"Thank you, Mr. Tucci." Sherri said.

He led them through the house and front door. He closed it behind them and everyone got into the car. They drove to the University of Arizona and followed the other cars to the parking area. They met the rest of the family inside.

"Sherri!" Shelly said. "You look lovely, I am impressed. What a beautiful gown." She walked up and they hugged.

"Thank you, Shelly. You look beautiful too! And Bella and Rosa, both of you look amazing!"

They replied almost the same time, "Thank you, Sherri."

All of the cousins and Sherri stood together and talked. Edward walked up. "Edward," Angie said, "You look handsome tonight. Is that a new suit? Tails, I am impressed."

"Yes Angelina. We just bought it. I thought I would look good in tails." He had black pants, a cream dress shirt, a blue silk ascot, a cream silk vest and black tails.

"You do Edward." Angie said.

Edward had a big smile. He valued Angie's opinion very much. He went to tell his mother. "Mother,"

"Yes, Edward."

"Angelina said I look handsome!" He was smiling.

"You do Edward." He walked back to his cousins. She turned and told Kristina, Lizzy, Maria and Sofia, "I had been somewhat astounded when he came to me and said he wanted to impress Angelina. He told me that if Angelina approved what he wore he would know he looked good."

Maria said, "That is interesting. I overheard him on Thanksgiving saying that he kind of looked up to her. He said he saw that her friends looked up to her and understood why. I believe that is amazing."

"He said that? I never would have expected that from him.

"Sherri," Grandmother Kristina said, "you are enchanting my dear! What a lovely gown! It is elegant and tasteful."

"Thank you. Ma'am. My mother helped me decide which to buy."

At that point everyone there began walking into the auditorium. Shelly gave all of the cousins their tickets. As usual, she had small packets of tissues for each of the ladies. Everyone sat. The lights came down and the overture began. Just as the last two years, Sherri already had tears in her eyes. Again, she could not believe that the symphony could still have such a profound effect on her.

Shelly noticed and smiled. She knew exactly how Sherri felt.

The orchestra and ballet can be very passionate. Some are deeply affected by the experience. The combination of the ballet and music that feels as if it comes from everywhere is an experience in itself. And the Nutcracker to some, is very moving. All of the ladies in the family were affected similarly.

Intermission came and the lights came up. The cousins got up and went walked out to the lobby. Sherri said, "I can't believe how this has affected me again just as it did the last two years. I am choked up."

Shelly went over and hugged Sherri. "This exhibits that you very much appreciate the ballet and orchestra, Sherri."

"We could say you are nearly a connoisseur." Bella said.

Angie just stood back and witnessed this play out. She was delighting in the discussion. She smiled and thought about how well Sherri interacted with her family.

Sherri said, "I don't know how to respond." She looked somewhat overwhelmed.

Angie put her arm around Sherri and squeezed a bit. "Sherri, do not get too flustered. You are learning about your deep feelings. And everyone is sharing in your experience. This is wonderful. The lights flashed. We need to return to our seats."

Sherri smiled and they all went back to their seats. The second act began. Everyone was fully enjoying the performance.

As usual, when Pas De deux began Angie got tears in her eyes.

The ballet ended and everyone made their way to the lobby. Shelly went to Angie, "Cuz, it affected you quite a bit this year, did it not?"

As they were all walking to the exit, Angie replied, "The music always has a profound effect on me."

"The symphony can affect you in amazing ways." Shelly said.

Angie smiled and they joined Sherri and rest of her cousins. Dominic, Lizzy, Lilly and Carl, Jack and Sofia and Grandmother Kristina and Grandfather Joseph walked together towards the cars. Angie, Sherri, Shelly, Edward, Bella and Rosa lagged behind talking as they waked. As they walked across the parking lot, a group of what Angie thought were college guys were watching them. She kept an eye on them. They were talking loudly and were being obnoxious. Then they started to walk towards all of them and Angie had a strong feeling that these guys were going to be trouble.

The guy's got close and one said, "Look at those girls! They are so hot. They look like fun. What do you think, guys?"

They said, "Yeah, you're right!"

As they got close the first one, A tall muscular guy reached for Shelly and grabbed her arm and said, "You can come with us. We will have lots of fun tonight."

Edward immediately grabbed the guy's arm and pulled and said, Let go of her!"

The guy wasn't expecting that and his arm was pulled away. One of the others ran behind Edward and put his arm around his neck and pulled him away. Edward remembered what Angie had taught him and immediately grabbed one finger of the guy that had his arm around him and pulled as hard as he could and bent the finger back all the way. He felt the bones break.

The guy screamed and let go grabbing his hand. Edward turned and kicked the guy in his groin as hard as he could, and the guy bent over. When he did this Edward grabbed the guy's head and smashed his knee into his face as hard as he could. The guy flew back and landed on his back screaming. His finger was distorted, and his nose was bleeding.

By this time Dominic, Jack and Carl saw what was happening and turned and ran towards them.

The guy that had grabbed Shelly's arm went to grab Angie and said you are even hotter! You're coming with me."

Angie grabbed his hand and put him in a wrist lock and he went down onto his knees onto the pavement screaming. Another went to help and Angie hit him in his nose with a palm heal punch with her other hand and broke his nose. He screamed and stepped back holding his nose.

Angie said to the guy she had in the wrist lock, "Are you finished, or do I need to break your wrist?" As she was holding his wrist, she slipped off her shoes and pushed them aside from under her gown.

Uncle Jack ran into the auditorium to get a U of A security officer.

The guy Angie had in the wristlock said, "Let go, sorry. I'm done, please!"

Angie said, "You guys are drunk. I can smell it. Go home and sleep it off." She let him go but she had expected him to try something else.

He stood and rubbed his wrist and swung his arm back at her and she blocked it, grabbed his wrist and hit him in the stomach hard with her knee. He bent over and grunted. After a few seconds he stood again and was going to try and hit her again.

Angie grabbed her gown and pulled it up and did a 360 degree reverse roundhouse to the side of his head. He fell over and hit the pavement hard.

Just as she did that Uncle Jack and the security guard came running out and saw Angie kick the guy. The security guard was shocked.

Everyone else had gathered around. Jack and the security guard were just getting up to them and the guy with just the broken nose turned to run and the security guard screamed, "It won't do you any good to run Steve." And the guy stopped. "You thought I wouldn't know it was you?"

He didn't say anything.

The security guard called for help on his radio. He looked at Angie, "Are you alright? I saw what you did."

"I am fine sir," Sherri handed Angie her shoes. Angie put them back on.

Shelly said, "Edward, you saved me." And she hugged him. "I never saw you stick up for anyone. That was exceptional!"

Edwards blushed. "I could not let that guy do anything to you. You are my sister. Besides Angelina taught us those cool moves and they worked just as she said."

Carl went over to Edward and said, "Edward, I am so proud of you. You saved you sister. I am astounded! I never thought that any of you would use what Angelina taught you."

Everyone stood around talking about what they saw Angie do. Most had never seen her fight. Grandmother Kristina said, "Angelina, I am astonished! Even after everything I have heard and been told about you, I still cannot believe it! And look," She reached and turned Angie and looked at her, "It does not appear that you have done anything! And you did it in a gown!" She was just overwhelmed.

Grandfather Joseph put his arm around Kristina and told her, "Sweetheart, now you know just how special Angelina is. She just ended something that could have turned out poorly. We should all go to the restaurant now. We do not need to remain here.

A few additional security guards showed up. They knew these guys well as they had been in trouble many times in the past. They ushered them to the security office for first aid.

Everyone got into their cars and left for the restaurant. As they drove Angie and Sherri talked. "I can't believe you did that in a gown!"

"As long as I can move, I can do that in anything I am wearing. You did see that I pulled the gown up did you not?"

"Yes, I saw that. You know, I can't believe how choked up I got again. I thought that after I heard the symphony a few times I would be used to it. I guess not."

"Sherri, The Nutcracker still does that to me, and I have heard it many, many times. I am so moved by the music each time I hear it."

They arrived at the Palomino, parked and met everyone and went in.

They were brought to their table and were seated. As usual, the men all put the napkins on each lady's lap and pushed in their chairs. They had a full dinner with fruit cocktail, salad, fresh baked bread.

Sherri did not feel uncomfortable as she did the first time she ate at the Palomino. She had learned how to be proper at the table. She recalled the first time she had eaten here. She remembered that she had been sweating and shaking but today she did not feel out of place.

The evening went well. When everyone was finished, they said their good byes and everyone went home.

43

They had Christmas at Dominic and Lizzy's house this year because Lizzy wanted to show off all of her new tableware and linens. She was excited because this would be the first time since they moved that they didn't need to rent at least some of these items.

During the past year, Lizzy bought a large set of ornate fine Italian China including serving dishes and bowls and real sterling flatware along with a set of Italian leaded crystal goblets and water glasses. The goblets and water glasses had gold around the edges. Lizzy had also bought a fine linen table cloth and napkins. She found a vintage set of gothic napkin rings. Dominic had bought 3 ornate gothic style antique candelabras, for Lizzy's birthday, each held five candles. And Angie had found some ornate antique iron trivets that she gave her mother for her birthday as well.

The table looked better than the tableware that they had rented for Angie's 18th birthday. This was the first time Lizzy had the family over and used all of this. Kristina looked at Lizzy and said, "Elizabeth, your table is exquisite! I am almost jealous! You chose a wonderful combination of items."

"Thank you, mother." Lizzy said.

Lilly, Maria and Sofia all went to see the table and they were all amazed. "You even found candles to go with your candelabras!" Lilly exclaimed. "Where did you find those?"

"Believe it or not I found them at S. H. Kress downtown." Lizzy said.

"Really? They look as if they came with the candelabras when they were new!" Lizzy was always astonished at what Lizzy could find. You have such a knack of finding things. Maybe I should go shopping with you more often."

"I cannot take credit for everything. Dominic found the candelabras and Angelina found the trivets."

"All of you are amazing! I will have to ask Dominic where he found those. I would love candelabras such as those. They are beautiful!"

"He told me he found them in a place that was kind of a junk shop. He said he saw the place and he thought he had to check it out. He was surprised to find them there."

"All of you are always finding these wonderful places with interesting things hidden around the city."

As was a custom now with the family, Lizzy contracted a server. She would be heating all of the food as well as serving everything.

This year, Lizzy bought two large prime rib roasts which still had the bones. She slow baked them most of the day to make them extra tender. She also made the salad.

She made an Italian style salad with Romaine lettuce, radicchio, red onions, pitted black olives, croutons, shaved parmesan and a mix of oregano, thyme, rosemary, basil, parsley and a little minced garlic. Then she tossed it with very light Italian dressing made with extra virgin olive oil, vinegar. She also bought fruit cocktail.

Lilly brought green beans Almondine and homemade buttermilk rolls. Kristina brought crusted rosemary scalloped potatoes and chocolate truffles with brown sprinkles. Maria brought a large assortment of her own recipe hors d'oeuvres and a large amount of authentic Italian cookies. Sofia brought a Ricotta Pistachio roll cake. It was her first try at making a traditional Italian desert.

They brought everything to the kitchen and showed the server. She would be preparing everything to serve. The server heated the hors d'oeuvres and put them out on a table in the Arizona room. Lizzy announced that the hors d'oeuvres were served. Everyone walked over and got some.

"Maria, these hors d'oeuvres are exquisite!"

"Thank you for the complement, Lillian." Maria. said.

Lilly asked, "Maria, would you consider sharing your recipe for these? They are amazing!"

"Of course, Lillian. I am delighted everyone likes them. It a recipe I found in a magazine."

"Really? I believed these were a family recipe." Kristina said.

Everyone visited and talked about what they have been doing lately. Dominic had served drinks.

The server was working on readying everything for the dinner. She had the rib roast in the oven heating along with the vegetables and potatoes. She tossed the salad and filled bowls. Then she filled small bowls with fruit cocktail. When she had these done, she went and told Lizzy these were ready.

"Everyone, dinner is served." Lizzy said. Everyone moved to the dining room. As usual, all of the men pulled out the chairs and got the ladies seated. Edward did this for Shelly. She was surprised as he had not done this previously.

"Edward, I am impressed!"

"I wanted to follow all of the men and no one has done this for you."

"Edward, you are learning to be a fine gentleman." Angie said.

The server brought out the fruit cocktail. When everyone was finished, she picked up the bowls and served the salad. She began to bring out the mail courses while everyone was eating their salad. Then she picked up the salad bowls.

The server brought out the vegetables and scalloped potatoes along with the rolls. Then she brought out the prime rib roasts. She had already sliced them. This way, it would not be required to carve the roasts at the table.

The serving plates were passed around and when everyone was served, Dominic said grace. "Our Heavenly Father, please bless this feast we are about to partake, may it nourish our bodies. Thank you for the opportunity to celebrate this day, the birth of Christ. Thank you for this time of fellowship with our family. We ask for your blessing for all of us and everyone in the world, especially those less fortunate. In your name we pray, Amen.

Everyone said, Amen. The server put on the background music and lit the candles and dimmed the lights. The server poured the wine for everyone and everyone began to eat. When they had finished, the server cleared the dishes. She brought out coffee and the Ricotta Pistachio roll cake, the Italian cookies and truffles.

Afterwords, everyone moved into the Arizona Room. The server changed the music to Christmas Carols. Everyone had put the gifts the brought under the tree earlier and now was time to pass them out. They opened their gifts and every talked about each and thanked each other.

Angie and the cousins decided to sing along with the carols. Angie led. After the first, Grandmother Kristina said to Angie, Angelina, you have a beautiful voice. I do not believe I have heard you sing until now."

Lilly agreed. She had not heard Angie sing either. Angelina, I am astonished!"

"Thank you." Angie replied. Again, she was surprised because she still didn't believe she sang well enough for complements.

Lizzy said, "Dominic and I went to hear Angelina sing karaoke at a bar she and her friends frequent. Dominic and I had a date night and also had fantastic cheeseburgers. But we were both taken back when we heard her sing. When she began to sing, Dominic thought they were playing a recording. But it was Angelina. Evidently the crowd enjoys her singing. They roared as if it was a concert."

Angie was sitting there feeling slightly embarrassed because she doesn't believe she is that good.

They all sang along with the carols for a while.

44

Christmas passed and it was New Years Eve. Dominic and Lizzy went to celebrate with the family at Lilly's house this year. Angie stayed home and celebrated with her friends. She had bought paper plates and napkins with New Years printed on them along with soda for everyone. Lizzy had bought a bottle of champagne for Angie and her friends.

Angie had ordered pizza early in the day to be certain they would still be able to have it delivered. She had planned on all of them watching one of the New Years Eve television shows in the Arizona room. She got out the TV tray tables and arranged them so everyone would be able to sit on one of the couches and see the Television that was in the Arizona room.

Then she decorated with streamers and balloons that said Happy New Year. She put the soda in a cooler with ice that she bought earlier in the day. Then she brought it into the Arizona room.

About 7:30 everyone came. Gina brought a variety of noise makers and cardboard Happy New Years hats. Most of which her mother had given her that she had from previous parties she had had.

Dominic and Lizzy left around 8 PM and Angie hugged them and wished them a Happy New Year. Everyone else said Happy New Year to them.

Angie had already put the plates and napkins on the table on the side of the room. Around 8:30 the pizzas came. Angie paid for them and brought them into the Arizona room and put them on the counter next to the plates.

Everyone went and got pizza and soda and sat down. Angie had already turned on the Television and had it on the channel that was broadcasting New Years parties from cities around the country. They ate and talked and watched the television. They discussed things that happened over the year and all wished for a better new year.

It came to 11:30 and Angie went and got the bottle of champagne and Janet and Paula brought the plastic toast glasses that Lizzy had bought for them. By about 10 minutes to midnight Angie opened the champagne and poured a glass for each of them. They all picked up noise makers and put on the hats.

They counted down and they all screamed "Happy New Year!" and drank champagne. Everyone hugged each other and danced around to Auld Lang Syne. They talked and drank more champagne until it was gone.

When it got after 1 AM most of them were becoming sleepy and they decided to go home. Angie offered to everyone that they could stay there for the night if they wish, but everyone decided to go home. They said good bye and this took some time because they talked about how much fun this was.

When they finally left Angie closed and locked the door. She cleaned up the remaining pizza and brought it to the kitchen and put it in the refrigerator. Then she grabbed the remaining plates and napkins and threw them in the garbage basket she had put out. Once this was done everything else could wait until the morning. She turned out the lights and television and went to bed.

45

Coming Soon

Angelina's Reckoning
An Angelina Tucci Novel

Chapter 1

1978

"AAAHHH!" Lizzy sat up choking, sweaty, panicked and coughing. It was 2 AM and she had tears in her eyes. She thought, "When is this going to end?" she looked at Dominic and felt a little better because she didn't wake him this time. She pushed the blanket aside, slipped her feet into her slippers, stood and put on her robe. She went into the bathroom and looked in the mirror. She had dark rings around her eyes and her eyes were bloodshot. She felt that she was beginning to age quickly. She reached for the medicine cabinet, opened it and took out her Valium. The psychiatrist she was seeing prescribed these for her anxiety. She took one and went back to bed. She tossed and turned and finally fell asleep.

Lizzy woke the next morning with a terrible headache, feeling depressed. "Another day of this?" she thought to herself. She forced herself to get up and get breakfast ready for Dominic and Angie. She always got up before Dominic so she can have breakfast prepared. Now this has become a difficult chore. She walked into the kitchen and tears formed in her eyes and ran down her cheeks. "Why am I bothering, this is so hard." She was crying now. "How can I be thinking like this? It is tearing me apart. What is wrong with me?" She wiped her tears and prepared breakfast. She then prepared both Dominic's and Angie's lunches. When she heard Angie walking to the kitchen, she forced a happy face. "Good morning, Angie." She forced herself to sound normal. She hoped Angie couldn't see through her facade.

Angie said, "Good morning, mother." And kissed her on the cheek. She helped putting breakfast on the table.

Dominic came into the kitchen. "Good morning honey." He hugged and kissed her then went and sat.

They all ate breakfast. When they finished, Angie and Dominic said goodbye to Lizzy and he and Angie took their lunch and left for the shop.

Lizzy began to clean up.

Lizzy continued to relive the trauma of the kidnapping every night. Even though she had been talking to Lilly, Maria and her mother. It wasn't helping. She still wasn't sleeping well, and she was becoming short with everyone again. She was falling into a terrible depression. Before the kidnapping she almost never got cross. She had had a mild temperament and never lost her cool. She was always sweet and upbeat around everyone. She always had the unique ability to turn any negative feelings or experiences into something positive. But now with the lack of sleep she is a wreck, and she is developing a temper and was no longer happy and upbeat.

She was having these dreams nightly since Angie saved her. Usually, these would wake Dominic up as well but last night it did not, and she felt somewhat relieved. When these nightmares woke Dominic, she always felt worse. She felt that Dominic should not have to be troubled with these nightmares as well.

She would dream that she is lifted by her neck with the rope, but Ash doesn't shoot it and she remains hanging, choking and kicking her legs. The dream is very vivid, and she feels the terror and choking each time. And she sees Angie shot and killed as she is hanging there.

She was worried that it is causing harm to her relationship with Dominic, Angie, and all her family. All of this together is consuming her.

She has talked to Lilly, Maria and her mother about it many times since Thanksgiving, but it was not helping. She mostly cries and constantly apologizes to them because she always ends up snapping at them when they talk.

Lilly and Maria both understand that what she went through was very traumatic. But they don't feel that they have been helping her and it has significantly affected their relationships as well. At this point it has affected everyone in the family.

Lizzy discussed this with Dominic often and she has been seeing a psychotherapist. But she hasn't felt that she has been improving. She constantly tells Dominic and Angie she is sorry for hurting them and that she feels she is destroying their family.

Dominic continually tells her, "Please do not worry honey. I love you and want to help you. I will do whatever it takes. I understand what the kidnapping did to you, and it was a terrible thing. I am here to help you. Maybe we should sit down with Angie and discuss this."

"I hesitate bringing this up to Angie. I fear it will bring back the memories she had from that incident with Mike. It would kill me if that happened. I would never be able to forgive myself."

Lizzy felt reluctant to discuss it with Angie. Both Lilly and Maria suggested that she talk with Angie as well. They told her the abduction likely gave her the same feeling of trauma that Angie had when she had been tied up during the incident with Mike. Angie had terrible nightmares from that. Lilly suggested that sharing like experiences may help her. Lizzy still worried that this may bring back the trauma that Angie had after the confrontation with Mike, and she could not bear to even think of that. Angie had suffered terribly from nightmares from that trauma, and she did not want to bring those thoughts back to her.

The next afternoon she was cleaning some things in the kitchen and just could not continue. She sat down at the kitchen table and tried to look at the newspaper, but she couldn't get herself to read anything. She was just to upset and was just staring at it. Her hands were shaking. She looked at the clock. It was 2:00 PM. Dominic and Angie were at work. She needed to begin preparing dinner soon, but she didn't have the energy to get started. She sat there alone worrying that someone would come in and kidnap her again and maybe this time they would succeed in killing her. She put her head down and supported it with her palms on her forehead and began crying.

Then she heard the door open and close. She immediately thought of her abductors and began sweating and shaking, her heart was pounding, she was breathing hard, and she was almost paralyzed with fear. She frantically looked around for somewhere that she could hide herself. She was about to scream.

"Mother? Mother? Where are you?" It was Angie. She walked into the kitchen. "Mother. Are you OK?" She went up to her and sat town across from her. When she looked at her and she could see that she was frightened and crying and she looked like a wreck. "Why are you afraid mother? I came home because I saw and felt that you were upset and terrified. I was worried."

"Angie," she hesitated. "I did not want to burden you with this."

"Mother, you have always been here for me I want to be here for you. Please tell me what is going on. I know something has been bothering you and I want to help. I felt and saw you feeling extremely afraid. And I feel as if you are choking. I do not like seeing you like this. Please talk to me mother. You have not been yourself since your abduction." Angie was becoming teary eyed. She pulled her chair around to the other side of the table and reached and put her arm around her. She looked very concerned.

Lizzy turned and looked at Angie and cried. She tried to talk through the tears. "I...." she sniffled, "I have been having bad nightmares about what happened. I did not want to tell you because I did not want to bring back memories from the incident with Mike. I know you had dreadful nightmares. Now I understand how you felt from those. I do not know how you could possibly have dealt with this."

"Mother, I am past those you need not worry. I dealt with those partly because you were always there for me. You sat and listened to me many times. I know you suffered very traumatic events. I have not told you, but I saw some of those events. I felt what you felt."

"You saw? What did you see? They did some horrible things."

"Mother, I saw and heard them speak and torment you in the room where they were holding you. They told you that they only asked for $10,000 and we would not pay. Then I saw one of them put a gun to your head and pull the trigger. I saw that two different times. Each time I jumped and almost died." Now Angie was crying. She sniffled, "I saw them pretending to hang you lifting you off of the ground with the rope."

"You saw that?"

"Yes mother, and I felt your fear as well. I felt so terrible. That made me feel angry, no, livid. I felt as if I could literally tear them apart at those moments. I do not know if I could tell you what I thought about doing to them. I prayed for forgiveness afterwards for thinking those things. I did not like the thoughts I had."

Lizzy looked at Angie with very sad eyes, "I did not know that. Now I feel terrible for you." She reached out and hugged Angie.

"Mother, we haven't talked since that night. I had a very vivid movie playing in my head each time I saw you. Just as we discussed after Mike, it was full in color as if I was watching it. And when they put the gun to your head, I saw through their eyes just as Sherri and I did before saving all of those young ladies. Oh! I just remembered. Mother, I have something I have to tell you. Father cried when I told him."

"What is it dear?" Lizzy looked concerned.

"Mother, I saw Grandmother Caroline! She told me that I knew exactly what I needed to do. She said, this is what made father cry, that I should not wait for the police because time is of the essence. I never had heard anyone say that phrase, but father said Grandmother Caroline said that often, 'Time is of the essence.' And she was so beautiful and was glowing. She said that she was proud of father for taking charge when she died and taking care of Aunt Maria. She also said she was proud of me. Then she said that you were father's savior. She said you are very much like she. She also said she would always be with me. This all happened in an instant. I am positive in just a few seconds. That was when I decided that I was going to go and get you back immediately by myself." She then realized that they had both stood up and were hugging tight.

"Mother, I want us to talk about this. Your talks helped me a great deal after Mike, and I wish to help you now. It is possible I have learned enough to help you. I feel that I need to try."

"Angie, I am so fortunate that I have you. It is possible this is what I need. I wake up multiple times each night. Usually, I am reliving each time they pretended to shoot me or hang me. The dreams are so realistic. It is just as if I am there, and I feel the same emotions. I choke when the rope tightens. Then I see them shoot you. I do not think I told you, but the doctor gave me Valium to calm me. It is an anti-anxiety medication."

"I know exactly how you feel. That is what I felt after Mike. I kept reliving those moments when I was tied up and beaten. I meditated many times in the attempt to free myself from those memories. I prayed every night. And one day I realized that I was running these thoughts through my head. I was dwelling on them. I was allowing these thoughts to control my life and dominate my thoughts. I decided that I needed to put all of it behind me. I told myself that these were memories, and I was not going to let them continue control my life. Every night when I went to bed, I said to myself that these dreams were going to stop haunting me and I was going to take back my life."

"Did that work?"

"Not exactly. I then fell asleep with the thought that I am finished revisiting this day and I have learned all that there was to learn from it. Then I thought to myself, "Angelina, you will stop revisiting these same dreams, there is no more to learn. If you do not end this, you will put it out of your thoughts completely and you know how that will hurt you for the rest of your life. These will end now. I also read about something called Positive Visualization. You create a detailed mental image of your desired outcome or where you desire to be."

"I began this by visualizing myself feeling good about myself living a full life without the thoughts of what Mike did. I incorporated all my senses. I created some positive affirmations and repeated these whenever I began to feel the stress from the incident."

"I also did this every night and after about two or three weeks the nightmares only happened one or two times each week. I kept it up until they were completely gone. Then when I meditated, I began with "my past is over, and it is time to move on." I found that after this the fear I had continued to vanish."

"I wondered how you ended those. You had been very upset many mornings. I could try something like that. Then could you teach me to meditate?"

"Of course, mother. I love you. I will do anything to help you, you know that."

"I know sweetheart."

At that point Dominic came home. He walked into the kitchen to say hello and saw Lizzy and Angie in tears hugging. "What happened? Angie, are you alright? I thought you left because you felt sick." He looked very concerned.

"Dom, Angie came home because she felt my fear and troubles. She is helping me attempt come to terms with my nightmares. She is doing what we have always done for her. I never thought I would be in a position such as this, on the receiving end."

"Has it helped?" Dominic asked.

"Very much."

"Thank you, Angie. Your mother has had some extremely bad nights since her abduction. I have not been able to help her." He walked up and hugged both of them.

Lizzy said, "Oh, I need to begin dinner. I have not done anything yet."

Dominic said, "It appears that you have had a rough afternoon. How about we all get cleaned up and we can go out somewhere for dinner?"

"That sounds nice Dom." Angie agreed. It was a Monday, so Angie did not have training. They went to clean up and change.

They ended up going to El Corral on River Road. They took their time and relaxed and talked. They each had beer with dinner which was a first for everyone. Dominic and Lizzy had had drinks together when they went out, but Angie never had a drink when they went out. Now she was old enough. The beer helped them all to relax a bit.

Lizzy called Lilly the next day to tell her about her talk with Angie. After they talked for a while Lilly said, "Lizzy, I can hear a difference in your tone. That is amazing!"

"I feel so much better as well. I even slept through last night. I haven't slept the whole night since this happened. You, Maria and mother were right. I am so sorry for how I have been acting." Lizzy was beginning to cry. "I caused everyone so much grief. Can you ever forgive me?" She was crying now. She knew that she had caused so much grief for everyone since the abduction. She felt as if it was all her fault.

"Lizzy, you cannot blame yourself. You suffered terribly from what happened. You cannot take blame for that."

Lizzy forced through her tears, "But I feel as if I caused everyone hardship. I feel so guilty." She continued to cry.

"Lizzy, I am going to come over. You have suffered greatly, and I feel as though you need someone there now. OK?"

"Alright Lilly. Thank you." Lizzy knew she needed support, and that healing would take time. But she still felt guilt.

Lilly spent most of the day with Lizzy talking and crying. It had been some time since they both sat and talked so openly and from their hearts. They decided that it had been too long since they had done this. It seemed that life had been becoming very complicated in recent years and they had been drifting apart somewhat. They still talked every day, but they had not really opened up to each other. They both decided that it had been far too long and they missed those talks.

They talked about Lilly's recent arguments with Carl and how Lilly thought she had not been talking to him as much lately. She said that they had always been so open and honest with each other but lately they haven't been talking. Lilly and Lizzy decided that the strain from Lizzy's problems had been affecting Lilly's relationship with Carl. Until today Lilly had not realized how much.

Lizzy said, "I think I need to spend some time with mother and then Maria as well. If this had caused this much trouble for you it must have caused trouble with both of them as well."

"I agree, Lizzy. I am relieved that you have discussed this with Angie, and it has helped you. I was very worried about how you were acting, and it made me feel sad."

They had spent the whole day talking. The day was more like it had been before Lizzy's abduction. Lizzy thought she would just go and visit her mother tomorrow. For once she was looking forward to it.

Late the next morning Lizzy went to visit with her mother. Her mother knew something had changed when she opened the door and saw her. "Elizabeth, hello. You look different. What happened?"

Lizzy said hello and reached and hugged her mother tight. Kristina hugged her back. Lizzy was crying. "I am sorry for causing you pain mother. Can you ever forgive me?"

After a minute or two they let go of each other. "Elizabeth, you have nothing to be sorry for. You suffered a very traumatic event. You sound different now. What changed?" They walked into the solarium and sat down.

"The day before yesterday Angelina came home from work early because she felt my pain and fear. She said she was very concerned. We talked for quite a while. She described how she got past her issues from Mike. And now she is teaching me to meditate. I feel much better than I have since the abduction."

I had been feeling that Angelina would be able to help you. That is why I had been suggesting you talk to her. I had an extremely strong feeling. It felt odd."

"Mother, maybe you share some abilities with Angelina as well. She did what Dominic and I have always done for her and what you and father have done for me. She listened and gave me things to think about. I feel blessed that I learned this from you and father and have been able to use it with Angelina. It has already made a difference. The last two nights I slept the whole night, and I haven't slept like that since before this happened."

"Angelina is such a good-hearted person. She has helped an amazing amount of people and now she had helped you as well! That is amazing!"

They talked and had lunch together. She left in plenty of time to prepare dinner for Dominic and Angelina. Lizzy thanked her mother for standing by her and supporting her. Kristina replied that this is what family does.

The following day Lizzy called Maria. Maria already knew something had changed. She had felt it the day Lizzy talked to Angie. She was expecting Lizzy to call but she wanted her to call when she was ready. They also had a nice talk. It was the first positive talk they had since the abduction. And because of this Maria felt relieved.

Over the next few weeks, Angie and Lizzy would go into the Arizona room and meditate. Angie explained what to do and how to work on clearing her mind. Soon they were both meditating. Angie had never realized how meditating with her mother could be so different than meditating alone. She found it more calming.

After they had been meditating for a few weeks Lizzy's nightmares began to lessen. After about a month they stopped. The only time she felt anxious was when she thought of the time that she was abducted. And after some time, these did not bother her anymore.

Lizzy was returning to her old self. The crabbiness disappeared and her sweet disposition returned. Dominic hadn't realized how much this had affected him. He was feeling much better since he was not awakened during the night anymore. And his worry had subsided.

Angie could feel how her mother was feeling and she was happy that she wasn't upset and tormented any more.

Lizzy also ended the visits with the psychotherapist. He could not believe the transformation in such a short time. He assured her that if she felt she needed his help she could always come back.

She thanked him.

Chapter 2

One Saturday afternoon, Angie went to the bank to withdraw some money. As she was sitting with her banker a man came in with a gun to rob the bank. He walked up to the banker Angie was with and pointed the gun at him. "Give me all of the money or I will shoot you and maybe this girl here too!"

Angie said, "Maybe I should move away" and stood up.

The man turned and pointed the gun at Angie and said, "You don't go anywhere."

He kept the gun pointed at her. She looked at the banker and rolled her eyes then turned back to the man and took the gun away with one swift move. She grabbed the barrel and stepped aside and grabbed the back of the gun with her other hand and twisted the rear of the gun up while pushing the barrel down. When she did this, it broke the finger he had on the trigger. The man was shocked and screamed, "you broke my finger, bitch." Angie pointed the gun at him and said, "Get down on the floor, now!"

He laughed and said, "A young girl like you won't shoot." And stood there smiling.

Angie handed the gun to the banker then turned and immediately hit the guy with a palm heal punch to the nose. Bam, he fell holding his nose as it blead. She had just broken it. "Next time listen!" she said sternly.

"You broke my nose bitch!" He sat up.

"Move again and I will break something else."

The man stood up quickly and tried to punch her. She used her usual Aikido move and broke his arm. "AAHH, Shit! You broke my arm."

"Move again and they will take you out of here in a body bag." Angie was angry now.

The banker just sat there with his mouth open. They heard the sirens. The guy said "Screw you!" and cocked his other arm back to punch her.

Angie quickly got into her stance and kicked him in the side of the ribs hard twice then kicked the back of his legs and he fell hard just as the police came in with their guns drawn. "Over here officers." Angie screamed.

The officers ran over just as she kicked the guy's legs and they saw him fall. The banker handed one officer the gun. They looked at the guy laying there with blood running from his nose, holding his arm and wheezing. "What happened here?" one of the officers asked.

"This man pointed his gun at me so I took it from him. Then he would not listen. I broke his nose, then he tried to punch me. At that point I broke his arm sir. Then he was going to try and punch me again, so I kicked him in his ribs which likely fractured them and knocked out his legs."

"You're Angie, Dominic's daughter, aren't you?" One of the officers asked.

"Yes sir."

"Ok," the officer said. He turned to the man and grabbed his unbroken arm and pulled him up and walked him out to one of the squad cars. He put him in the back. He put hand cuffs on the wrist of his unbroken arm and closed the other end on the screen that divides the front and back seats and closed the door.

The other officer asked him, "That's the girl that killed those guys using Martial Arts?"

"Yes, that's her. Hardly looks like she could do something like that does it?"

"I would never guess. She looks like she could be a model but Martial arts?"

"Well, she just messed up this guy pretty bad. If you really want to know what she can do just talk to Lieutenant Edwards. He told me that when he showed up at the place where all of the girls were being held, he got shot but he saw her fight. From what he told me I wouldn't want to run into her in the dark. He said one guy came up behind her and put a rope around her neck and she ran up the wall and flipped over him and got out of it in seconds."

"Ran up the wall? How does someone run up a wall? She said this guy pointed his gun at her so she took it away. Like it was no big deal. Then she broke his nose, arm and maybe cracked his ribs. She didn't even look shaken up. Did you see the banker guy? He was shaking like he saw a ghost. Maybe you're right. If she can do things like that, I wouldn't want to run into her in the dark either, or during the day for that matter."

When the police left, Angie turned and sat back down. She looked at the banker and said, "Try and relax sir, you were never in any danger."

"I, I can't believe what I just saw." He was shaking. He was looking at Angie like she was some kind of superhero. His eyes were wide open, and his mouth was quivering."

"Sir, can we get back to my withdrawal please?"

"Ah, ok, um, where were we?" He looked for his pen and the withdrawal form he had picked up just before the guy walked over to them. Now, you wanted withdraw money from this account?" His voice was still quivering.

"Yes sir. I would like to withdraw $7500 from this account, it is the one I use for investments." She handed him the passbook.

"Ok, Angie. It appears that you have been doing quite well with investments. Your Grandfather is teaching you well."

"Thank you, sir." She already had made $30,000 from investing. (This is equivalent to about $160,000 in 2025 money) "I am looking at a very special 1970 Trans Am I would like to purchase."

"I see. I will make the withdrawal and come right back." He walked to a teller to make the transaction. He came back counted the money on the desk put it back into the envelope and handed an envelope to Angie. Normally he would ask if she was ok with carrying this much cash but after what had just happened, he felt there was no need.